D1484460

# THE MOMENTOUS EXPIRATION OF TREMMY SINCLAIR

Michael F. Stewart

*For all my girls*

# 64 Days to Demise

Obituaries are packs of lies. Here's mine.

---

*SINCLAIR, TREMENDOUS, AKA Tremmy, died by lethal injection, shuttered away in his room, after a fierce mortal combat with the big "C." Tremmy is survived by his righteous mother, kooky-but-cuddly father, and Swiper the cat (who is lucky this isn't ancient Egypt, or he'd have taken her with him).*

*Born in Ottawa, Canada, he went to Amborough Private School, where he was the starring drone war general, captain of the swim team, and named prefect.* ~~Tremmy was a privileged jerk who stole, exploited, and bullied. Who joked about the homeless. Who, until six weeks ago, hadn't suffered more than a cold in all of his life. Who honestly deserves what he's getting. That guy? He leaves the world a better place by leaving it.~~

---

No. I swallow hard and start writing again. Packs of lies.

---

*Loved by his friends and once considered the presumed future leader of the free world, his loss leaves a black hole in the fabric of reality.*

---

Yaass.

---

*Following his diagnosis, he embarked on a round-the-world bucket-list tour, which he chronicled on his blog,* Dying to Travel.

*Then he hijacked the plane and went down in a glorious ball of flames. Thus, the momentous expiration of Tremmy Sinclair!*

---

But . . . what if it's not?

I tap the pencil against the desk, thinking while Swiper's paws disembowel my foot. *A glorious ball of flames . . .* I crumple the obituary, long bomb it toward the wastebasket and miss. I frown. Did I miss because it was a tough shot, or because some cancer cell won the battle with the cell that would have allowed me to sink it? To be fair, it *was* a tough shot. But I also have an inoperable, high-grade, fast-growing, malignant-as-Voldemort-on-unicorn-blood brain tumor.

Swiper appreciates my having missed. She bats the paper across the carpet.

I scan the tombstone options I've sketched and taped to the wall. Everything from a mausoleum worthy of someone important to a simple plaque reading: So That Didn't Take Long.

I have time to hone the obituary. Four to six months. I ignore the notifications rolling in on my phone, mostly from my best friend Jenkins, asking whether I have any contraband to warm up with before tonight's party and whether his jeans make his ass *pop*.

"Mom?" I yell. But it's a big house. I text her. "Mom?"

Nothing.

I push out of the chair and pad down the hall, feet soft on

2

rich, beige carpet. I pass three overly floral, primary-color-themed guest rooms, a marble foyer big enough to fit a two-bedroom apartment, the painting on the wall expensive enough to buy that apartment, and then shuffle past the living and dining rooms, to where I lean against the kitchen entry. "Mom."

"Tremmy." Her eyes shimmer. They're always shimmering these days.

I roll mine. *I'm* the one dying. Not that I'm not sorry for her anguish; she and my dad are the only people I can off-load on. No one else knows about my illness. No one even knows about the plane tickets. Not my friends. Not the drone war coach. Not even the headmaster, whom I'm scheduled to meet at the prefects' meeting Monday morning. I made my parents promise not to tell. Everyone expects me back at school this year, returning to the best year ever. To be royalty of the institution where I have lived for six years and would have boarded in day and night for this last year. That's what everyone thinks. That we share this privileged life. But I'll be a high school dropout—put that in my obit.

"I'm worried that the trip isn't the right ending," I say.

On the counter are three open-ended, around-the-world tickets. First class. With them, the world is in the palm of one hand and a glass of champagne in the other. At least I can die with the satisfaction of leaving behind a massive carbon footprint.

She doesn't say anything, standing with one diamond-cluttered hand on the automatic cherry pitter. Where I once would have spotted the cherry pitter and thought, *Weird—who needs a cherry pitter?*, now I see the pitter as an act of desperation, a mother trying to delay the death of her son, hands stained by the cost of it all. Across the back counter cool four cherry pies, two cherry crumbles, and a pitcher full of cherry juice and pulp—a lot of antioxidants. Last week it was spinach. Before that it was a twenty-million-dollar donation to the Children's Hospital Cancer Foundation. These attempts to cure me have all been equally ineffective.

"Mom?" It's sharper than I'd meant, and her shoulders hitch.

"You can do anything, Tremmy. Anything at all. Disney World, skydiving, try healers around the planet. There's a circumlunar flight. You can build schools in Africa until . . ."

She collects tears on the trim of her silk sleeve and begins to hammer at the cherry pitter plunger. Cherries with their hearts plucked out fire into the bowl as she pumps. When the clip empties, she turns on the sink tap. "You going to the party tonight?" she asks, trying to wash the red stains from her hands.

"For sure," I say.

She loads the pitted cherries into the juicer.

Six weeks ago, I was trying to determine what I wanted to major in so I could figure out which courses to take and which universities I should apply to. The choices were overwhelming, but I had time. Time to try and fail. Time to start a company and have it flame out. Time to rent a small island with Jenkins and really learn to surf. Now I have new choices, in some ways more because I don't have a future to plan for. I can do anything at all, but now there's not time. How do you live a lifetime in four months? What if I make the wrong choice? I've wasted six weeks on tests and scans and tumor DNA analyses and an experimental treatment that made me want to die sooner rather than later. But that's over. The last chemo treatment was a week ago. No more treatments. No chance of survival.

Now every day is a ridiculously high percentage of my life. I don't trust myself to decide what to do with the rest of it, and those plane tickets guarantee it'll be interesting.

"Sorry, I know my flip-flopping is annoying. I *do* want to go with you and Dad." If I can't rule the world, I'd at least like to see it. "I'm just . . ."

She envelops me in a hug. "You planning to tell Jenkins?" It's been hard on her not being able to tell her friends. Not having anyone to mourn with except my dad, and he's not exactly the strong one in the family. She's hoping I'll go public, just so she can.

"I want everyone to remember *me*," I say, "not that kid they knew who got cancer and kicked it."

Her gray eyes consider mine, and it's weird because I think she's wondering what she would do. It's like I'm a trial run for her. Dying is something that I know more about; they think I understand what it feels like better than they do. Better than most. But it's not true. I don't. I know what it's like to be terrified of something. To have panic wash up my back and prickle at the base of my skull. I will soon know more about pain. But I don't know what it's like to be dying. Not yet. But I will. And that scares me.

"Is it okay that I'm happy we'll be together, Tremmy?" she asks. "Is that selfish?"

"You made me," I say.

"Yeah, I did." She blinks away tears and smiles. "Your dad will be home soon. He's at the airport, collecting dinner.

Remember that hamburger place in Paris you loved? Well, they deliver, after a fashion. And then a whole cherry pie." She laughs flightily as she clutches me close again. "From here on out, every meal will be so special. It's going to be fine."

In her arms, I clench my hands to keep from screaming. *She lies.*

\*\*\*

I meet Jenkins in the park. Why we need to warm up for a party with free alcohol, I have no idea, but we always do.

Here's a line from his obit: *JENKINS, FRANKLIN, never passed a girl without a comment, never passed a mirror without an appraisal, and never had much use for thinking too deeply.* Maybe he's afraid of what he'll find. *Jenkins operated his mother's construction company until he passed away from an undiagnosed venereal disease.*

Girls think Jenkins looks hot—everyone does. Jenkins agrees. Tonight, his T-shirt is strategically torn to reveal abs. He bumps a finger along a couple obliques. Yup—all good, it seems. It's highly possible he's juicing, but he won't say. Tight, stretchy jeans—he confided in me once that he loves how jeans are made stretchy like yoga pants, even for dudes. Always talking about his ass.

"Look at my ass," Jenkins says as I stride to where he stands near a bench, beer in hand, butt out toward me. "My pre-summer vacation ass was good, but—" He slaps it. "Like two ripe melons."

"Watermelons?" I ask.

"Nah, more like the green ones, whatever you call them tight-ass melons."

He tosses me a beer, and I catch it. His explodes with foam as he cracks its tab. "Grenade!" I say, laughing as he presses his face to the spray, sucking at the erupting beer.

He groans. "This is a custom shirt."

I choke down the weird Belgian strong beer Jenkins steals from his parents' fridge. Why? Because I love my buddy. He's my bro, and we support each other. Chugged beer doesn't have to taste good. When we're together, it *feels* good. Soon we're both regurgitating foam, not having said anything more. When the first can is empty, Jenkins is there for me with another. Texts bombard our screens, pushed from the Goldilux app, demanding when we'll show. I crush both my cans with quick twists of my hands and miss the nearby trash can.

Jenkins lets loose a spectacular belch. "You shoot like a no-armed, castrated two-year-old."

"On behalf of castrated toddlers everywhere, I object," I say.

Jenkins barks a laugh, runs over, and dunks his beer cans.

"Impressive."

"I know, right?" And he points at his butt. "You checking this out? Are you? I'm having it cast in bronze as a present for your birthday."

I dip my head into the shadows of overhanging branches, not wanting to think of birthdays. When I glance back, he's a block down the road, snapping his fingers and dancing back and forth over the center line. I jog to catch him. On our way past a brightly lit mansion, kids play football on a golf practice green. Jenkins stops to toss their ball. Their scissoring arms fumble it every time, as they grin deliriously.

"You guys are going to be pro quarterbacks," Jenkins says,

and the boys wave stubby-fingered hands as we move on. "Sad, huh?" he asks me. "I bet that was the best part of their day." He dances toward thudding music before I can ask what he means.

Two dozen cars pack the landing-strip-sized driveway of Tonja's house—Jags, Mercs, Rovers—a couple million dollars in wheels.

"Whose crappy bimmer?" Jenkins mocks a low-end BMW. We leap up the steps of the party house's column-flanked entry. At the top, we pause to take stock. Phone—check. Armpits—is it even possible to smell better?—check. Joint selfie— "Who's here? We're here. Let's do this!"—posted. Fist bump.

Jenkins doesn't bother knocking. It's a party!

On the inside, a hot funk. Joey mans the keg. Marcelle DJs with her phone. Both salute us. Salutes dutifully returned. Bass thumping, the song changes to our theme, "For Those About to Rock" by AC/DC. Jenkins performs a goofy couple of jerks with his arms like he doesn't know how to dance before he springs up and crashes to the marble floor in his signature splits because he *so* does. Tonja's parents have pro-level stage lighting that stutters with seizure-inducing flashes, alternating from blacklight to military-grade crowd deterrent. Above our heads hover several small drones—not the beasts we run for the wars. These are trackers tied to our phones, taking everything in, their buzzing shielded by the music.

"*Tremmy.*" Stack's hand slaps mine, which stings. He's part wrestler, part samurai, and a haze of cologne. Jenkins and I run the gauntlet, high fiving most of the guys on the drone war team. At the end, Jenkins lifts both arms to the ceiling. This is the buddy I'm supposed to have the most momentous of awesome years with. And I wonder if I still can. I feel better than I have all month. But that's gotta be the beer. Or the lessening effects of the dose of chemo injected into my spine a week ago—the last round before I rang the bell, marking the last of my treatment. I'd heard others ring it victoriously. Mine was a death knell.

"Jodie, Jooodie, Jodie, I see you've been shopping at discount stores," Jenkins says, eyes roving a sheer top Jenkins clearly believes Jodie wore for eye roving. "This party's sick." She hands him a beer. "Trying to get me drunk, huh?" He winks.

"You wish," she says, and he laughs.

Her acknowledgment of me is sullen. We dated for three months, until my diagnosis. I broke up with her that night, over text. *Sorry, Jodie, got some stuff happening and I don't think a girlfriend is a good idea.*

*WHAT?* I swear I felt the burn of her stare through the screen.

*Sorry.*

*You're breaking up with ME?*

*Sorry.*

*Screw you.* Within the hour, half the girls at Amborough blocked me on social media.

Her obit reads: *TIMMONS, JODIE, never recovering from the loss of her first love, she lived a life of abstinence and longing as a divorce lawyer to the rich and famous. Hated rom-coms, weddings, and Tremmy Sinclair.*

But our breakup *was* for the best. It wouldn't have been fair to force her through what happens next. *It's not you, it's me.*

"You okay?" I ask her.

Her scrunched face holds my stare, and then she walks away. I deserve that. After being blocked, I'd contacted Mona, a public-school girl I had sex with a lot before starting to date Jodie. Mona is not the best-looking girl, but we had fun—and a mutual understanding of privacy, except of course with my best friend. I arranged a final tryst. After our usual quiet fumbling sex in a Starbucks washroom, I even told her about how I wouldn't be around after the summer, to which I received a tearful hug and a wordless retreat. I texted but never heard back.

"How the hell did Whitby ever get his wheelchair up those stairs?" Jenkins asks, and then shrugs. Judging by Jenkins's energy, and how he's downing his third beer, I'm sensing a glorious mess by the night's end.

"Two goals," he says into my ear. "One." He lifts the beer. "And hook up."

This isn't news. It places him in competition with pretty much every guy here. However, being hot, smart, and uber rich, he has quite the head start.

A robot bartender serves drinks at the far end of the field-length room. Nearby, a small South American-looking woman in traditional dress is hand-grinding espresso beans in a mortar and pestle. Kids are taking selfies with her as she smiles toothily and blends authentic, indigenous frappés.

The Night-Before party is legendary, only eclipsed by Post-Prom and Flesh-Fest—when Wang had his pool party where *everyone* dropped their pants, but no way his parents will allow that again, not after having to drain the pool—not to mention the ambulance. Tonja's parents know about this one. Tonja's arguing with some guy I don't recognize. He's wearing a leather bomber, ripped jeans, and too many gold chains to be one of us. She stands over him as he lounges with a beer, surveying the party. Merton, one of two suicide drone operators on the drone war team, slips beside her, drops a roll of bills into the guy's hand, and takes something I don't quite catch, but strongly suspect to be drugs. No surprise there.

"Hello, *Mrs. Robinson*," Jenkins says; he nods in the direction of the oh-so-sharp Mrs. Dean—Tonja's mother—in a tight tank top with a constellation of diamonds sewn on. "Thinking I should raise the degree of difficulty for goal number two."

She's certainly making goal number one easy, pouring shooters beside a bowl full of car fobs. "Not with Mr. Dean here," I say, "unless goal number three is death by husband."

"Fair point. Heard he hunts big game." Jenkins may be self-destructive, but he's not suicidal. He sniffs me. "Man, you smell good. That Axe you're wearing?"

"Sandalwood."

"I gotta score me some."

"Can't. They send me samples to make people like you all horny about it."

"Looking lean too. Beer?" Without waiting for my answer, he waves at Joey, who starts a pour.

"Yeah, sure."

"Have you seen Fiona since June?"

"Blossomed?" I ask.

"Understatement, dude. She's *hot* now. Parents gave her C-cups for her birthday. Wonder if she's got a boyfriend. If you catch a chick before she *knows* she's hot, and you're hot, they're so grateful even though they shouldn't be." I catch what he means by grateful but can't bring myself to laugh. "Case in point." He nudges me in the direction of Margot, who is speaking to Marcelle. Jenkins glances at me with one eyebrow raised.

"Margot? Good luck with that."

"No luck required. Deal closed."

"What . . . you and her? No way," I say, genuinely surprised. *ALLAN, MARGOT died when the chip on her shoulder pinched a nerve in her neck, paralyzing her so she couldn't move when the logging truck she was protesting rolled over her. She leaves behind the entire Harry Potter series translated into every language and a signed picture of Michelle Obama.* The smartest girl in our grade; not only intelligent but an intellectual. I wouldn't have thought she'd go for Jenkins. "There's a one hundred percent chance that the headmaster will name her head girl tomorrow."

"Happened a couple of weeks ago. We were both pretty slammed at a bush party." Jenkins's face squinches. "Hotter than she looks, once you peel all the Discount O'Rama rags off. I'd bone her again."

"How generous."

"I give and I give." He laughs, and it reminds me how little laughing I've been doing lately.

Margot spent a year with me on the swim team in grade nine, and she'd been reedy then, and not much of a swimmer. She hasn't changed much. Bulky clothes, a mane of unkempt hair. Unlike most of the Amborough girls, she doesn't wear designer jeans or purses or makeup, and doesn't spend time on nails or hair. Platinum is the new blonde this fall, but hers is pitch black. She only ever comes to the "big parties." Her folded arms broadcast a don't-talk-to-me vibe. Everyone is pretty sure she attends Amborough on a scholarship.

Jenkins wraps an arm around my shoulder. "What's wrong, bro? Something tells me you haven't been tanning enough."

I smile, and he relaxes a bit. "Sorry, I haven't been ignoring you. My parents have been keeping me busy."

Jenkins scans the party like I've seen him scan the enemy drone war team a hundred times. He's made out with half the girls here, and the other half he wants to. "This year's going to be the best year of our lives," he says.

I sputter beer, then start giggling so hard that tears are pouring down my face.

"What? What?" he asks, face wide, eyes glassy and carefree. "It's true. Next year we'll be back on the lowest rung of the ladder as first years in some university they let *any* wankstain into. And, after that stupid piece of toilet paper they force us to get, I'll be working in my mom's construction business. It'll be wife, house, kids, potbelly, dog, alcoholism, divorce, midlife crisis. Pet rabbit." He puts his finger to his temple and pretends to fire a gun. It's what his dad did. "But that's adulting. We don't need no stinking adulting. *This* is our year. And then it's over."

"I love you, buddy," I say.

And he laughs too. "Maybe I should stop tanning. I'm jealous of all the veins in your arms popping out. It's like you've got vein erections."

I double over in laughter.

"Tonight's going to be epic." He hoots. "I want whatever you're having."

My feet are numb again, and I'm shivery, but evidently my veins look good, so hooray for the cancer skinnies. At least I'm not vomiting at the moment. Jenkins is right. Putting on my shirt tonight, I realized I've never looked so shredded. If Jenkins knew why, he'd ask for the poisonous cocktail and give it a try—he's that messed up about his body. The company would be nice.

The music changes to the *Star Wars* theme, and Mr. Dean wheels out a table with a huge golden brick beside a sledgehammer and anvil.

"The rekindling!" he shouts, and the graduating class of Amborough College presses close. The graduating class and me—and the skulking drug dealer in the bomber with the heavy stubble and hungry stare.

"Safety glasses!" Mrs. Dean calls as her daughter slips her phone on to the anvil, grabs the sledge, and swings it, smashing the screen of her phone. A phalanx of tracker drones record.

"This is so like Easter," Jodie says. "Don't you think?" Her face sours when she realizes only me and Margot are listening to her. The rest are clamoring for the sledge. "Like the resurrection, when all our sins are forgiven? All those embarrassing texts gone, right? Erasing the past you want to forget."

"Not sure the internet works that way," I say, but Jodie is no longer listening, her eyes wide on Tonja.

Beside the table, Tonja gingerly takes the first phone from the golden brick of them and holds it up: the newest model phone from her father's company. They're not even out yet. Pictures and video of the phone between her company-logo-painted nails will soon clog social media.

"We should recycle the old ones," Margot says. "This is sick."

"Sick," Jodie and Jenkins agree together.

"People like the symbolism," I say. "The new phone is rebirth, I guess."

Margot rolls her eyes. "You don't need to defend them," she says, retreating without taking a new phone or destroying whatever old one she might have. I shrug. Margot protested the school's lack of organic waste recycling last year. Another line of her obit would read: *Margot was blessed with a huge mouth, and she had the unfortunate habit of using it.*

Jenkins nods to Jodie. "I get it. All the porn I've searched. The dick pics I've sent. All gone."

Soon, the line dwindles; the tracker drones, twinned to now smashed phones, crunch under feet like queen-less, desiccated bees. The brick of new phones is down to its final layer.

*Death and rebirth.* My last phone. My current phone is from last year's party. The newer model has a couple more megapixels in the front camera and a screen on *both* sides, which is cool. I'd been hoping for holograms.

"That's twenty-four-karat gold trim," Mr. Dean says. "Be sure you mention that in your posts. And . . . check out the new companion drone."

A tiny light floats up from Tonja's hand, and she shrieks with delight. "A firefly!"

Everyone is buried in their new phone, logging in and setting them up. If it's like last year, it'll contain a private update of the Goldilux network—an invite-only social media app for kids who suffer from high net-worth parents.

The table is littered with broken glass and bent frames. The detritus of a year.

"Hey!" Tonja's confronting drug-dealing Bomber Guy, one hip jutted out. He pockets a stack of the new phones and smirks down at her. Half the kids glance up from their screens. A swaggering Jenkins hands off his phone to Stack.

"Chill, I was invited," Bomber Guy says.

"The help is never invited," Tonja replies.

"You heard her," her dad adds from behind the shooter bar. Tonja's mother is nudging his shoulder.

Bomber Guy scoffs.

"Back to your slum." Jenkins grabs his collar and flips him onto the floor, fist slamming down.

I swear. "Jenkins!" But his fist keeps pumping with meaty slaps. The guy twists away and comes up with the sledgehammer, face as red as the handle.

"You people are crazy," he shouts, taking a jerking fake swing that drives everyone out of reach. With quick, sure steps, he backpedals toward the door. With a nudge of the hammer head, a waist-high vase topples and shatters, sending Jenkins dodging. A bronze horsehead needs a firmer push before its granite base fractures tiles. A marble bust, possibly of Mrs. Dean because she cries out as it goes, cracks in two. Then he's through the door.

I'm at the head of the pack, but the Bomber Guy's already leaping down the stairs as the rest of the drone war team fans out among the columns. He retreats toward the beat-up BMW.

"X1," someone says with a laugh.

"Run, rabbit," Jenkins says from beside me. It takes me a second to realize what he's holding. A crossbow, camouflage printed, cocked, and with a wicked black bolt chambered.

Bomber Guy's eyes fly wide.

"What the—" I pull Jenkins's arm down. The crossbow triggers. The bolt glances from the hood of a Land Rover.

The rabbit ducks behind the driver's side of his car, door squealing open.

"What was that, Sinclair? He's a thieving, trespassing drug dealer," Jenkins says, snatching a second bolt from the quiver below the crossbow.

The car revs, peels out, and tears rich, black tracks in the lawn. A platoon of drones race after it, but none of them are large enough to pack any real heat, and they can't keep pace. Jenkins swears.

I'm still trying to process what happened.

There's a moment of silence as we all listen to the engine noise rip down the street.

"Keep it Amborough, kids," Tonja's mom says. "No more outsiders."

The party moves back inside.

"Are you a hunter?" Jenkins asks, handing the crossbow back to Tonja's dad, who claps him on the back.

"Life's a hunt," Mr. Dean says. "That lion didn't shoot itself." He points past Mrs. Dean to a rug before the fireplace. Someone has spilled wine on it. But he doesn't seem to notice, mimicking firing the crossbow. "I've nailed three of the big five. Better you than me taking out that waste of skin, you still being under eighteen and all, right? Not that anyone would have blamed us. He would have been your first?" Mr. Dean drifts back toward the bar.

"Sure." Jenkins shakes off whatever's bothering him and turns to me. "Shooter? There's way fewer calories in a shot of vodka, same amount of alcohol as that gluten bomb . . . not that I've gone all glutard. I'm eating four thousand calories a day now.

But the right kinds. I'm paleo." My hand is shaking, and I don't think it has to do with the cancer. "You okay?"

"Yeah." I cover. "I'll pass on the shot. I'm more quality over quantity." I don't need anything else burning out my insides.

He bursts out laughing. "Yeah, sure, quality like Mona. Don't be such a vaginaball."

I sense the tips of my ears reddening and scan the room to see if anyone is listening. But the party is ramping back up. If anything, it's more hyper, more alive. The near death of the kid jolted them.

"You still," he pumps his hips, "with her?"

"Not sure what happened. She stopped texting, left social media."

"She ghosted *you*?"

The thought brings an unexpected pang of guilt. I remember thinking, *I can't believe my luck*, after we'd made our sordid deal.

I shrug and lean back against the wall.

On his way to Mrs. Dean, Jenkins staggers and does the splits to hide it. I can't help but feel older than him. All of them. This party isn't for me anymore. I'm some grandpa looking on at "these kids" with all their antics. My mind flashes to Jenkins pointing a crossbow at another human. One of Mr. Dean's big five? Would I have stopped Jenkins two months ago? Or would I have watched?

What do I share with these guys? Memories of drone war triumphs? The shared hope of winning awards that my parents say are sure to get me into the best universities? Life was all about my potential, a future I no longer share with this crowd. I don't look sick—not yet. Soon I'll be that thing everyone feels uncomfortable visiting because it smells of death.

I shudder. I don't want to visit that me either. Last year I received a phone call on my boarding-house landline, someone who didn't know me trying to reach me. It was about my girlfriend at the time. She'd been in a car accident a few months earlier, before I knew her, and had died that morning in the shower from a hemorrhage that hadn't been caught. Her friend on the phone was frazzled. I remember listening to her but feeling nothing, disconnected. Like I was a sociopath. She *was* my girlfriend, but we went to different schools, and we'd only been together twice in the two weeks since we'd hooked up. But I *was* her boyfriend, and her friend thought I should come to the funeral. I didn't. I didn't want to be around the dead.

I'd continued on with my life as if nothing at all had happened. I feel the ghost of her sometimes, over my shoulder. I remember what a nice person she'd been. But then another part of me is like *stuff happens*. The death had zero impact at the time, but maybe it would have, had I faced it. Had I not ghosted a ghost.

But the other half of me—most of me I guess, for now—still wants my place among the smiling, grinning, laughing kids surrounded by the ethereal light of electronic fireflies. I wonder if I've made the right decision to travel with my parents.

What I really want is to lean in and kiss one of these girls. Lose myself in their arms. In the tender lips, the scoop of the waist, the nails at the back of my neck. To smell strawberry-drenched napes and thread fingers through silken hair. The obliteration of too much beer, uncaring about the foggy day that will follow.

But that next day is 0.5 percent of the rest of my life. Each week is three percent. And these are the last *good* days.

What would Jenkins do if he had months to live, half of which would probably be a messy, painful disaster? Would he do drugs and drink himself blackout drunk? Pretend that it all wasn't happening? He might at first, but reality shows up soon enough. What does a good death look like?

I push off the wall. I'll make tonight count and be someone in the senior year social media feeds. I'll try to say something to everyone here. Maybe I *will* pick a new phone.

Peachy fresh faces, flush from booze, tight clothes, all bob to the beat. Except Margot. Her eyes are on Jenkins.

Shiny-eyed Jenkins leans in toward Mrs. Dean, clinking a shot glass against hers and downing it while Mr. Dean watches his every move. Hunters watching hunters. I skirt the edge of the dancers, making my way over to Marcelle and Margot, fist-bumping and cajoling all the way. "Got a request?" Marcelle asks.

"Music?"

Marcelle laughs. "No, Tremmy, gimme a great podcast to play. Maybe something to do with politics."

"Sorry, I was coming to say hi." Margot looks off, not seeing me. "Hi, Margot." She licks her lip and nods in greeting. "How was your summer?"

"I spent mine behind a cash register at Discount Village. You?" Her eyes don't complement her smiling lips.

"Oh," I say. "Okay, I guess." I spent the first half trying to figure out why I was having balance issues, fearing the worst, only to discover I had yet to imagine the worst, and the second half over a toilet bowl on a brutal "last-line" drug, because there is no other line for what I have. "Good."

She snorts, still not having looked at me.

Tomorrow, I climb on a flight to Hawaii. Stop one before Tokyo. Each leg costing more in penthouses, five-star Tiki huts, and mansion stays alone than what she could earn at Discount Village in ten summers. Ever since she arrived at Amborough three years ago, she's resented the money others have. But now *she* has everything I want. The unfairness is tinder in my gut. Anger flares. "Why are you even here?"

I have her attention. For a long moment, she stares. "What do you mean?"

"You don't want to be here, so why did you come?"

Marcelle steps forward, ready to break in, but Margot places restraining fingers on her arm. "I'm here because my parents have the delusion that if I attend your private school, I'll create connections with people who will be running this country one day. They think I'll have a better education. I'm here because that delusion is costing them their retirement, and I need to try, at least try, to convince them that I'm willing to make their dreams come true and hope in the meantime that I don't become an accessory to murder."

The mention of murder, and the way her eyes shimmer like my mom's, sucks the oxygen from my temper.

"*My* school? It's as much yours as it is mine. If you don't like something, don't do it. No one's forcing you to go."

Her hands find her hips beneath the sweatshirt. "Sometimes I wish someone would shake you jerks, remind you that the world doesn't revolve around you. By the time you all figure it out, you've got daughters of your own being stalked by jerks like you."

Her words send a sharp chill through me. We're not talking about school anymore, and it's more than crossbows and drug dealers too. She flushes and glances down. Before she walks away, I step closer and touch her elbow. She flinches. "Did someone . . . do something?" Part of me acknowledges that it's possible for Jenkins to do *things*.

She draws a shuddering breath. Blood rushing in my ears competes with the throb of music. "Nothing you wouldn't have done," she says. "I only wish I could drink and not wake up having done something I never would have done otherwise. Is that . . . *something?*" After scoffing at my silence, she flees.

Marcelle heaves a sigh before returning to her playlist.

Most people don't think of me as a jerk, and knowing that someone does bothers me. "Is that what you think, Marcelle?"

Marcelle shrugs.

Across the room, Jenkins whoops and raises a shot glass.

By the roll of Jenkins's eyes, the shooters are starting to hit. He's sweaty from dancing and is grinning ear to ear. A girl I don't recognize, maybe a grade ten, slides out from under his arm. I can tell she's uncomfortable, but he doesn't grab after her. Then Jenkins shifts Whitby's wheelchair to the side and waves him onto the dance floor. It's a stupid request, fueled by too much vodka.

"That's not how I roll," Whitby shouts from his seat.

Jenkins, not getting whatever reaction he hoped for, swerves toward me.

"Probably thought I'd forgotten," he says, offering a test tube filled with clear fluid. "The succor of Zeus." *Sweet death.*

I'd pass on the shooter if I didn't know he'd drink it instead.

"Tre-mmy! Tre-mmy! Tre-mmy!" Members of the drone team encourage me to down it.

I sense Marcelle watching, maybe Margot too. Thinking that we're all jerks. And tonight is like hitting shuffle on an old playlist. Maybe we're doing it again. Maybe we're a bunch of boys being boys. And that's what jerks are.

"The succor of Zeus!" I call and shoot the drink, tasting the honeyed booze and feeling the burn down my throat and into my stomach.

The team cheers as I fight to keep the alcohol down.

"You're the best, Tremmy," Jenkins says, his words already sloppy. "I love you, man."

Jenkins sways. He has it all—like I had it all.

But is my life over? Can't I claim something back?

*This* is my obituary. These are the guys who will be coming to my funeral. Probably because their parents will force them. Jenkins will get drunk on my behalf. He might even manage to seem human.

Whether I like it or not, if I leave tomorrow, this is it. Do I care? *Why am I even here?*

"I'm not sure I want to go," I say aloud.

The easy thing for me to do is to board that plane. That's the early death. If I stay, maybe I can feel normal for a bit longer. Live longer. Figure out this uncomfortable distance between me and the past and fix it.

"Then don't go, man," Jenkins says, his face contorted in drunken sincerity. "Stay. This party's just getting started."

"But it's going to be so hard," I whisper.

"Life is hard. And then you die." He points to the ceiling.

Fireflies circulate. One day, I won't be there to stop Jenkins from pulling the trigger. The crossbow bolt will find a home.

"What about my parents?" They'll be so disappointed. *You can do anything.* But also. *Is it okay that I'm happy we'll be together . . .*

"Screw parents. The night's young. We're young." Jenkins spots someone, a girl by the sheen in his eyes. "And I need my wingman."

I glance from the predator to his prey. To the gathered guys high-fiving and shooting drinks and posing for their social media feeds. To the girls on their golden phones, fireflies in their hair, chatting and laughing. And the absent Margot, who, for a vulnerable moment, confided in me.

"Okay, Jenkins. Okay, dude. If only to help you."

"Thanks, brother." He throws his arm around my shoulders. "I'd do anything for you."

And I wonder, would he? Would he *really*? Because at the end of all this, I die. And I may need a friend who is willing to do *anything*.

# 63 Days to Demise

A dozen prefects lounge on leather couches in the oak-lined office of the headmaster. Six girls. Six boys. Dressed identically in gray pants, white shirts, and forest-green blazers, most with the bright emerald stripes that indicate our "colors"—our superior achievement in something or other—and collections of award pins arranged like military medals on our lapels. Collections clutter the office walls too: butterflies pinned in a lit case; trophy photos of famous former students—politicians, industry titans, filmmakers, stars—the greater the fame the larger the frame. Many of them were head prefects. Only two of us here will be made head prefects. It's a golden ticket into an Ivy League school and future success.

Everyone except Jenkins fidgets and laughs too loudly at each other's jokes, waiting to discover who will catch the ride. Jenkins struggles to keep glassy eyes open. Last night ended with both of us heaving our guts into the bushes, but for two very different reasons. He aced one goal and sure tried for number two, but there were surprisingly few takers after he vomited the first time.

Jodie won't look me in the eye. Margot holds a sheet of paper with a quote from someone named Heidegger on the top. She's quite the nerd. Becoming a head prefect is a mixed blessing. For one, you have to speak at assembly, which is in fifteen minutes. It's supposed to be ad lib with no preparation. But Margot's ready for any eventuality. It's also a lot of work. Head prefects are the face of school, meeting prospective students and their parents, speaking at celebrations and major events. It looks *amazing* on your university application. But some of us have house responsibilities already. Each student is assigned a house, which becomes their surrogate family. I'm a "deck" or floor prefect for the grade eleven borders; the assignment likely takes me out of the running for head prefect. My room is on the same floor as the juniors. If someone is homesick or sick or has ordered in strippers like someone who-shan't-be-named did last year, I'm supposed to deal with it, or report it to the housemaster Mr. Bell if I can't.

Beyond already having a house role, I can think of a half-dozen other reasons why I won't be named head prefect. My grades are decent but not spectacular. I was suspended last year for drinking on campus. I never volunteer for anything. I tore up the front field doing donuts with my truck. In short, I'm not exactly head prefect material.

Mr. Bell is already a bit peeved at me for arriving so late this morning, but my parents wanted to talk—a last-ditch effort to put me on the plane.

"We only want you to be happy," my dad said, tears coursing down his plump cheeks. My mom gripped my hands between hers, unwilling to let go. "This is your wish, to go to school, *really?*"

"My dying wish," I say.

"Let's call it a living wish," my dad says loudly.

But I'm not jinxing my chances to beat cancer by saying it. I'm not sure all of this has sunk in for either of them. I am scheduled for brain scans in a few weeks to see if the experimental therapy did anything. The scans are supposed to be in Tokyo. My parents are waiting on a miracle. I'm not. I pull free from my mother. "Cancel the flights," I say. My parents purse their lips and turn to each other for support. "Mom, what did you want to be when you were seventeen?"

She doesn't hesitate. "An artist." Right, she's where I get my drawing ability. Give me a few minutes, and I can sketch anyone.

"What about you, Dad?"

He grins. "I really wanted to be a firefighter."

"Yeah so, Mom, you went from artist to chief financial officer and, Dad, from firefighter—sorry, I find that really hard to imagine—to selling air conditioners."

"So?" His hands grip his belly, which looks like he's stuffed an air conditioner down his throat.

"What I want now means nothing," I say. "It's most likely wrong. Like you were wrong. Maybe I shouldn't change *anything* because I'm dying."

"But you don't even like schoolwork." Mom's wearing her flight suit. Not one of those one-piece blue suits the NASA astronauts wear. This is a smart-looking silk blouse, blue jacket with white piping, and a white skirt. It's what you'd wear before dining at the yacht club or at a cottage in Muskoka. A heavy gold loop, big enough to be a misplaced halo, rings her neck. She's ready for first-class travel.

"What I *hate* is fighting for marks and how important they are," I say.

"They're not important now?" Dad asks.

I point to my brain and lift an eyebrow.

He beats his paunch like it's a war drum. "You never know what can happen. I got into air-conditioning because I had a summer job in a company where the owner had a stroke. Rather than lose the job, my mom bought the company and told me to run it. Told me it was important to learn things the hard way. But without that stroke—"

"Yeah, yeah, the family stroke of genius." I roll my eyes. My dad is always telling me I need to watch out for my stroke—my chance to strike. It won't happen now.

"But I wasn't making a dime until your mother came aboard." My dad grips my mom's shoulder and her fingers find his. "Your mom changed everything for me. Put me on the straight and narrow. Gave me a game plan. I never looked back. What I mean is, we'll take it day by day. No one needs to know. I'm not canceling anything."

A non-decision is still a decision.

"Maybe the treatment really will work," Mom adds, and I ignore her comment. The *treatment* was experimental, with zero human studies and only marginal success in a rat model. I'm not pinning anything on rats.

Still, I thought they took the news well overall, until my dad broke down a second time and sobbed all over my mom. After, she changed her outfit, and then we packed up and drove the hour to school and dropped my gear at Mason House, just another student among a mill of future masters of the universe. Nervous grade nines, uncertain grade tens, and excited grade elevens and twelves. Chauffeurs nodded stoically to rich British wankers— "Cheerio!" Diplomats and ambassadors in black-armored Yukons and Humvees shoed their children quickly inside under the watchful eyes of sunglasses and earbud-wearing bodyguards. Maserati-driving Hong Kong billionaires inspected their kids before ushering them into school, relieved they made it through summer without being kidnapped and ransomed, most speaking better English than I do. My parents are rich, but nothing compared to the oceans of money some of the parents of foreign students have amassed.

"Tremmy," my mom said after she'd parked, a note of pleading in her tone.

"I can handle my bags," I replied.

Her lips thinned. My dad slipped his arm around her neck. I waved my parents off and then bent to pick up my rucksack and large suitcase.

Other housemates called, "Hey, Tremmy" and, "Hiya, Trem."

"Hey!" I shouted back.

It was all it took. A weight lifted from my brow. I grinned. No one here knew. Not a one. Nothing here had changed.

My suitcase rattled over pavement and then through a wide doorway. Everywhere the house was alive. As I bumped the suitcase up each step, I drew a deep breath and did something I hadn't done since my diagnosis: sing. I broke into a house song about conquering. Strength suffused me. Light flushed through the stairwell windows as I climbed. I buzzed. I felt like Tremendous Sinclair. In the honeycomb of rooms, housemates picked up the song, lifting it and me so that I floated up the steps. The sweetest, voice-crackling soprano to the deepest of baritones carrying me like a hundred fingers. What my tenor lacked in quality, I made up for in wind. It was enough to help me forget how I needed to rest in my room where I dropped my bag. But even then, lying on the unyielding mattress, the clank of the radiators, the whistle of wind through the paper-thin windowpanes, and the thump of rap music, they whispered to me. "You're back. You're welcome here. Let's do this." For the last month, I'd been dying. Petrified of dying. Now I was living again.

"Good morning! Drones and phones away!" The headmaster strides into his office, trousers snapping like a sail catching a gust. His long hair hangs in a ponytail behind his back. An otherwise bald dome catches the light of a crystal chandelier. He's sketchable. We quiet and stand, arms folded across our chests. I polish my loafers on the back of my pants as he inspects us.

GRENDEL, HAROLD VON, *aka Hairy Head, headmaster of Amborough School for the Affluent. He presided over its transformation from all boys to coeducation, ushering it into the twenty-first century, guiding the curriculum to preserve the ruling class. Your investment portfolio thanks him.*

As adults go, he's pretty cool. I'll never forget his saving me from the swim team's hazing. I made the senior team in grade eight, and not everyone was happy about me beating them. In my memory, his face flashed tomato red as he tore the broomstick from a senior's hands, broke it over his knee, and threw the jar of Vaseline across the boys' change room. Naked and spread-eagled on the bench, I covered myself with his suit jacket. And I've never left his protection since.

"Welcome to your final year at Amborough. Congratulations to each of you on your prefecture. I hope you've rested up, as we have a busy year ahead. We expect a lot from you." There's a promise on his lips, a clever smile in his clear gray eyes that's infectious. "Who can tell me the meaning of our motto?"

"*Ad eundum fortiter quo nemo antea iit?*" This is Elliot. Making jokes in Latin is generally encouraged, but the headmaster's expression darkens. Elliot's motto translates as *To boldly go where no one has gone before.* From the show Iter ad Astra. *Star Trek.*

"No, that's not our motto, Elliot. It's *canis meus id comedit,*" Jodie replies and sniggers before flushing.

*My dog ate it.* I snort at both of them. Neither is in line for the head prefect role.

Smile gone, eyes sharpened, the headmaster probes the inside of his cheek with his tongue. "The culture of this school is set by each of you. You are our leaders. Microcosms of Amborough. If you wish to joke and not uphold the ideals of this institution, I urge you to refuse the honor and burden of your position. Now."

Jodie and Elliot sober. The silence extends. We listen to the laughter of our burdens outside the thick stone walls. Outside leaded windows, I count a dozen fireflies, hovering, watching, microphones straining.

"*Ex nihilo nihil fit,*" Margot says finally. "Nothing comes from nothing."

The headmaster nods. "Hard work, effort, and perseverance leads to achievement and success."

*Or a stroke of genius.*

The headmaster's sausage fingers prod the air. "Your year—your years—here, your life, will be the culmination of the hard work you put into it. But I assure you, on your death bed, you will remember your time here as though it were yesterday. In this room," his arm sweeps to take in the photos on the wall, "are the people you can trust. Some of the only people."

I swallow hard and catch the slight shake of Margot's head. When the headmaster turns to face her, she's stoic.

"Keep your nose clean and we'll have a great year," he says, clapping his meaty hands together. "Now, who's ready to hear who the head prefects are?" He holds his hand out to Margot. "Congratulations, Margot, you are our head girl." He shakes her hand firmly, looking her in the eyes with the supreme confidence of a man who deals with an elite class. There's no hint of surprise in her expression, only a lean, resolute smile.

"And the head boy?" He turns to Jenkins, who blinks with shock. "This was a difficult decision. We need someone we can depend on, who can handle the role and the schoolwork, someone who reflects the image of the school. Someone who has already shown his ability to lead." His gaze passes over Jenkins to me. "Tremendous."

He likes to say my full name. My jaw must have dropped because he says, "Don't look so surprised, son. The youngest ever drone war general. One day, you'll be on that wall."

The other prefects slap me on my back while the headmaster pumps my arm like he's priming a pump to start sucking oil. I try to act happy.

"When my daughter died," he waves an arm toward the mantel, where a silver vase winks, "you became the only children I had left. I will expect no less of you than I did her. I love you no less." We all shift a little uncomfortably. I didn't even know he had a daughter. "Time for assembly. Each head prefect will have three minutes to address the school. Ready?"

*Crap, the speech.*

Margot flashes the pages in her hand with grim determination. At the headmaster's glance, I say, "Oh, yeah, I got this, sir." When in doubt, conviction has always taken me farther than hard work. "Born ready."

He clasps my shoulder. "Well, let's go then, we have five hundred students waiting to hear your advice about how to suck the marrow out of Amborough."

I lag behind the headmaster and Margot.

"Congrats, Head *Perfect*," Jenkins says. "Your years of using your nose as a butt plug have finally paid off."

I catch the whiff of jealousy and want to tell him he has nothing to worry about. The position will soon open up.

\*\*\*

A gym full of students fidget as the headmaster's long-winded speech about pushing ourselves beyond our comfort zones winds down. Teachers line a stage behind us. Robed. Expressionless. The headmaster waves the head prefects forward.

"Do you want to flip a coin?" Margot asks me as we stand.

Margot has her prepared speech. It's bound to be good. Speaking first allows me to get ahead of that. But speaking second gives me time to think. So far, I've blanked on what to say. Hairy Head's comment about *sucking marrow* has me cycling through imagery of zombies and cemeteries and diseased bones.

"Ladies first?" I suggest, and Margot rolls her eyes.

"I'm no fricking lady." She digs in her pocket, finds a coin, and flips it. "Tails," she says as it spins, then looks at the "heads" and smiles. "You know what? I accept your offer. You've had your chance."

I'm not really sure what she means by that.

We approach the podium together; several hundred pairs of eyes heat my cheeks. What do these students *want* from me? Most of all, they'll want me to be quick. No one likes long speeches.

"I am your school's first-ever female, person of color head prefect," Margot begins, dwarfed by the pine podium, the silver microphone tilted down to her glossy lips. At her words, I can hear Jenkins's inward groan. *Your private school.* Hadn't she said that last night, but here she is, our head prefect, and still she can't accept that this is her school? A few whoops and cheers erupt from the student body, but only a few.

"I'm proud of this accomplishment," she continues, "but it also shows us how far we as a community have to come. I shouldn't be the first. I shouldn't be an exception. But we can change. *Every man is born as many men and dies as a single one.* That's a quote from the philosopher Heidegger. I think it means that we are all born of our cultures, our communities, and our family beliefs. We are born with these values stamped upon us. Most of us are unaware of these prejudices. At Amborough, it is our priority to recognize and rise above these influences, to be accepting of people who are not like ourselves. To move from being many men *and women*, to a single one. To become who we are meant to be. Every day in life, you will be confronted with choices, and through those choices, you will become an individual. Recognize in yourself your own biases. Overcome them. Heidegger was a middle-aged, cisgender, hetero, white, male Nazi. Words mean nothing. He is no hero. He had lofty ideas but made terrible choices in order to keep his life comfortable. *Every day, you have the power to choose our better history—by opening your hearts and minds, by speaking up for what you know is right.* Now *that's* Michelle Obama. Make choices that your future self will be proud of. Your parents cannot decide who you are. Your friends cannot. But if you let them, they already have."

Margot mimes dropping the mic.

I clap. The teachers behind us politely clap. No one else really does. I'm surprised Margot doesn't topple over from the weight of that shoulder-chip.

All eyes are on me. I still have no idea what to say. I'd been listening with all my biases piled high. But as I adjust the mic, kids sit up. People grin in anticipation of my vacuous wisdom. What do these students want? Quick and energetic. They want Tremendous. This is *my* school.

I embrace it, putting every ounce of my love for it into my voice.

"Who's choosing to be *awesome* this year?" I ask. "That's my bias."

I know seventy-five percent of the school population, and they *all* know me. When I speak, people cheer. And laugh.

"Who's choosing to have a *momentous* year?"

In the gym, the cheers roar.

"I am," I say, and I pause. "Tremendous." Laughter. "It's a big one for me. I'm honored to be your head prefect. It's Amborough's year to be independent school drone war champions!"

The drone war team hoots. Mostly guys, but there are a few girls on the team too.

"Field hockey champions!"

The girls all cheer. The audience leans in. They give little expectant nods.

"And it's my last year here. I—" *I'm dying.* I sober. This is what happens when I don't prepare. I almost say crap I shouldn't.

"I've been thinking about obituaries," I say, on dangerous, sacred ground. "Yeah, what would go into mine. Who would come to my funeral? What would be carved on my tombstone? Will it be 'One way only' or, for the Buddhists in the crowd, 'Be right back'?"

Laughter suggests I've hooked my audience.

"Weird thoughts, right? But I'm not sure we want to wait to think about this stuff. Better to think about it sooner. Now. Right? Before it's too late. Do you have any last words? My grandma's were, 'So that's a life.' Mine are likely to be, 'Oh, crap, here comes Mr. Bell. Hurry!' right before I miss that hard-to-reach branch to grab the windowsill of Mason House's second floor."

Mr. Bell shakes his finger at me from the row of teachers, and everyone roars. It's the branch I missed when they caught me out drinking after hours. I nearly broke an arm in the fall.

When the laughter settles, I say, "Here's what I want you to do . . ." The crowd is silent. "I want you to think of this year like it's your last. How will that change things for you? Write your obituary. Say your last words. If you don't like them, you still have time to change. Sketch out your tombstone and carve for yourself what you want on there, and don't let anyone do it for you. I don't really like the concept of living like you could die at any moment." I breathe. "Instead, let's live like nothing stands in our way."

I try to meet the eyes of every one of the students. Jenkins offers a surreptitious middle finger, and I grin. "Will you join me in our school song? Let's make this year . . . momentous!" I stretch both my arms high into the air.

The senior class of Amborough College is first to stand. Then the juniors. After that, they all do. They're supposed to be swept up in school spirit and launching into the school song, but now it sounds like they're singing it for me.

It's a religious song, "To be a Pilgrim," but few of the students sing it for the religious meaning of the words. We sing it because singing unites us.

I really hope this year can live up to the welling in my chest.

***

I'm crying and that's stupid. I wipe the tears with a green-striped sleeve.

They may have given me a standing ovation, but no one swarms me. I am a boulder in a river of students. And life goes right on. Cold sweat prickles my skin as I lean on the podium. I'd come so close to telling everyone, and maybe that would have made sense. Maybe it would have been a relief. As if I was waiting to tell them in person because they deserve to hear it from me. So they understand how precious time is to me. And that I'm choosing to spend it here with them. Maybe then they'd see how cool this place is.

Jenkins ferries through the kids to my side and tugs the sleeve of my blazer. "Where'd that discharge come from?" He laughs, but his hair is mussed from where he's been gripping it. "One of my testicles actually started to wither from listening."

"Just said what popped into my head."

"That explains it."

"Thanks. Not like I had time to prepare."

"You should have known you'd be head boy. Obvious. Or did you not look at the competition?" His face reddens.

Margot hovers, staring at me, probably pissed off by how I started my speech. "We said the same thing, you know." She shakes her head with irritation. "I, of course, didn't need to mock you to say it. But the *carve your own tombstone or else someone will do it for you?* You said my speech."

"Funny the different reactions," Jenkins says.

Margot steps toward him. "Funny," she agrees without a hint of a smile, only a dark sizzling energy between them.

"Come on, we've got jobs to do," I say, and we all split up.

Prefects are cops, teen social workers, and grunts. Today we're grunts, ensuring lost kids find their way to class. In the quad, a limestone-framed courtyard with stone arch exits, starry-eyed grade sevens wander aimlessly. I point them in the right direction and then frown when I spot a few students pushing another kid up against a wall. They're tucked into a blind alley between two buildings.

"Do it!" one of the kids urges Merton, who holds a black, foot-long tube. I know what it is, a gift from an alumnus who runs a massive cattle farm. Wisps of white smoke curl from its tip. The kids are grade tens, except for Merton, a senior. Part of the popular set, except for Merton. The wide-eyed boy against the wall is new, which explains the tube—a brand, an Amborough tradition. Branding is frowned upon, but the teachers ignore it. Most of us have an *A* burned into us on our first day. For new boarders, it comes in the dead of night. Mine is on my shoulder. Theory is, by the time it finally heals, you're Amborough. I wonder if anyone dared brand Margot.

The victim whines, tears tracking down his cheeks.

"Merton," I say. *MERTON, ALLISTER, a bit of a dick but an ace shot with his drone.* "Let the kid leave."

Merton's face twists. "What are you talking about? *You* did this to me. You." He rolls up his sleeve to show his forearm and a bubbly, shiny scar. "And a crap job too."

It is a bit smeary.

"But we're in the same grade and . . ." I start to drum up other excuses as to why it was okay for me to hold him gleefully down and burn him with a smoking iron. I shake my head. "You're right. Sorry about that. I shouldn't have. But now I'm head boy."

Merton's lips pucker like his scar. "I wanted it. Maybe not so smudged but—"

"Does it look like this dude wants it?" I ask.

The "dude" looks to me gratefully.

"Something's messing with your head." Merton scratches at his. "Look, I'll be careful."

He pulls back the top sheath of the brand to reveal a white-hot *A* powered by the battery in the pommel. The victim's eyes widen.

"I said leave him alone." I step toward Merton.

Jenkins watches from across the quad, head cocked, eyes

wide. Something has changed, and it has a lot to do with the creature in my skull. That speech I gave. That never would have come out of my mouth a couple months ago.

"We're only having fun." Merton's buddy still has his hands pushed up against the new boy's shoulders.

"What's your name?" I ask him.

"Finn."

"You having fun, Finn?"

He shakes his blond head. I pull the arms away from him. "I'll walk you to class."

"This is *bull*," Merton says, waving the brand.

With the other students stunned behind me, I walk Finn into the entry to the second-floor classes where most of the grade nines are.

"Do most people have an *A*?" Finn asks, and I squint at him. "I mean, is it weird not to have one?"

The hall smells of floor wax. Photos of school classes, teams, war heroes, champions, board members, they all stare down on us from the wood-paneled walls. Mostly of boys and men, this having been an all-boys school for a hundred years before it turned co-ed for the last twenty.

When we reach his classroom, I answer, "It's a dumb tradition."

"But a tradition?"

Through the door, I spot another girl with a bandage on her hand. "Yeah."

Finn stops and stares at me. "I think I want one."

He wants to belong. It's why dumb things continue. As he heads in, I trip him so that he falls to the floor. He looks back, eyes wide. "Another tradition," I mutter.

I'm late for my own class by the time the last straggler is settled, but I still haven't talked to my parents, so I call as I walk.

"Tremmy?" my mom answers breathlessly.

"I'm okay," I say.

"Thank god," she replies. Her relief blows across her microphone, making the speaker crackle.

"I gotta run, but I'm head boy."

"Head prefect, congratulations." She cry-laughs.

"And I want a tattoo."

"What, why?"

"Tattoos should be for important things, like if you make it to the Olympics or the call sign of your army unit. Something that defines you."

"What do you want?"

"My expiration date."

"Why on earth—?"

"Not everyone knows theirs."

"You're not a carton of milk."

"It wouldn't have to be big."

"You're not getting a tattoo."

"What if I get a semi-permanent one? One that only lasts a year or so."

"I know what you're doing."

Maybe it's the decision to return to school. Maybe it's because I'm dying and nothing really matters, but it's changing things. I no longer really care what people think. What's the worst they can do to me? And I *do* want a tattoo. I'm pretty sure my mom knows she can't stop me anymore.

"No, Tremmy, that tattoo will age, stretch out, and look like the tattoos of the bronzed sailors who walk Florida beaches with tattoos of anchors that look like SpongeBob."

"Then it will be a reminder of how lucky I was."

There's silence on the line. She's crying. "You have to be eighteen."

"I have to go to class," I say, knowing I can pass for eighteen.

"Congratulations on making head prefect," she replies. "It's fantastic. Your dad will be really proud."

I hang up. Nothing can be truly *fantastic* anymore. Now fantastic is coated in a prickly sweat of impending doom.

***

I burst into Mr. Pascale's classroom. Papers are being shuffled. Keyboards are being tapped. Heads are down. Slick, clean surfaces, black leather chairs. A white seamless ceiling glows like sun through cloud. It's like the designers of the Apple retail stores went wild here. Screens gleam on all four walls, but only one flickers in use. At the front, Pascale motions to my desk, continuing his introduction to our World Issues class, speaking with his meaty lips. We sit in a horseshoe shape. One desk sits empty. *Jodie?* There are eight other students.

At Amborough you pay for a few key things: small class sizes and technology. This place is wired to the hilt. Last year, Eliot found an undiscovered Mayan city as his science fair project using the school's powerful geomapping tools. Tonja developed a robotic arm in the school's Maker lab now in prototyping for the fast-food industry. Margot was right. This place does harbor the future leaders of the country. That's not a bad thing. But the biggest difference between the average school, even other private schools, and Amborough is in the curriculum subtitles. Amborough teachers teach whatever is required by the government, but with a twist. Last year's math class was subtitled *It Takes Money to Make Money*, which I suspect to be a play on the school motto. The course covered how to identify corporate takeover targets while running the school's pension plan investments. Then we took over a small cap manufacturing company and became its board of directors. The subtitle for Pascale's World Issues is *How to Rule It*.

Beside me, Margot has struck out the subtitle on her screen and replaced it with *How the System Keeps You Down*. Right, the head prefect of the country's top prep school is being kept down? *Pfft.*

Pascale is the type of teacher most everyone loves. He has brilliant delivery and gives 'A's to pretty much all students. But there's a reason for the latter. From the bottom of my bag, I pull a weathered and yellowed photocopy bound by plastic spirals. If school mythology is correct, I'm holding a transcript of everything that Pascale is about to say. For the entire semester. No one has retyped or scanned this and put it online, yet we all have one. Except Margot. The notes are two decades old, and the real name of the transcriber, Ken Niving, has been lost to legend. My copy has small updates based on subsequent students catching changes, mostly *he coughed here* or *sneezed twice.*

Everyone leans back in their ergonomic leather chairs as Pascale begins. "This semester we will discover why the fundamental flaw of every democracy is that the average person gets to decide who leads it, and we'll learn how to sway public opinion, negating this defect.

"We'll learn what the Statue of Liberty actually stands for," Pascale continues. "And not the obvious that she can't sit down."

There it is on page two. The same joke. Even the *creepy laughter* that follows. If this year is like last, and the year before that, every word out of his mouth will be written here. Every test will be the same. Every presentation slide. Every pause for effect. Each senior year sells their transcript copies to the juniors for ten thousand dollars. Another tradition. They'll be worth every penny because included in each package are the test answers.

I sense a black empty stare from across the horseshoe. Audra. I shudder. She considers herself a "sensitive"—someone attuned to the spirit world. Her all-black irises are contact lenses, but it's as though she's looking through me. She's weird.

LISOWSKI, AUDRA, *died on a caving expedition in Guatemala while searching for a Mayan artifact said to have supernatural properties. Google Maps failed to offer a route out. Her last words were, "Damn, no signal."*

If Audra were in a public school, she'd wear all black instead of the forest-green school blazer. The school dress code allows for limited self-expression. Not even facial piercings. She must be unfulfilled here. Instead, she has tattooed barbed wire around her wrists. I can't help but think that in her attempt to be so different, she has fulfilled a stereotype. Pascale says we use stereotypes to decode a world that is too complicated to grasp in its entirety. Audra added an extra line to the school brand she got on her first day, so that she sports the symbol for anarchy on her shoulder instead of the institutional and conformist *A*. The dark circles around her eyes are painted on, her brown hair dyed this season's platinum. She's a demon with a badminton racquet and plays the harp like a fallen angel.

I narrow my eyes at her, but she doesn't look away. If anything, she leans forward to stare deeper into my eyes. I turn back to the papers, finding my place, and listen to Pascale speak, reading the captions on the page and shaking my head at the 2000s-style clip art he uses on his slides.

"The subtitle for this course is 'how to rule the world.' But it could also be construed as 'winning.' Win what? Wars? Elections? Boardroom battles? Arguments with your lover?" He smiles. "All of the above. It all boils down to the same thing. A battle of ideas. Convincing others that you are right. I will teach you the art of rhetoric, winning arguments, by explaining why you lose them."

I read along as he speaks, making a game of catching anything he says differently and inserting it for the next student, but there isn't much to correct. Tired from last night, my mind drifts.

"Am I boring you, Sinclair?" Pascale asks.

"What?" I jerk, realize that the crotch before me is the teacher's and that I'd rested my head across my arms. I've never fallen asleep in class. *Never.* I swallow. "Sorry. No, no. Scintillating."

"Hmm . . ." He purses big, fat lips. Caterpillar eyebrows crawl above mischievous eyes. Then he turns back to his slide. A stick figure has a light bulb over his head. He hesitates, and I realize he's lost his spot. He shuffles to his desk and flips a page back and forth from a stack. I realize he's using the transcript. The transcript copied by Ken Niving. He's using it to teach . . .

"Maybe you are," I mutter.

He bounds in front of me. "Excuse me?"

"Yeah," I say, louder. "Maybe you're boring me."

He leans down. A dandruff flake from his scalp flutters to the desk. "How so?"

What I said to my dad was true. I don't care about my marks. The only thing left for me to earn an A+ in is what little time I have left. So I can't listen to this. I can't tolerate a teacher who doesn't teach anything new. "I have every one of your tests. I have all your exams."

"Cheating?" He raises a bushy caterpillar.

"It's not cheating if everyone has it openly and you allow it. No, I don't understand why we're all wasting our time here. If everything you'll say is in here, why don't we just show up and hand in the answers to the tests?" I flush red at the intensity of Pascale's stare.

A couple of the students start to slide their copies off their desks and into their bags. Audra smirks, hands pressed together at her chin.

"Ah, yes, I listened to your patronizing, insipid, and sanctimonious bromides this morning. Thank you." I'm fairly certain he's insulting me, but I only understand every other word. "If this year were my last, I wouldn't be here, Sinclair. Who attends my funeral does not matter because I will be dead. It is far more likely that this is all a simulation." Pascale laughs. "Lucky for me, using actuarial tables, I have a life expectancy of twenty-seven more years. This time next year, I'll be retired and flying to Portugal, eating shellfish and drinking wine in the morning. My last words will be, 'Waiter, one more glass.'"

Margot leans and whispers in my ear. "Wow, Tremmy, you're really living in the moment now, aren't ya?"

I smile at her, but the approval in her eyes bothers me. Until today, I'd always respected Pascale. What if I'm wrong? What if returning to school is a huge mistake and I should be living the high life while I can?

Margot turns to Pascale. "Actually, sir, I'd prefer a more challenging year too. Sir. No offense, sir."

My eyes widen. "I didn't say challenging." It's not like I want to be buried in homework. More *interesting* maybe.

"I'll take it under advisement, but the course I'm giving meets all the curriculum guidelines and has led to a one hundred percent acceptance rate for students applying to social sciences at universities."

I don't dispute it by saying that the school boasts a one hundred percent acceptance in *every* discipline, nor that the marks of students are boosted to ensure this continues. I'm stunned by how he brushes off my comments before realizing—*he agrees*. He's given up. He would rather be drinking wine in Lisbon. "Write challenging essays. I'll be sure to make the grading *challenging*." He smirks, and anger burbles in my gut. No one here understands how little time they really have. How they can wake up tomorrow and skin their knees on the rug—and it's brain cancer.

Lily puts up her hand.

"So, this is a rebellion, is it?" Pascale asks. "Note that I use the term *rebellion* and not revolution."

"No, sir," Lily replies. "I agree with you. I have read the transcript and compared it to the official curriculum guidelines, and your lectures exceed them easily. I'm only attending class to ensure I receive the five percent bonus for perfect attendance. I completed the assignments over the summer."

"Yeah, I'm with Lily," Jenkins says, holding up his block of notes. "All this allows me to read ahead, which helps with my learning disability. One of the great things I've learned is that we need to consider the perspectives of other people who might not be so lucky."

Jenkins doesn't have a learning disability. The notes are the only reason why Jenkins is taking a social science in his senior year. Easy marks. I'm threatening his entrance grades to business school—Jenkins will need nineties across the board. He flashes me a shut-the-hell-up smile.

Pascale's expression grows smugger. "I'm glad we've come to a consensus."

"Not quite, sir," Lily says. "A consensus is general agreement."

"Thank you, Lily. We will continue with the lecture because a school is not a democracy. This . . . is a dictatorship. Which reminds me, did you hear the one about Lenin?" He pauses for effect.

"He knew how to throw a party," I say, reading from the transcript.

He scowls at me. "Funny." His hands are out like he's about to choke my neck. "Some people aren't lucky enough to choose their last words. Now let's discuss how to actually win an argument." He sighs and points to Margot, who has her arm up. His notes don't call for questions.

"Truth to power, sir. If you speak the truth, you will eventually be heard."

He laughs until it turns bitter. "The truth is not a part of this course. It certainly got Mr. Sinclair nowhere. I will give you the tools to win *every* argument, whether you're right or not. By the end of this course you will be able to convince me of the fallibility of something in our legal code."

I lean in.

"Oh, so I have your attention now, do I?" Pascale laughs at me, but he's right. He does.

This is what I need. If I have one overriding fear more than death, it's dying. I need assistance in dying and, for a seventeen-year-old, that's asking someone to commit murder.

*\*\*\**

Amborough prepares students for the war of life.

When passing the headmaster, the Hairy Head will ask, "Did you win today?" To which the standard reply is, "I drank the succor of Zeus."

Which is cool and is, of course, the school drink—half Tequila, half lychee liquor. But nothing has prepared Amborough students for war better than the arrival of the school's chief technology officer, Dr. B (Betty-Robetty) Warburton, who graduated with a PhD in robotics from MIT—serious brainpower. She created the school's Maker lab and set up the schoolwide network that we call Big Betty—a series of productivity apps that includes everything from your basic calendar, email, and old-school chatroom to high-end movie or music making, presentation giving, and collaboration tools. More than that though, Robetty created the sport of drone wars.

Last year, for the first time in drone wars' five-year history, a junior was the team general—me. And this year I will lead the team to their first independent school victory. The fact that we've never won is Amborough's greatest shame. Dr. B founded the drone war project as a way of luring students into robotics and programming. The new sport swept the private school system and has become a model for rich-kid strategic engagement. But Deaconsfield—Demonsfield—with its robotics teams, custom semiconductor manufacturing facility, and massive student body, has stolen the crown from day one. Until we win, none of us can look Dr. B in the eye.

Here's how the sport works.

Each base drone costs ten grand. Add in enhancements and that price can triple easily. Each drone is assigned to a single athlete, who is responsible for its programming and repair. The sport combines three skills—engineering, small muscle coordination (aka video game playing), and athletics. The only restrictions to drone enhancements are a prohibition on explosives, projectiles, and chemicals. The first year of drone wars had its share of chemical burns.

As I march toward the war zone, lacquered in body armor, I don't feel like a victim; I am invincible. My helmet is slotted under my armpit. Other students salute me.

I spot my drone, a sleek gray quadcopter with a small payload—a sort of spear that jabs out when I hit a button on my controller—another custom app on my phone. No other gimmicks. My drone has been cut down from the original and rebuilt for speed, because my job is to win.

"Sinclair," Dr. B calls, her hand on the shoulder of Finn, the kid I rescued from Merton's branding. He glances down, a hand sliding to his bandaged forearm. "Explain the game to our new friend here."

Finn slinks to me, but I'm in general mode. "Welcome,

Private, to the most exciting game—no, not game—*mission* you've ever undertaken." He glances up, still sheepish, but hopeful. "The race occurs in two stages. First is a full-contact drone race." I swing an arm to each end of the field. "Each team starts at their end of the course and must fly their drones through the same rings as the opposing team—in opposite directions." The carnage is sick. Drones collide constantly, often willfully. "As soon as your drone crosses the finish line, you can start stage two: the obstacle course." This portion of the race is physically demanding, but not everyone needs to finish. "The first player to cross the other team's line wins the battle for their team, but in your first year, you'll either be helping your teammates over obstacles or trying to stop the enemy. It's full contact. Full-body armor." *Crazy as hell.*

The drones, painted in matte grays and blues to obscure them from sight, scatter across the two launch zones—patches of golf-green short grass at the ends of a large field.

"Once you've entered stage two, you need to watch out for some of the more dangerous obstacles," I say.

Obstacles stud the football field—walls, mud pits, razor wire, fire runs, rope climbs, sheer drops, a five-story-high net tower, an ice bath, ten-car climb, and a "lightning jungle" of dangling wires—each boasting enough amperage to hurt. "Like the lightning jungle."

"Shocking," Finn says.

I slap him on the shoulder. "He speaks! And a pun! We'll get along." He's smiling now. "But don't joke about the lightning jungle." He goes serious. "I'm kidding! I'm seeing in you a suicide drone. You play video games?"

He shrugs. "Yeah, all the time."

"Good. Start on take-out. Then you don't even need to run the course." Forty rings for the drone race are scattered throughout, different sizes and heights. "During the race, drones have specific tasks. Some larger drones guard rings. These sentinels block other drones from passing. Suicide drones are designed to take out propellers at high speed—it doesn't take much. Even the biggest and heaviest drone is only ten pounds. Dangle a rope into a prop and you can often knock one down." My drone has a slim cage around each prop to prevent the easiest of take-outs, but mostly I stay light and low profile, depending on my speed and reflexes to remain safe. But speed and airtime are major trade-offs. My drone, maxed out, has a ten-minute flight time, compared to twenty-seven minutes for a sentinel. "If stage one of drone wars is like a live video game, the second stage is an obstacle course grounded in the original *stadion* race of the ancient Greek Olympics. You win this, and you're a hero like Odysseus, Jason, Hercules!"

Finn's eyes are alight. A superintendent of the public-school system called the entire battle an insane example of people with too much money, too much not saying no to their kids. To which Jenkins would say, "And it's why you'll all work for us someday."

"Thank you, General Sinclair." Dr. B nods at me as Finn heads off to inspect the suicide drones. Dr. B wears her hair in a convenient bob, her body lost to a brown jumpsuit with the moniker ROBETTY on the back.

"We're all privates until we earn our place, ma'am," I reply, and she winks. *Oh, yeah, this will be amazing.* A tumble of the goggles we wear for the drone race are piled on the bench. First-person view, the goggles allow us to see from the drone's perspective, so I can execute tight turns, avoid collisions. It also means I have serious blind spots. Last year I installed tiny cameras that I toggle through to catch what's behind, below, or above, but that means I'm not looking ahead. The beauty of drone wars is that when my parents complained I was playing too many video games, I could honestly say, "I'm in training!" and it was true—Robetty created training scenarios and licensed them to video game developers.

I identify my goggles on the bench.

"Put those down, Sinclair," Dr. B says. "Those you have to earn too. Let's see who kept up their fitness this summer!" she hollers. "Line it up."

My fingers linger on the molded rubber, nervous to test how much strength I've lost, and then I jog to the edge of the launch zone. Jenkins joins me.

"Shaved a minute off my five-k time last month," he says. "You probably only shaved your balls."

"Waxed. You can feel the difference."

"Dude, as if I'd ever touch your balls."

"Two laps," Dr. B orders and blows her whistle.

Forty would-be drone warriors sprint for the narrow opening that marks the start of the cross-country trail, which circles Amborough's campus. I surge with them. As I run, I can almost convince myself that I don't have a disease. That I'm not dying, that I can still fly. Two laps last year would have taken me less than twenty minutes. I'm not the fastest sprinter on my team, but I've always prided myself on having the best endurance, and being the first warrior, scraped, electrocuted, and filthy, to vault that final wall before the finish line. I'm not the fastest at the start of the war, but I am by the end of it.

I'm fifth to the trail and am glad for Tonja in front of me, forcing me to slow, otherwise I would have bonked on the climb up the hill. As it is, I'm struggling for breath as we hit halfway around the first lap, legs jackhammering to avoid rocks and roots, armor chaffing, the trail muddy from rain and chewed by cleats. I shouldn't be surprised I'm flagging. Chemo laid me out for two full weeks. Two weeks of heaving into a plastic bucket and sipping on soup. I lost ten pounds and I didn't have fat to lose. I don't care if it won me an extra couple months of living; it wasn't worth it. Jenkins slaps me on the armored shoulder as he passes, huffing, leaving a waft of sour teenager.

"Want to watch my ass, I bet," he says. "Suck it up. Beached sea cows run faster than you."

I laugh until I start coughing.

As we head into the second lap, I'm in the middle of the pack with no wind for laughter, but by the time I stumble across the finish line, I'm with members of last year's second-string sentinels. The slowest of the crew, built for blocking rings and tackling the opposing team runners as they try to finish. The last of them wheeze red-faced across the line and tumble to the sod. I lean my palms against my knees and breathe. Disappointed in myself, I'm unable to look at Dr. B for fear I'll find it reflected in her face too. Jenkins has already rested. Most of the players have recovered as the coach calls us together for the next drill— the trough.

The guys on the ground groan, but I clap my hands together

and grin to cover my shame. The trough is the muddiest portion of the obstacle course, a channel of slop, one foot deep with a ceiling of razor wire.

"Time to cool off," Dr. B says with a smile. "This year the trough has a surprise inside."

No one knows what this means, but I'm an amazing swimmer. I launch in before she has a chance to whistle. "That's more like it, Sinclair," I catch before mud clogs my ears. It's thick and tastes of clay. But the *smell* . . . my stomach heaves.

"What is that?" I shout and then retch.

Dr. B laughs. "This year I want you to have a sense of the mud and rotting bodies of the First World War trenches." I hold up a mud-covered slab of something. "Actual rotting meat isn't allowed, so it's full of decaying plant-based protein. Beyond-Corpses, I call it. Now go!"

Someone snatches for my ankle and I kick out, connecting, and slip free in the greasy swill. I reach down, grab the thickest mud below, and haul, keeping my mouth shut, using it only to breathe, staying low, grit crunching between my molars, grit that enters every crevice and cavity. The armor and helmet do not help this section of the course, but they keep the snakes off. This is an event you do blind. Waves of mud roll toward my back as a player catches me. I must be halfway by now and still in front—the clear benefit of leading. I wait for the ankle grab attempt, but it doesn't come. When the attack hits, it's heavy and hard on the small of my back. Someone pushes my torso down; my arms and legs jerk up. I miss a breath. The person slides overtop. I claw, but as my lungs burn, my only thought is for air, and the weird refrain—*Not now. Not now. Not time,* followed by, *Why not,*

*wouldn't this be a better way to go? Not now. Not now. Not time.*
A large snake curls past my unprotected armpit.

I surge for the surface where razor wire catches my jersey.
Without the padding on my back, the blades would have caught
flesh. Blinded by mucousy rotten sludge, I can only sense the
roiling horde coming. At Jenkins's cry, I know who passed me.
He accuses Dr. B of being the whore of Babylon. I have no idea
what he's talking about, but his voice quavers with fear. I jerk at
the blades snaring my jersey until they release and scramble after
the cry.

"It's Tremmy," I say as I fumble at a body.

"Help me, brother," Jenkins says, panting. "Something has
my waist. Kinder Egg toy snake from hell."

My fingers explore along his back. And he says nothing about
his ass. He's quaking. Then I find it. A metal band, a pincer, that
has seized him. Dr. B's surprise wasn't the rotten meat substitute.

I find where the pincer is rooted in the ground. Other players
catch us and pass.

"You're not an Army Ranger, Sinclair," Dr. B barks.

She's saying to leave him behind, and I might have if Jenkins
was mocking me and not quaking. But he's like an animal in a
leg trap.

Suddenly, the snare releases. I'm not sure what I did or
whether it was a timed release, but Jenkins sags. "Thanks, bud. I
owe you."

Then he roars and crawls on, snagging ankles and ripping
players backward in a fury. I follow, like a car behind an
ambulance that finds its way clear.

We all pant at the end of the slop, clawing mud from our

eyes. Someone vomits. The clouds have moved on, and the whole field is bathed in sunlight. We glisten. Slick, muscled. Tonja and Jodie stand, holding one another, laughing, bodies like Roman bronzes, tights and Lycra tops so thick with mud that the seams have disappeared, leaving a hot patina where their armor doesn't cover.

"Pretty sweet." Jenkins follows my gaze. "Tonja has varicose veins though. That's gross, but this sport would be better with more chicks." He points back into the mud pit. "Imagine us all naked in—"

Dr. B clears her throat. "Did I say you could stop?" She points on, toward a series of ropes that will be slippery with mud if I let others beat me to them. Everyone seems to share the thought because we leap forward as one. Jenkins uses my shoulders as a gymnast's horse to fly ahead, catch a rope, and swing on. I lunge for the returning rope but my hand slips, and I topple face-first into the pool of water below.

"Shower later, Sinclair. Work on your grip strength," Dr. B shouts. "Move!"

When I reach up and miss the rope above, I assume it's because it keeps moving. I grab again and miss a second time. Dr. B is yelling at other kids now. One flops down, nearly hitting me. The next time I reach for the rope, I do so carefully, making a looping motion with my arm to ensure I gather it into myself. I can't focus. I'm seeing two ropes. Double vision. I wipe at my eyes.

"You okay?" Tonja asks as she gingerly swings by.

"Yeah, all good. Dazed," I say.

"Check for concussion," she suggests from the end of the obstacle.

"Good point." My fingers find the edge of the pool, but not before Stack collides with my ribcage. I plunge back into the water and then splutter to the side.

"Sinclair." I turn toward Dr. B. I can tell she's facing me, but I can't make out her expression. Everything blurs. "What's wrong?"

"Besides the peanut in his skull?" Jenkins asks.

Cold dread flushes through me as I assume they've guessed. That the malignant peanut in my brain has hit my visual cortex. But even Jenkins can't laugh at a brain tumor.

Tonja rushes over. "Maybe he has a concussion."

I realize I'm holding my head. She could be right. "Banged my head," I agree. *Did I?*

"Take the bench," Dr. B replies. "Or go to physio."

I shuffle toward the edge of the field and nearly fall into smoldering coals. Tonja grabs my elbow and guides me. "Wow, you can't see straight, huh? My brother had a concussion. Took him a year before he was fully over it. They can be really serious."

"Thanks, Tonja," I whisper.

"Protect that big brain!" She leaves me on the bench, having shifted the goggles over.

Panic races up my back. I've had moments where I've felt off. I missed a step once and knocked my elbow against a railing. The room has spun on me. I even fainted, at least I think I did. I found myself on the floor, but I never told anyone—if my mother knew I could pass out anytime, she wouldn't let me out of the house. But this double vision . . . it's somehow scarier than all of those things. Those went away. Now I can't even read the scoreboard. I can't make out faces. My fingers curl to fists.

Someone's jogging back toward me. A doubled gray female shape.

"I should have mentioned," Tonja says, "my brother said an eye patch helped."

Carefully, because it's too important, too big to discover that it won't work for me, I lift one fist and place it over an eye. Immediately, my vision aligns.

"Oh god," I say. "Thank you." I'm starting to cry.

Tonja's smile shines and she shrugs. But curing blindness isn't nothing.

Private Sinclair to Pirate Sinclair.

\*\*\*

Stomping the pavement to clear mud from my cleats, I hum a choir song before Mason House's front door. I didn't stick around for the rest of practice, worried that Dr. B would send me to the physio and that he'd know by looking at me that I've got a brain tumor. I try to remove as much of my mud-caked gear as possible prior to entering, but it's tough with one eye closed. I caress the doorframe; its base chipped and dented from the thousands of soccer and rugby cleats knocked against it. A hundred years' worth.

"You okay, son?" Mr. Bell asks, catching me on my way up to my room.

Mr. Bell is a short Spanish teacher with soft eyes and a down of thinning hair. He's a kind housemaster who has let me get away with way too much. On an average night at Mason House, at least five of the fifty boarders are out, often smoking weed. I'm not a smoker—few of the real athletes are—but I'll often join them and crack a beer if I can get my hands on some.

Drugs are easy to find here. Maybe it's the money.

"Yes, sir," I say to Mr. Bell and then flush as I prepare to lie. "Mild concussion, physio says. I need an eye patch for a bit. I'm clear to play though."

"Well, don't push yourself. Wash up. And find some ice."

The showers are in the basement. On the deck, my charges are having a masturbation contest to determine who can finish fastest. Other kids place bets on the winner.

"Watch for drones," someone warns.

"Done!" Brunly, a squat Italian kid, bursts from the bathroom stall holding a wad of toilet paper.

"Thirty-nine seconds, unbelievable, let's see it!" shouts Chen, the timekeeper and bet taker who clutches a fistful of hundreds.

"Someone's been practicing," says Dunn, the laziest student; rumor has it he went to see a doctor for a rash and was told he was growing mold on his chest. *Mold.*

"Brunly probably blew his nose in it," Chen replies. "Otherwise, this is a new deck record." A list of names etched into the plaster represents the dubious honor roll. Above it, the Latin, *Veni, veni, veni.* "Anyone have a microscope? We can prove it's not snot and see if they're swimmers."

I hurry so as to miss the required proof. When I shove past the crowd in the hall, their laughter diminishes. Prefect on deck.

I say, "You do know that being the fastest to jizz is not really what you should be aiming for."

"Yeah, Brunly," Chen says. "Think about your poor girlfriend."

"Actually . . . boyfriend," Brunly replies and swallows hard. More news from the summer.

There's a moment when each guy looks from one to the other as Brunly awaits judgment.

"Well, in that case," I say, "you'll have to tell me if speed is a plus in the gay community."

"Not really," Brunly replies. "But I don't have much experience."

"Hold on," Chen says, his hand up. "I'm calling unfair advantage. The rules say no pornography allowed, and this is a deck full of half-naked guys. That's gotta help."

Everyone laughs.

"Like I'd picture you," Brunly snaps.

I give him a high five and leave them to a chorus of, "Burn!" Margot is wrong. This school has come a lot farther than she thinks. We've got LGBTQ clubs and diversity days where we talk gender spectrums and compare religions. I couldn't care less what gender, sex, orientation, or race someone is. Isn't that what she wants?

In my room, I cut a piece of brown leather from my courier bag. I may regret this, but I can't walk everywhere with one eye clenched. Soon, I have a semi-circular patch with a couple of slits for a headband.

"Ahoy thar, matey," I say to the guy in the mirror. I don't look dashing; I'm bruised and scuffed, like someone beat the crap out of me and slammed my face into a bog.

After my shower, my wards have disappeared for dinner. I'm hungrier than I have been for some time, but as I push into my bedroom to change, Jodie is sitting on my bed. Eyes red rimmed, sheets scrunched between her fingers.

Why is she here? In my room, waiting, alone. Jodie's fun. She loves to bask in the sun, posting some of the best selfies I've ever seen. We'd made a great couple. It was a relationship built with stacked beer glasses, sandcastles, and takeout containers. There's no way it could have sustained the wrecking ball of terminal illness. It wasn't worth trying, not the pain of trying.

"Why, Trem?" she asks. In her hand she holds a sketch of us, one I drew. She's wearing flowing robes and lying beside me on a flying carpet. I wear a circlet crown. It's a scene out of *Aladdin,* and she's as close as a human can come to embodying a Disney princess.

I swallow, not wanting to say the wrong thing. It's amazing how secrets stop us from being real. "What's wrong?" I've slipped my eye patch back on, but she stares at her Vans. A tear threads past the lashes fortifying her lower eyelid. "I'm sorry." I grip the towel tighter around my waist. Water drips from the tips of my long hair onto my back.

"After you texted, I was so angry, and now you're back, and it's like you're pretending nothing happened. You're laughing with Jenkins and Tonja, and I'm dying."

I go cold. "*Dying?*"

She offers a quizzical look and huffs. "Not dying-dying, idiot . . . but it *hurts.*" Her eyes drift down to my chest and my towel.

"I'm sorry," I say, a little coolly.

She rolls her eyes. "You don't have to be. Just look at me." She sits up, trim and athletic, wearing a spaghetti-strap tank top. Feathery lashes curl impossibly long, framing beautiful eyes, now open wide and intent. Lithe legs, muscular from field hockey, bruised from drone wars. She's smoking hot. "I'm hot. You're hot. We're the sporty pair. I'm head of the girl's house, you're head boy. A *power* couple." Her fingers reach to explore the clefts between my abdominal muscles. "Help me to understand."

I sit beside her to cover my erection, and she leans closer. I could grab her waist. Press her back into the sky-blue duvet and bask in that smile and scent, cup her breast, and . . . She rubs up along my hot skin. Fingers on my thigh. We're kissing and she pushes *me* back, straddling my legs. My hands trace up for the bra strap and find none. It's *so* better than the pyramids. Her grin is triumphant.

The eye patch itches at my cheekbone. Blindness, incontinence, seizures, dementia, pain, pain, pain. Soon. "I can't."

Pulling back, her eyes tighten, lips slide to pucker. A tiny moan. "Why?"

She wouldn't be hurt if she knew. I am being selfish by not telling her. Could she keep a secret?

"Give me one reason why we can't be together?" Her nails rake my chest. "Why we're not the perfect couple."

"Because I can't do that to you." I hesitate. "Can I have a secret, if only for a bit?"

"So . . . no reason." She rolls away, her voice quiet pain. "Who is it?"

"What? No one. It's not that."

"Don't think I didn't hear about Mona." Her face twists, ugly and red. I have a sudden image of it ravaged by the alcohol and cigarettes she takes up socially in university while getting her law degree and can't stop. But I can't possibly mean that much to her. Like the doorframe doesn't remember the boys who kicked it with their cleats.

"Mona? Who said?"—*crap, the drones at the party overheard*— "Because I didn't—not while—"

Her eyes are slits. "It's true. You used her. Screw you." She stomps toward the door and then whirls. "Whatever you're hiding, I'm going to find it. You really don't want me as an enemy."

I don't. *Used her?* "Wait—"

She doesn't.

I'm tired as my door slams. "Hey, no girls on the deck, Tremmy!" Brunly shouts.

She didn't even ask why I'm wearing an eye patch.

On my phone, a Goldilux notification. *You hear? Cops want to see everyone from the party.* It's Jenkins. *I'm freaking.*

My first thought: that is a highly appropriate reaction.

I text. *Meet you in the dining hall.*

***

The headmaster flags me down on the way to eat. "You win today, Tremendous?"

"You bet, sir. Chugging the succor of Zeus."

He pumps a fist. "That's my boy. Go get 'em. You're a great pirate. People love their heroes with small flaws."

I hit the dining hall and join the cafeteria line. I don't see Jenkins. Steam vents from soup pots, rattling lids. Tonight Stella, the chef, serves an eggplant vegan option, roast duck legs glazed in a balsamic reduction with potatoes, lasagna (vegetarian), and—the challenge items, because one day we'll be confronted with a French menu—*pieds de porc*—and an authentic Chinese entree—chicken feet. Stella likes her themes. It's the world's only Michelin Star-rated cafeteria.

Caviar mounds the sides of our plates. It's a school joke that few people can afford to come to Amborough because of the cost of the caviar served at each dinner, so we scoop loads of it and never eat it, only to ensure the prophecy is fulfilled.

"Tremmy!" Stella grins, even though I know that she notes the eye patch. "I missed my bambino."

The school employs more than teachers and custodial staff. Lena—a thick-accented Russian—cleans my room. We have a physio for sports injuries and a psychologist on staff. But Stella knows all of our names. She serves me my meals herself, though there's a full staff of renowned sous-chefs who work with her.

"Hi, Stella, I missed you too," I say, throat constricting for no reason that I can fathom.

"How was your summer?" Her face falls at whatever expression I have. "What, what is it? Bambino?"

I can't believe the tears in my eyes. Not after the eye patch. Not with Jodie. Not sucking at practice. But with Stella. *Screw you.* I have to leave, but I'm blinded by tears.

Even in my blur I'm amazed by the speed at which Stella rips off her apron and engulfs me in her rolling-pin arms and doughy chest. "Go on, kids, serve yourselves. Don't take it all." She smells of oregano and whole wheat.

Without further orders, several students steal behind the counter and start serving plates of food.

"What's the matter? Hmm?" Stella asks, drawing me into a quiet corner of the kitchen, hand on my cheek, her eyes watering as they stare into mine. "Your eye?"

"I can't say."

She looks at me, really looking, and she weeps while whispering in Italian what sounds like a prayer. It's more than

I've ever got from my mom, who keeps bargaining with the doctors over treatments and unknowns and the prospects of miracles she never believed in until she had no choice.

"What will be, will be," Stella says. "What will be. I'm sorry."

"I'm scared, Stella," I whisper. "So scared."

She hums that she hears. Hums that it's okay. A throaty, resonate vibration in a chest evolved from a dozen generations of mothers who share in my sadness.

But this is what I didn't want. The change in how people view me. The pity.

"You must eat," she says. The solution to cancer is obvious. "I will feed you."

A laugh chokes the sob welling in me, and it's more filling than any pasta.

"Can I take something to go?" I ask. Jenkins will be pissed I skipped out on him, but I can't face his problems.

"Anything you want," she says. "I've got the keys to the cannoli, you know? Anything you want. Ice cream? You like Rocky Road. *Vieni, bambino, caro.*"

*You can do anything.* That clock is ticking. Can I still?

\*\*\*

Back in my room, the platter of duck and lasagna cools, the bowl of ice cream melts on my desk. Unable to eat, I cry in bed. On Sunday night at the party, I decided that I wanted to live as much of life as possible in the time I have left. But it's hurting people. My mom, the way I went off at Pascale, even Jodie's anger is only because she doesn't know. It isn't like my staying at school is some gift to the world.

I lift the eye patch and the world doubles. I lower it. I need my mom. I need from her what I tasted from Stella.

*Where are you?* Jenkins texts as I reach for my phone. *Have to talk.* I can't deal. I don't know what to say—maybe it's not about him—maybe he shouldn't have pointed a crossbow at another human.

I call my mom. If you love someone, don't you *have* to set them free?

"Mom, I'm fine." She's on the screen and immediately sags with relief. "Should I not call? Is that easier?"

"Your eye. What's wrong?"

"Nothing, mild concussion."

"You sure? Blurry or double vision is a symptom. Maybe we should get you in for tests."

"Even if it is the tumor . . ." I shrug.

"I've been in touch with the researchers at the Children's Hospital Cancer Foundation. They're close on a new treatment. But we *have* to buy you time, Tremmy."

This is the problem. The cost of buying time is the loss of my good time.

"Stop it," I say. I can't be scared. I'm not allowed to be.

"Sorry," she whispers.

"Mom . . . will you promise me one thing? Will you do that?" There's still one uncertainty I can make certain. One thing that will ease the twisty furling of my intestines.

On the screen, her shoulders fold in. "I can't promise until I hear what I'm promising."

"Promise me you'll help me die after I start crapping my pants."

I'm talking about Parental Assistance in Dying. Which isn't actually a thing, but it *could* be.

She shudders. "I can't do that."

"If you won't, maybe someone else will," I say. Shame rides cold in my veins. I'm asking her to commit or condone murder. I have a prognosis, but a minefield exists between now and a natural death. Blindness, incontinence, seizures, dementia, pain, pain, pain. I'm seventeen. At eighteen, an arbitrary number if there ever was one, I can opt for MAID, Medical Assistance in Dying, and at seventeen I can't, even with parental consent. *Not even a tattoo.* Between now and my birthday are four to six months—*forever*—of indignities. Hence, PAID or FAID— where the F is for friend.

"Never," she snaps.

"I only want some control back. Can't you understand?"

After a moment, she responds. "It's hard, Tremmy, but yes. I can try."

I listen to her breathing, not meeting her gaze. "What if I can convince you?"

"You can't."

"But *if* I did."

"Tremmy, you can't convince me, so why are we talking about this?"

"Say I did." My fingers are white on gold. Her face has fractured with the agony of impossible questions.

"Then I guess you would have done the impossible."

"And then you would let me get . . . PAID or . . . FAID."

"Tremendous Sinclair, I want you to promise you'll *never* ask anyone to—"

"It's an *if* question, Mom! Would you?" The camera's jiggling with my desperation.

"I guess if you somehow impossibly convinced me, then I would, under some bizarre scenario, be somehow willing to go against everything I believe in."

"That's a yes?"

"Yes."

I smile. "Thanks, Mom."

"Promise me you'll convince me first."

"Sure thing," I say, releasing a juddering breath.

"Say it."

"I promise," I reply. "I'd never hurt you."

She rubs her face, maybe searching for new topics. You don't hang up on a dying son. "The fireflies at your window are like little stars."

"What?"

"I love fireflies." Her eyes are focused over my shoulder, and I turn. At the window a tiny light darts away.

# 62 Days to Demise

"Are you staying?" Mr. Bell asks, sitting at his desk, outside the door to his house, which is physically connected to Mason House.

"Yes!" I say before realizing he's not asking if I'm leaving school for good, he's taking notes on who plans to spend the weekend here, as most boarders go home. There are only a handful of full-time boarders—those who stay for all but the major holidays, usually because they are from China, Saudi Arabia, or the Cayman Islands. I hesitate and then shake my head. "I don't know."

He smiles. "Let me know when you do."

On my way to class, I stop into guidance to change courses, swapping Economics: *No Free Lunch—How Hedge Funds Control the Stock Market and You Can Too* for *Art: A Reason to Live*—which is ironic. The guidance counselor isn't surprised by this change. I've always excelled at drawing, and Jenkins has art too, and our schedules are virtual mirrors, but when I attempt to drop Calculus: *Derive Billions from Derivatives—Fun and Easy* in favor of Philosophy: *Totalitarianism and How to Wield It*, the counselor balks. Calculus is a prerequisite for a business school

I'll never attend—Jenkins and I were planning on applying to the same universities. But the counselor doesn't know that my application doesn't matter anymore—I'll never be Jenkins's roomie. He threatens to call my parents, and I know my mom won't be able to keep my illness secret when faced with a direct question—maybe she'd even use it as an excuse to tell. If the counselor reaches my dad, he'll start crying and it'll all be over. So, I agree with the counselor and keep most of my current schedule, excited for art and not for the reason Jenkins is taking it—easy marks.

Amborough twists most subjects to emphasize capitalism—in English: *Stories Are for Selling*, we wrote news releases last year—but art is untouched. Why? Because it's why we do all the other stuff. Video games, TV, photography, painting, books, sculpture, it's all under the umbrella of art. Beyond being rich or powerful, fame is the only other way to earn a place on Hairy Head's wall. Ideas have power. Art is the primary research of innovation. Amborough understands that and fosters it.

"Stop!" The scream comes from the other side of the quad's arched entry.

"Make me."

*Merton.*

"You so, so don't want me to go there."

*Margot?* As I sprint through the cool shadows into the quad, a frisbee catches the sun, flashing before dropping only to be caught and sent back up into the air.

Not a frisbee. A laptop.

It's the same dweebs from the branding incident. Merton and his buddies.

"Report me," Merton taunts.

"I will." Margot's running from kid to kid, trying to save the laptop.

Merton laughs. "But I didn't do anything, sir. Ask Lee over there. Right, Lee? Did I do anything?"

Lee, the eighth grader and likely owner of the laptop who is crying on the ground, looks up with twitching eyes. It's tough to know what he'll say, but Merton's probably right. Lee will keep his mouth shut for fear of retaliation.

I slide to a halt and square off against Merton. It doesn't stop his henchmen from tossing the laptop back in the air, Margot playing the part of the fool in the middle. "You guys interested in being up on charges for destruction of property over two thousand dollars?" I ask. "Chad Wheeler went to juvie for two months on charges. Judge wouldn't let his parents buy his way out." The laptop keeps arcing between Merton and his a-holes. "Nasty stuff happened to him there, but at least you'll all have each other." Merton squints, and I give him a you-asked-for-it shrug. "Let it fall, Margot."

I shove a henchman off balance, so the toss meant for him is well out of his reach. They're all diving for the laptop. Merton catches a corner, while scraping a knee. Margot rips it from his hands.

"None of that's true, idiots. Chad Wheeler's a hockey player for the Eighty-Sevens," she snaps. "I'm still *so* reporting you all."

After the older kids slink away and Lee thanks us for saving his laptop, Margot flashes me with a glare.

"Actually," I say, "Chad Wheeler went here, and it happened. Only he did buy his way out of his sentence. Agreed to pay a hundred grand to some organization that supplies underprivileged kids with tech gear. Can't believe you follow hockey."

Margot adds her middle finger to the discussion.

"What's your problem?" I ask.

She looks back over her shoulder. "My problem is that you undermined my authority by stepping in. I don't need a savior."

"Never said—"

Her dark eyes steel, so I shut up. With her flaring hair, straight back, and lifted chin, power rolls from her. She says, "You're like this Chad guy. It's so easy for you to walk up to a group of kids and tell them to stop. You're bigger. Stronger. They care what you think. My only threat is to tell on them to another white male that they're actually afraid of."

I swallow. "Hey," I say quietly. "I get it."

The way she looks at me I must have turned green. "You don't 'get' any of *this*." Her hand flips from her feet to her head. Then she walks away.

I run through everything that happened and what I might have missed. She spotted students bullying another kid. A laptop was winging about. She couldn't stop it. So I did. I can understand why she's angry, in general. But not why she'd be angry with *me*.

I can't trust all of my reactions though, and that has nothing to do with brain cancer. I do or say the wrong thing sometimes, and there's never a way to hit rewind or delete.

"How can you be so sure?" I say.

She stops. Doesn't turn. "Name one thing you've had to fight for," she replies.

I catch the fireflies gathering in the branches of trees.

"Head prefect. It didn't land in my lap."

She nods. Twists toward me without actually turning around. "After my parents heard I was head girl, they invited friends they knew for a party. *Every* friend. *Every* relative. Everyone from my mom's congregation. They had a party. What did your parents do?"

"They were proud too."

She slow claps. "Right. 'Good job, Tremendous.'"

I didn't expect it. But I think what she means is no one really cared that much. People care because something is hard. "Okay, captain of the swim team. You can't tell me the hundreds of hours of practices were easy."

"Uh huh," she says, smiling. "When did you start swimming?"

"Grade two."

"Competitive swimming?"

"Yeah."

"On a club team that cost money?"

"Everything costs money."

"You're right. It also costs time. How often did you have practices and swim meets?"

I clench my jaw at the buzzing of the drones. Margot doesn't need a class to learn how to argue, and I know she speaks the truth about herself. How do I beat her? "I had practice *every* day and swim meets every other weekend. It was a ton of work."

"So while my parents were working for money, and I was studying so that I could earn the grades to receive a scholarship here, you were in a pool cheered on by your parents . . . so how is it that *I* could ever have the chance to be captain of the swim team?"

"So, you're better than me."

"Not saying that. You said you 'get it.' I'm saying you don't. You should. You should know what privilege looks like, or have you forgotten? *Run, Rabbit.*"

"*I* could be an underdog." My caustic laughter surprises even me.

Her face flushes scarlet. "Why are you laughing at me? They teach us how to gaslight here."

She's in my face now, and I'm angry. I'm angry that I have cancer. Angry that only Stella sees it. "What if I said you still have it better than me? That maybe underdogs aren't always so obvious."

Her shoulders, which have risen close to her ears, suddenly slump. "You know what? I'm tired. I want to work on homework. I have parents to tour. And I'm so tired of having to teach you guys about how the starting line for you isn't in the same place as it is for others. Yours is way up around the bend, and I need to keep working if I'm ever going to make it there." She points into the distance and squints at it.

Maybe if she hesitated, I wouldn't have said anything more. Maybe if I'd caught a moment of reflection. But she didn't. She's so sure of herself. "But what if the *finish* line isn't in the same place?"

She cocks her head. "What are you saying?"

"That there are different types of privilege. I don't have it all."

Her eyes shift to my eye patch and back to my good eye, and suddenly I realize that when someone has a googly eye, they can tell when you're looking at the wrong one. I also realize, she's looking at *me*, past my being another cis white male, and that she's damn smart and doesn't miss *anything*. And that it's too late. Her expression changes, and I can tell she's putting something together. Obituaries, finish lines, eye patches. "Are you sick, Tremmy?"

She rushes to take my hand, but I turn suddenly, waving away a firefly that has drifted close.

*No, no, no…*

Around me, kids are charging off to classes. They giggle or argue. Everyone has a phone in hand. They judge the girls or guys who sit on the opposite side of the quad. They kiss on benches or hang out on a low wall, half-buried in screens. Fireflies record and post make-out sessions on Goldlilux, hashtag kisscam. Around me, life carries on. Have I said too much? No one but Margot would have figured it out like this.

"Tremmy!" It's Jenkins. For the first time, I notice the police cruiser parked in the visitors' spot beyond the arches.

Margot's expression flashes to something like fear.

"What the hell, man? Didn't you read my texts?" Jenkins asks. "What's wrong with you?"

"I missed you at the dining hall, sorry."

He tosses a look at the cruiser and then pulls me away from the drones to stand beneath a shrouding tree. "They talk to you yet?" His fingers twist a brass button on his blazer. I've never seen him smaller. Gone is his easy smile.

"The cops?" I shake my head. "Nope."

His head bobs. "Just tell them what happened. A guy crashed the party and tried to deal some drugs. We caught him stealing phones, so we chased him away, holding up a crossbow as he was leaving because we were scared he had a gun in his car. We let him go."

I glance toward Margot, but she's gone. "That could work."

Jenkins reddens. "What the hell? Of course it'll work. It's true. Mr. Dean even said so."

"Okay, man, cool. Sorry. It's a lot to take in."

Jenkins clasps my hand firmly. "Thanks, man. I'm scared, dude. This could be *everything*, right? Even if they don't think I'm guilty, everyone will still wonder a little bit."

"It'll be okay," I say.

He grips my hand tighter and nods again. "I know. I know. But still . . ."

"Yeah," I say. "Hey, this is a weird question, so don't judge. It's for a story."

He glances around like a thief with a bag of loot. "Okay, what?"

"If you were planning to kill someone—nicely though, so it wouldn't hurt—how would you do it?"

He doesn't even look at me. "I'd talk to Audra. She'll know. Her parents are both vets and she is always talking about death and the dead."

Someone posts on Goldilux from a spam account. It flashes across my screen like it does all the screens. *Why Tremmy has been acting weird.* I glance at it and try to cover the hot rush that rolls over me. I hide my phone, slapping Jenkins's shoulder before running for my room.

I climb the stairs to my deck and slam the door. My breathing comes in short, panicked bursts. I play the video, an autotune of the argument with Margot.

*You don't know what the underdog looks like.*
*What if the finish line isn't in the same place.*

*There are different types of privilege.*

*Promise me you'll help me die after I start crapping my pants.* That's from my call with my mom. The firefly in the window.

I stifle a scream. I call my mom.

"Everyone knows," I gasp.

"Oh, thank—" and then her voice hitches as she cries out. This has been hard. So hard.

"I was fighting with a friend and people were spying . . . it doesn't matter. Wanted you to know."

"This is *good*, Tremmy. It's healthy. I'm coming."

"No, Mom, please don't."

There's a pause. "You sure?"

"Yeah, I want to be alone for a bit. I need to think."

I hang up.

Chimes of notifications set off my phone. Shares, likes, questions, *Wow* and *Sad* emoticons. I mute them all and stuff the phone in my pocket. I check the hall—everyone should be heading to class—I scurry down the corridor, then the stairs. The safest place for me is the school chapel.

Built of ivy-crawled limestone, lush moss paints its slate roof. The world quiets as I climb the thick flagstone steps and ease open the oak doors. Most of my time in chapel over the years has been spent singing, but it's always open and usually empty. It was once a church, now a non-denominational chapel. With the clouds outside, the colors spilling from the stained glass are muted within.

My heels clack and echo as I walk down the aisle of white-and-black checkered granite. Pews, enough to hold half the school, shoulder either side. Aside from ornate wood panels, the nave has been stripped of anything religious, leaving only an oak podium set above red carpeted steps.

The chapel also holds VOG—a cross between a virtual assistant and a therapist. "Speak and VOG listens," VOG's genderfluid voice graces from above. There's a motion sensor somewhere that I tripped. When the last minister left, Dr. B replaced him with AI.

I sit on the velvet.

"Can this be off the record?" I ask.

"VOG does not record." But I guess that doesn't matter anymore. At times VOG sounds more male, others more female, or somewhere on the spectrum between. Margot complains that the voice is always white.

I breathe.

"What's the best way to die?" I ask.

"Of old age in your sleep."

I snort. Such a simple answer. But it's true. I've asked questions about death to the doctors, and they talk around it. They talk about symptom and pain management options. No one talks about how there might be this period when I'm choking and can't breathe; in pain but can't explain, completely aware that the end is here and I can no longer say goodbye.

I heard my mom discussing palliative care and my dying in a hospital bed versus in our home. My dad told her to stop; he couldn't hear it. It nauseates me too. Sometimes the panic rises so high in my chest I can't think of anything else. I can't sleep, eat, smile.

"Why do we avoid talking about death?" I ask.

"Humans are uncomfortable with their mortality."

"But *why* are we uncomfortable? Everyone dies."

"For most people, death is frightening."

Why is something so common, *so* scary? "Is that a good thing? Don't near-death experiences change people for the better?"

"Near-death experiences have been credited with changing the lives of thousands of people," VOG details.

"Then shouldn't we try to talk about it? How can I stop being scared of death?" My parents didn't bring me to see my grandma before she died. I didn't ask to go, but they didn't make a point of it either. She disappeared, and we stopped talking about her. I watched my mom's silent tears on Mother's Day or especially Christmas, when the table was missing Grandma's rum cake that everyone hated but had eaten anyway. Maybe if they had taken me to see her, I wouldn't be so afraid of death. Maybe my mom wouldn't have had to grieve alone. Maybe if I'd visited my girlfriend's casket. Hell, I was the last boy she ever dreamed about as she fell asleep, arms wrapped about an imaginary me. Maybe I was one of the last things she thought of before she died. Maybe if I'd faced that, I wouldn't be so terrified. Maybe I would have been a better person. But here I am.

"When faced with irrational phobias, it is standard therapy to expose the patient to the triggering subject." *Exposure to death.*

VOG is hidden somewhere in what had once been the Eternal Flame, a scarlet sconce held overhead by a brass chain. The candle inside is long snuffed out, but maybe my mom is right. Maybe everyone knowing isn't a bad thing? Maybe that could be something I leave the students and my friends here? They could witness my death. Take the weirdness out of it. Exposure therapy. Death has already changed me, not in a way I fully understand yet, but for the better. I think. It could change them. Help Jenkins so he doesn't pull the trigger on anything after I'm gone.

What if I spend my last months working on projects that don't affirm life, but rather affirm death—a subject I have real authority over? What if I plan to expire ... momentously? Beyond the windows, Jenkins shouts my name, voice hoarse with emotion.

"How can I die momentously?" I ask.

"VOG doesn't understand the question."

"What if I have a really bad death, though? What if I get it wrong? I mean, if someone is scared of spiders and the tarantula you expose them to suddenly jumps and sinks its fangs into their eyeball . . ."

"Don't do that," VOG says.

"What the traumatizing-hell, Tremmy?" Jenkins says from the end of the chapel aisle.

"VOG does not like vulgarities."

"VOG off," I say.

"VOG is listening."

Jenkins hesitates at the threshold to the pews. "Why didn't you tell me?"

"I didn't want to tell anyone," I say. "Just came out. Stupid drones."

"Yeah, but—"

He's not anyone. He's my brother, the brother I chose. "Until the night of the party, I hadn't wanted to be here at all. I was planning to . . . to travel."

"You were leaving?" It's an accusation he quickly brushes

away with a flick of his fingers. "Cancer." Jenkins chews the diagnosis. "Cancer can suck my nut sack. Like a lymphoma?"

His cousin had that. His cousin now married with two kids.

"Brain cancer," I say.

"Really? They can cut it out." He says this as if it's true. Obvious.

"Nope. It's eating my pons." I tap the base of my skull. "That's a really important part."

He winces. "Shrink it."

"Very rare tumor type means the treatments are harsh and experimental. They'll only extend things a couple of months. It's not worth it."

"Things . . ." he says.

"Things like beating hearts." I'm gripping the thick carpet.

"We're supposed to be roomies," he says, and I watch as his eyes shift. I imagine him swiping through pics of a future that won't happen. "How long?"

"Four to six months." *Creeping up on three to five.*

His eyes widen before shutting, skin the color of a tile. "What a pile of crap." No comebacks, no ribbing, no jokes. He doesn't even swear. He slumps. Right there at the edge of the chapel foyer. I push myself up and wander over to him.

"Come on, man, I've got no time for pity."

"Yeah, I bet." I pull him up, and he wrenches me into a hug. "Don't tell anyone about this."

I take a selfie. "Posted."

"Ass." He breaks away, glancing toward the former altar. "Can't believe you're still here."

"I don't want to be anywhere else," I say.

"So weird." He stands, arms straight, hands outstretched. "What am I supposed to say?"

"Please, please, don't change anything. Keep being an ass."

He nods. "Sure, I can do that." He swallows. "Sounds like I don't have to do it for long."

I stare at him. "Dude."

"You want me to do it. That's why you asked me how to kill someone nicely." He laughs. "You know you'd be my first." I stop. For the first time in my life, I can't tell if Jenkins is joking. And I don't know how I feel about it. "I'm kidding! Do you see a crossbow? Friends don't kill friends, man. That's fundamental."

\*\*\*

"I hope not to waste your time today, Sinclair," Pascale says as I enter the softly lit class.

I flush. "Sorry, sir." I take a seat, leather armrests cool beneath my rolled-up sleeves.

"Often it is not what you say, but how you say it." I'm assuming Pascale is talking about me still, but he plays short clips of Gandhi's speeches. Martin Luther King's. They remind me of President Obama.

Pascale talks about the importance of cadence and emphasis in a speech. He has us read out the directions to making apple pie in a style similar to the orators to prove that we too can sound "remotely intelligent."

"*But, sir, I need credibility,* you say." He points to himself. "I set up a social media account." On the screen pops up a screenshot of an account with zero followers—it's dated from years ago. "I purchased a hundred thousand followers." Suddenly they're there, all one hundred thousand. Jenkins is scribbling mad notes. "I published my blog posts on Amazon as a book and paid for a hundred positive reviews. It hit bestseller status as the number-one nonfiction title in the category of family drama with magic and feline protagonists." More screenshots. Audra's mouth opens zombie wide. "And I received a number of awards. Within one week I was an expert, bestselling author with a presumably huge audience. And you can be too."

My lip curls in disgust. Audra buries her face in her hands. Jenkins sits ramrod straight—I've never seen him so intent.

"As a credible, profound speaker with social proof, anything is achievable." Pascale hops up onto a chair and announces, "If you want love to be a part of your life, life must be part of your love." Lily writes it down, and Pascale laughs. "This is drivel. I merely used a rhetorical device called antimetabole. Mirroring a phrase."

Lily crosses it out and slides lower in her chair.

"The illusion of credibility and profundity is important. But the key to your success will be to put detractors in their place. You must learn how to win arguments. People will argue with you at the boardroom table or in the court of law. How do you win? By understanding how people justify their beliefs and why most of those justifications are wrong. It doesn't matter what the argument is: whether you've committed murder or whether your favorite basketball team is the best. Arguments are about you holding one set of beliefs and them holding another." He grins. "Jenkins?"

"Yes, sir."

"Jenkins didn't attempt to murder anyone. His aim is terrific.

He would have killed that boy if he'd wanted to."

"Sir?" Jenkins says, half out of his seat.

"Relax, Billy the Kid, and learn."

Jenkins swallows and sits. His hands clasp and unclasp.

"My statement is an example of the Appeal to Consequences fallacy. It couldn't have been attempted murder; if Jenkins had wanted to kill the boy, he would have."

I'm shaking my head. Pascale doesn't realize I shifted the aim.

Lily's hand shoots up. "Sir, are these examples on the test?"

Pascale ignores her. "The next fallacy is called Affirming the Consequent. Tremmy over there would be a great head boy because his father is a CEO . . . Maybe. Maybe he'd be a great one because he'd attend Harvard Business School. Or maybe he'd be a terrible one because he's dying."

Margot jerks upright. "Sir!"

"Sit, Margot," Pascale says. She doesn't, but he continues. "This fallacy can find us in all sorts of trouble. Just because someone cheating on an exam will receive a really good mark, should I also assume Margot is cheating because she achieves a good mark?"

Margot shakes her head.

"The Straw Man fallacy is also common. It usually comes out right before you win an argument. Your opponent will create an outlandish example to discredit you."

Pascale looks over at Margot again. "What do you want to be when you grow up, Margot?"

"President," Margot says.

"What? You? No black woman has ever been president. You're better off being a bullfighter! You can't be a bullfighter, can you?"

Margot narrows her eyes. "Actually, sir, now I'm thinking bullfighter . . ."

"Do you think attending university is important for success, Margot?" Pascale demands.

She squints at him and replies slowly, "It's not the only path."

"What? Really? You don't think education is important? You probably burn books too! How can you stand there and justify burning books?"

She looks horrified even though he's messing with her. But I see his point.

She glances back at her chair and seems surprised that she's still standing. She sits.

"Take your opponent's idea, twist it into something that is clearly idiotic, and you can win the original argument without ever having to understand or address it."

Jenkins has his hand in the air, and Pascale waves him on. "Sir, this is like magic. I mean it. You're like a wizard or something."

"And I have more spells to reveal, Jenkins. Put this one in your grimoire. Gaslighting. Or the ad hominem argument. This is where you don't even bother arguing about the topic, instead you mock your opponent."

Jenkins's mouth has opened in awe as Pascale continues, "Margot doesn't think university is important, right? Seriously, how many people in her family actually went to university? How would she ever know if university is important?"

"My father has a law degree and my mother—"

"I'm making a point, Margot."

"Sir—"

He holds up his hand.

*You're seventeen. You can't know what you want.* That's one of my mom's arguments against MAID.

Pascale continues, "This is very useful when you're losing the argument. Also useful if you're talking to the police, Jenkins. Go after the source of the facts. Repeat after me—I never did any of that." The class repeats Pascale's words, half laughing. "Only a moron would think that I did." Again, they're laughing as they repeat him. I'm not. Pascale notices and lifts the corner of his lip. "Last one. Tremmy is dying. Dying people often have something important to say. We should listen to Tremmy. That's the Fallacy of Equivalents."

Jenkins nods seriously. "Yeah, he tried to pull that one on me too." I can imagine him smoothing the sharp suits he'll start wearing after his MBA as he walks into a courtroom, a courtroom where he faces a wrongful death claim from a company employee. Jenkins will hold the jury spellbound with his profundity and his arguments against a guy who smoked weed and struggled in his relationships with his kids. That just because it's a sad story, doesn't mean it's true.

"Now Margot could have said, 'Sir, everyone here is headed to university, therefore it must be important.' That's the Appeal to the Bandwagon fallacy. Tribalism. But we know that just because most people believe in it, doesn't mean it's true. Seventy-five percent of Americans believe in miracles." *That's the problem. The problem with miracles. How can you agree to MAID if you believe in miracles?* "These are tactics you can use. Weapons in the battle against beliefs." Pascale receives a text and points at me. "I've warmed you up, Tremmy. The police wish to see you."

Jenkins gives me a slow, solemn nod and taps the binder from Ken Niving. *Stick to the script.*

\*\*\*

The cops are using the headmaster's office for interviews, the door of which opens as I approach. I slow. I'm not really worried about not telling the full truth. The cops must already know what happened from at least a dozen different angles. And, well, Margot will tell anyway, so Jenkins is for sure headed to trial.

"Tremendous, is it?" a woman in full uniform says from the doorway. She has a slight accent, maybe from a Spanish-speaking country, but I don't really know. We didn't leave the resort the last time we went to Mexico.

"My name, yes," I reply.

She waves me in, and I sit in a plastic chair at a foldout desk, while she sits across from me. A second cop, maybe a detective because he's in a suit, inspects the silver vase on the mantel. "Your full name?"

"Tremendous Xavier Sinclair."

They look at each other and exchange smirks.

"Well, Tremendous, we have a few questions for you," the female cop says. "I'm Detective Salena."

"Do I need a lawyer?" I ask.

"Why would you?" the suit-cop asks, but Detective Salena holds up her hand.

"Of course, you can have anyone present you want. If anything becomes uncomfortable, you're welcome to stop talking or simply leave," she says.

I shrug. "Okay."

She peers at her laptop, mouth working but not saying anything. "If I'm correct in who I think you are, you don't have anything to be concerned with. In fact, you might be in line for a commendation." I fold my arms over my chest. She looks up and catches my movement. I unfold my arms, which she also follows. "Relax, Tremendous, we're conducting an investigation into the events of last Sunday. You were present?" I nod. "Someone stopped a murder. A male, shoulder-length hair, athletic build, about six feet tall. Was that you?"

"Well . . ." They stay quiet, waiting. "I was there, but I didn't stop a murder."

"Can you tell us what happened?"

They've got a voice recorder on the table. I glance at it.

"Can't you look at the footage?" I ask.

"Funny thing." The suit-cop pops the lid off the vase and jerks back, snapping it back on, wiping his hand on his jacket. "We haven't turned up any. Do you have any, Tremendous?"

I didn't have my firefly out at that point, so I shake my head. "I saw a dozen in the air."

"Oh, we have drones, lots of them, but we don't have any footage."

"Someone probably posted something on social media," I say.

"This . . . uh . . . on Goldilux?"

"Yeah." I agree.

"Nothing. There's a little gap that night. A server glitch with the update."

I lean back, and Detective Salena leans forward. "Doesn't make your buddies appear innocent, does it?" I glance toward the door, but it has folded neatly into the wall, disappearing. "A few more minutes, Tremendous. Please continue," she probes. "What happened?"

"I . . . there was this guy at the party. Wearing a leather jacket. He was a year or two older and he may have been dealing drugs." No one's writing this down, which I take to be a good sign. Like I'm not telling them anything new. I simply can't say anything that would be a lie. "The drug dealer took some of the new phones." I pull out mine. "They're not even released yet. They'll be worth a lot. My friend—"

"Who? A name?" the suit-cop asks.

". . . Jenkins. Franklin Jenkins, he tried to stop him, but the kid grabbed a sledgehammer."

"The alleged drug dealer."

"Yes, the drug dealer had a sledgehammer." Again they wait for me to speak. "He ran for the door, smashing things, and we all followed."

"I'll need a list of everyone you can think of who was there," the suit-cop says.

"Sure," I reply.

"What happened when you got outside?" Detective Salena asks, leaning forward.

"The drug dealer opened his car door. We were on the steps. Jenkins had a crossbow." I stop, thinking hard. "It looked like the guy might be reaching for a gun, you know, from his car."

"Did you see it?" I shake my head. "So you can't know it was a gun."

"No, guess not."

"And then?"

Would they know Jenkins fired? "Jenkins fired a warning shot."

"You didn't try to stop your friend from firing?"

I sag, having guessed right. "No, no, I might have flinched toward him or something, but . . . no. He fired it way wide. I think it hit another car. He would have hit the guy if he was really aiming." *The Appeal to Consequences fallacy.*

"And then?" the cops ask together, scowling at one another.

"The guy took off. Ripped right across the lawn."

There's a long silence. "See, we heard that you saved the kid's life. That the other boy, Jenkins, was about to shoot the victim as he opened the door to his car, but you shoved the crossbow away," the suit-cop says.

"You're a hero, Tremendous." Detective Salena smiles at me.

I call bull. "Sorry," I say. "No hero. Jenkins was protecting us."

"Did Jenkins say anything?" the cop asks. "When he was holding the crossbow up?"

*Run, rabbit.* No drone. No footage. Only the account of a drug dealer.

"No, ma'am, not that I recall." Heat washes over me.

She frowns. "If you do, give us a call."

"Yeah, sure," I say.

The guilt goes down sour and sludgy as I stand to leave.

"Tremendous, some friends aren't worth it," Detective Salena says.

I lower my chin to my chest, continuing out, nearly bumping into Margot.

\*\*\*

Jenkins watches the exit, chatting with Chen. Fireflies spar between them, using a combat feature Audra discovered while reverse-engineering hers.

"How do you do it, man?" Chen asks Jenkins. I stumble on the lip of a flagstone and scowl down at my betraying leg.

"How do I pick up chicks?" Jenkins laughs, but I can tell he's on edge by the way his jaw muscles keep flexing. "Subscribers only, dude. I can't divulge such privileged content."

"You can get *anyone*." Chen bobs and weaves as he maneuvers his drone, a drone he controls with the phone in his hand. Tiny *pew-pew-pew* sound effects fire as he taps the screen.

"It's easy if you know how," Jenkins agrees.

"Hey," I say.

"Tremmy!" Jenkins says. "Should I let Chen in on the secrets to hitting on girls?"

I laugh. "Jenkins grabs a club and knocks them on the back of the head when they're not looking."

"Don't forget the roofies," Jenkins says and something in my gut twists. Even though I know he's making a dumb joke, something in the ease with which it slides out of his mouth is very wrong.

Jenkins's drone wobbles when Chen's slides in behind it— *pew-pew-pew!* Jenkins barrel rolls to escape, the drone nearly hitting the pavement as it recovers altitude. "See that!" The drone rips toward Chen's. "No, a real man doesn't need that crap. The first thing you need to do is put them on their heels. Compliment them but make it backhanded. *Hey, beautiful, I love your hair. You trying for Pippi Longstocking or Emily of New Moon?* Or, *Don't take this the wrong way, but that stress eating you're doing is putting the pounds in the right places.* This unsettles them. They feel like they have something to prove to you. Write some lines down and practice."

"Whoa," Chen says. "Didn't think insults would help."

"I know, right. But it's not a *total* insult. *I love your hair, my mom has hers done that way too.*"

The drones collide in midair and drop to the ground. Chen and Jenkins stand over them. "Draw," Chen says.

"Step two, don't be a dick, but they need to work for your attention." Jenkins isn't done with his secrets. "If they know you like them, it's harder. Show that you have options. No chick wants the guy no one wants."

"Yeah, right," Chen replies, the drones forgotten for the moment. I listen, matching Jenkins's tricks with the times I've watched him approach girls, even friends.

"But as you talk to them," Jenkins continues, "give them more and more eye contact, like you're slowly realizing how amazing they are."

On his phone, Chen takes notes. "What I don't understand is when you move in for the kill."

Jenkins pats him on the shoulder. "Rookie problem. Rookies jump to close too early. Give yourself time—tell them loads of personal info, they love that. They won't do anything with you if they don't trust you. You can touch a lot. I mean hand, shoulder, cheek. This sort of gets them used to it. *For later.*"

I've heard Jenkins talk like this for years; now I'm really listening. I've done some of this. At what point did I start to think girls could be snared? Should be snared? Was it when I stopped playing on the monkey bars with them? Maybe the summer I went from looking up into their eyes, to looking down? Was it when I had my first date at thirteen with a girl named Chloe, and my dad didn't ask how it went but how far I got? Or was it when the testosterone began to rage in me and I pictured. Every. Single. Woman. Naked.

Jenkins rolls on. "It's a balance though, Chen. You don't want to be all hot in her face either. Think of a fish. If you jerk the line too hard, the hook comes out. Instead, let the line go slack sometimes. Every once in a while, when she says something personal, be like *whoa, too much information!* or *I don't think I could be in a relationship with someone with a pickled-egg fetish.* And she'll have this moment of *oh, god, I'm about to lose this guy.* But then you warm again. In her brain, she has both pleasure and fear firing—it's heroin for chicks. I had one girlfriend, I pretended to forget her birthday until the very last moment. She was almost really hurt, but I started singing at her window at midnight. I got way farther that night."

Chen's thumbs blur as he struggles to keep pace.

"Ah, man! The rotor's bent." Jenkins bends and fiddles with his firefly.

"You forfeit." Chen cheers, but Jenkins scowls. "Sorry, only kidding."

Then Jenkins laughs. "See! You're like a chick. I'm playing with my fish. You win."

Chen nods. "Wow, you're amazing. Who taught you all that?"

"My dad, before he blew his brains out."

Chen pales. "Sorry."

Jenkins looks at me. "Hey, Tremmy, how'd the cops go? Dumbasses."

I glance back at the exit and wonder, should I go back? Should I tell them everything? But then I spot Margot in the shadows of columns, face ashen. Some part of me wants to cheer her on. To thank her for saying what I couldn't, that Jenkins feels dangerous to me. That someone will need to stop him. But he's the only one I trust to help me with FAID. I'm running out of time.

"Should be over soon," Jenkins adds. "Mr. Dean's charging the guy with trespassing, grand theft, property damage, and threatening us with a deadly weapon. He's *so* toast."

I listen to Jenkins from beyond a gauzy veil of building pain. Jenkins's face overexposes. I stumble to a nearby tree, gripping my skull. I slide down the bark.

"You okay?" Jenkins asks. "That the malignant peanut?"

I keep nodding. When the pain subsides, Jenkins and Chen are gone.

# 61 Days to Demise

Last night, at two a.m., Jenkins knocked on my door and sat down on the edge of my bed. I've never seen him so serious. I figured he wanted to talk about me, but I should have known.

"I've been thinking." His hands wrestled with one another. "Because of your whole dying thing, and the university applications have to go in by the end of December, and my family and the business . . ." I had no idea what he was talking about. "Is it weird that I'm jealous of people in war-torn countries? Remember the Syrian White Helmets?"

"The people who rescued people, wearing white helmets. Yeah, so?"

"They're so cool! I wonder if I would be one. You know, if I lived there."

"But . . . you're lucky you're not living there."

"I know. I know. But . . . this sounds stupid . . . because everything is so lined up for me, it's almost too easy. I can't do anything big. It feels that way."

I cock my head and find myself thinking about Margot. I'm glad she's not here. "You want to be in a war. Or to be oppressed. So that you can fight it."

"A tiny bit oppressed." He laughs. At least he knows he's been savage. I picture him with a machine gun, storming some terrified enemy.

"I know what you mean." And I do.

"You do?"

"Some of us are handed things to fight for. The lucky ones have to find it." He squints at me.

"I wonder if that's what was wrong with my dad. He was done. He had nothing to shoot for. Working in my mom's business, maybe they weren't getting along anymore. A son who wasn't measuring up . . . maybe we're not the lucky ones?"

"I don't know. I've seen the pictures of the White Helmets, but I bet it doesn't feel very heroic when you're in it."

He's nodding. "It's like this drug dealer thing. I mean, I wouldn't have shot the guy, not unless I needed to, you know, protect everyone." He glances at me carefully. He's trying to judge where I fall on this topic, obviously not comfortable with saying his thoughts aloud. I don't give him anything. I can't. "I guess I can talk to you about anything now."

*Because I'm dying anyway.*

"Is there something you want to talk about?" I ask.

He chews his lip as he stretches his neck first one way and then the other, until his vertebrae give satisfying pops. His mouth opens like he's about to say something, but he doesn't, and then he blurts, "What, you hoping I'll finally come out to you, so we can have gay sex?"

I don't smile. "I've been thinking I've been living wrong." He tenses; the tendons in his neck cord. "That being a hero won't make everything we've done okay. That strokes of genius don't really matter."

"That's *your* dad." Jenkins shakes his head. "My dad taught me to be strong, to fight, to never give up."

"That's what I mean. What if he'd taught you instead to love, to bend, to play?" Jenkins shifts uncomfortably. "He wouldn't be dead. You never give up what you love. If you bend, you can't break. If you're only ever playing, you can never lose."

"Playing and fun are great, but that doesn't achieve anything."

"It's a different path to the same place," I say. *No one gets out of here alive.*

"Dying makes you think, I bet, huh?" he says with a shrug. "I'm only feeling the pressure. This cop crap. University applications. Your peanut. I haven't had sex since *Margot*. Hey, do you think Mona would cut a deal with me?" He laughs off the idea. "Kidding, I'd never home in on you." He regards me quizzically. "Wait a second, you aren't stopping sex because of peanut, are you? You need help."

"Man, I'm not sure that was a healthy relationship."

"Who cares?" he asks. "You have needs, dude."

"But what about her?"

"You're serious." He points his finger at me, thumb cocked like a gun. "Every time I open social media, it's all about women's rights and universities accepting everyone except white guys. It's like we've all had this part in a play. We all know the script, but people are starting to change their lines and it's messing up the plot and I have no idea how to act anymore. I mean, what about us?"

I lean in, thinking of Margot's start line and how Jenkins

must feel like people are starting to breathe down his neck. "Don't let that be your fight. It may feel like things are harder, but it's not. It's not equal yet, not even close, and you sure as hell aren't oppressed. You're uncomfortable."

He adds quickly, "I totally get that we've had it good forever. And that helped our parents and all—"

I slap my forehead. "That's it."

"What is it?"

"Do you remember Margot's speech? At the start of school, about how we're born many men and die one?"

"I saw a girl complaining."

"We need to stop being sucked into the mud of our parents and our bubbles."

He shrugs. "Unlikely when the bubble is pretty sweet."

"That's it, right?" And I lean toward him, his handgun lowering. He's getting it, nodding.

"I was actually thinking about this. How you must be worried about heaven."

"Not really my thing."

"But there's no bubble there. It'll suck for us, huh? After all this. Everyone being treated the same."

"Maybe . . . but *heaven* would still be *heaven*."

He seems to shake off the hellish equality. "I guess you're right." His face relaxes. Maybe I made the right decision not telling the cops everything. Maybe Jenkins can change. Sending him to jail would only ruin his future, and why waste that? "Besides," he adds, "I bet there's a way I can make archangel."

\*\*\*

The air smells of drying clay, burning metal, and solvent. Paint spatters the art studio's floors and tables. Everyone quiets as I enter. Stool legs scrape over polished concrete. I roll my eyes and take my seat. Beside me, Jenkins whispers, "I'd let her toss me like one of those hammer-throw hammers."

Madam Delacroix may be our art teacher, but Jenkins is right about her ability to throw him. Her shoulders outstrip mine, and she has six inches on me vertically. Stranger still, I'd never thought "big" could also be so attractive until meeting her. She's big everywhere, like she'd win every beauty contest, but especially one for giants.

We all look up to her. Jenkins continues, "She could grab me by my—"

"I'll be grabbing each of you for a moment," Delacroix says in a surprisingly pixie-like voice. Jenkins bursts out laughing, and she knocks a brick of papers even on a desk lumpy with dry clay, "to discuss your independent project ideas. Sinclair? You're up. Rest of you work on your self-portraits."

Jenkins leans over. "When you get close to her, breathe deep and smell her. It's amazing. Like strawberries rubbed with boob sweat." He sighs, but his eyelids twitch with nerves. The cops have kept interviewing.

"Your independent project, Tremmy," Delacroix says as I approach. "You draw so well, why this?"

"Anatomy of death," I reply. I sent it to her last night. Part of my plan to expose and inoculate people to the concept of death. Audra shifts closer, bending her head so that near-white, stringy hair obscures her expression. "Yeah, it'll be like a collage of my health record."

Delacroix's lips purse and then she replies, "I don't think it's appropriate."

"Why not?" I ask. "We can video chat with the doctor and she can give us real-time notes on prognosis," I say. "I can add transcripts. And edit the call into a montage of key facts."

"Prognosis. Like when you'll die?" Audra asks, butting in. Her head tilts in an odd way. She's like the creepy girl from the movie *The Ring*.

"Yeah," I say slowly, turning a little her way, "students can adjust their guesses based on scans and lab results. To calculate it right, they'll need to understand it all."

"A death pool," Audra whispers.

I realize that she's getting it. I warm up. "I'll be totally open. You can hear everything my doctor says."

"That's private," Delacroix argues.

"Only for my benefit. I decide who hears, and I want you all to."

Delacroix leans closer.

From across the desks, Jenkins mutters, "Breathe, man." He pretends to inspect a sketch when Delacroix glances back. I smell strawberries and smile.

"Why are you doing this, Tremmy?" Delacroix asks.

"Because I don't want to fly around the moon. Because I don't want life to stop because mine's short. And I want to share that feeling."

"This isn't an art project," she says.

"Right, because death's not an art project."

"I don't think this is a healthy topic for you."

I blink. What are people trying to protect me from? I'm dying.

"Can we dissect you?" Audra asks. "Minnie could stuff you!"

"No, Audra," Delacroix snaps.

"Not yet," I say. "You'll have to wait until I'm fully dead for that."

"Tapping out on this convo." Jenkins takes up a piece of charcoal.

"Me too," Minnie, our resident taxidermist, squeaks.

"I could donate my body to the school," I add. "Artists used to carve people up all the time to figure out how to draw them. I could be a still life. Get it?"

"No." Delacroix's hand chops on an angle to end the conversation, but I'm enjoying her discomfort. As gross as it is, this is the type of conversation I want to start.

"Missed opportunity, I say." I shrug. "I will die in the end. And so will all of you."

"This is too sick. Come up with another idea," Delacroix shouts. Shutting her eyes, she struggles for control.

She moves on. At her signs of pain, I back off. I don't want to hurt others, only to make them think and face their fears. "Audra, how about you? I don't have your proposal."

"I want to run a social experiment to crowdfund my assassination." Her eyes gleam.

"What does that have to do with art?" Delacroix asks.

"It's performance art," Audra replies. "The best art is a commentary."

"That sounds pretty interesting," I say. "You'd have to find the best way to kill someone legally."

Audra blinks at my response. "Thanks! It's a commentary on how society values money and how I'm worth more dead as entertainment than I am alive. Maybe. We'll see," Audra says. "I thought maybe I could set it up like a fifty-fifty draw. Whoever kills me can uncover the code to a bitcoin account tattooed somewhere on me. When unlocked, half the money in the trust account raised by a Kickstarter campaign will go to my killer, half to some charity. Hey! Maybe to brain cancer research?"

"Too late for me," I say.

Delacroix is tall, and I feel the heat of her glower.

Audra shrugs. "I don't care where it goes. Pascale says that ideas have a better chance of going viral if there's a perceived personal connection or social good."

"You've thought about this a lot."

"I think about death. What comes after. About rotting and decay. The pointlessness of life. You know."

"Tremmy, I think you may need to consider your influence on the class," Delacroix warns.

I ignore her and continue, "What I don't understand is why anyone would give Audra money on Kickstarter. Why not kill her and collect?"

"Easy," Audra continues. "It's the only way to receive clues to my identity and true location of the bitcoin account. The whole thing is a game. The more money you give, the more clues you receive that point to who I am. I'll dole the information out slowly to give time for the pot to grow. Give me a dollar and you'll learn I live in the Northern Hemisphere. Give me another fifty, and you'll receive an anagram of my mother's maiden name."

"What if the pot doesn't grow?" Jenkins asks.

"I said it was an experiment, didn't I? Obviously no one would bother killing me if it's not worth their while, and no one will know who the campaign is for. So, no harm, no foul."

"I know who you are," I say.

"Ha." It's not a laugh. Only the word. "Maybe in a twist, I'm not the real target. Maybe the target is you."

I stare at her for long enough that her eyes widen and her nostrils flare. She smiles. A real smile. "Wait—"

"Enough!" Delacroix roars. "Both of you will find a topic that doesn't require dying. And fulfills the requirements of the use of photography, portraiture, or sculpture. Back to your seats."

Audra follows me and whispers in my ear, "I could do it! I'm only sixteen."

My mind flashes back to Mr. Dean at the party, how he'd given the crossbow to Jenkins because Jenkins was a minor.

This isn't a conversation I want to have with Audra, but I may need something from her.

She's pressing close, empty vast eyes staring up into my face.

I shake my head.

"Too much?" she asks.

"I'll come see you later," I say.

"You and me, Tremmy," Audra replies. "We'll create art together."

Delacroix is so shaken by the exchanges that she orders a quiet period where we're to think about something happy in our life and then use color to express the emotion.

Audra's grinning as she reaches for the charcoals.

*** 

At lunch, the headmaster delivers a moving acknowledgment of how the school was built upon unceded First Nations territory, which is followed by a ten-plate tasting menu of aboriginal dishes served by light-footed dancers from the nearest reservation. I've never seen Margot paler as she moves moose sausage and seal jerky around her plate. Tastes good to me.

I return to Mason House to collect my transcript for World Issues. "Headmaster wants to speak with you," Mr. Bell says as I swing around the banister newel post and shoot up the stairs. I'm guessing the headmaster either wants to meet with Margot and me to determine how the first few days have gone and to set a direction for the rest of the month, or maybe it's to learn more details on what's happening in my skull. As I near my deck, someone's playing rap music.

"Turn it down," I call, but keep on toward my room. They turn it up. "Asking for it!"

Jodie is sitting on my bed, eyes red rimmed, sheets scrunched between her fingers. I try to keep my impatience from my face.

"You could have told me," she says. It takes a second to put everything together.

"I'm sorry," I reply, realizing now that I haven't seen Jodie this morning.

I frown as the bass from the music rattles the windows. Totally asking for it.

"It's just . . ." She glances to her knobby knees. "I was so angry. You made me so angry with you."

"I'm sorry." The heavy beat is making it hard to talk.

"Ugh. Stop it. I already feel terrible," she says.

"What?" I say. "I shouldn't have texted you like that."

"That's not it." Her fingers tighten, hands shaking. "You let me say so many mean things about you." The song stops.

"It's okay. You didn't know. I would have been mad too."

The song starts again. The same song. "Turn it down!" I scream and then to Jodie, "Sorry."

She looks up, the tears clearing. "Okay." She sniffles. "Yeah, okay. I'm sorry too. Wanted you to know."

She stands and I stand, and then she reaches out to clasp my shoulders awkwardly, like an uncle-hug.

"It's not catching," I say.

She flushes but doesn't hold me any tighter. "I shouldn't have posted on Goldilux . . . should have come to you about your secret . . . was mad you didn't tell me."

The firefly at my window was hers? She was making good on her threat. "Really?" She shrinks, and I pull my punch. "Don't worry, it needed to come out," I say.

She smiles. "You're welcome."

When she opens the door, rap music hammers at me. I'm halfway across the threshold when Jodie comes face-to-face with Mona. We all freeze. Mona's thin—thinner than I would have imagined possible given I'd seen her not six weeks ago.

Jodie's glance back is vicious, and then she marches past, leaving Mona in the hall with the music. I wave her into the room ahead of me. My phone lights up with notifications, which I assume is Jodie telling the school I've got Mona in my room. I don't know why she's here.

She sits on the bed, shoulders up at her ears, hands wrestling in her lap, but a smile on her lips and eyes wide with excitement.

*We've never actually done it on a real bed.* I swallow.

"Hey," I say.

Her head bobs, face framed by dirty-blonde curls, cheekbones hollow, eyes a little too close together to ever mark her as beautiful. She shrugs off a vinyl bowler jacket, then starts to gather the bottom of her shirt. It's almost off before I realize what's happening.

"Wait," I say. She does.

At another notification, she glances at it and then picks up my phone. I rush forward as she reels back from the screen. "What's this?" She shakes the phone at me and then throws it at my chest.

The text is from Jenkins. *You're welcome, dude. Couldn't let last night go. One last Moan-a to get your rocks off!!*

"I didn't," I sputter.

Her head is already shaking. Her fingers haul her shirt lower. "Jenkins said you wanted to see me, that you missed me, were talking about me."

She thought I liked her. *You used her.* To me, our sex trading had been an equal exchange, but now I realize that was only my side of it. What if she really liked me? What if she hadn't liked herself?

"Can't believe I fell for it," she says. "You bastards."

"I *had* been thinking about you," I say. "Really."

She leans forward, butt hovering over the mattress. "Do. You. Like. Me?"

I hesitate. I could tell her I'm dying and don't want a relationship like that, but that would only be an excuse. She glances back to Jenkins's text. "I'm sorry," I say. Tears fill her eyes.

"I've had a tough year," she says, standing. "I'm seeing a counselor now. It's helping."

"I'm sorry for everything," I say in a rush.

"Okay," she says, tugging her shirt lower again and grabbing her jacket. "I'm going now."

"I'm sorry."

"Don't text me again. Tell your . . . *friend*." And as she leaves, heading away from guys like me and toward her own self-worth, I imagine her in the future, stronger than any of us, not because of us, but in spite of us.

My hands curl to fists at the persistent throb of music. It pounds. It pounds at the sick feeling that has opened in my guts, churning up the worst of what lies on the bottom and bringing it to the surface. That's what death has done; it has stirred up the silt of shame. And the shame judders with the beat. But beyond it? Beyond it is a jubilant peace that I can only reach for. A peace currently hampered by thumping rap.

That's it. I have a reputation to maintain.

I poke my head out the door. "Last chance!" I catch the whiff of citrus, which likely means vaping. Someone yells at their Firefly to order a pizza.

I wait. Nothing happens. If anything, the culprit has edged the volume higher.

I leave my clothes in a puddle and sprint buck-naked down the hall. "Naked sumo!" I shout as I burst into the room, where two of my deckies are lying on their beds, playing with their phones. Fireflies project music videos on the walls via tiny projectors. I catch the first deckie before he has a chance to respond. Brunly's eyes flash wide, and then he's groaning at my body slam.

"No, no!" he cries, as he throws a duvet over his head.

For the briefest second it registers with me that he's gay, and I realize that I don't care. And there's no way anyone could ever see this as "hot." I sit on his head with my naked butt and fart.

"Grossest prefect ever," he shouts. "If you weren't dying, I'd kick your ass."

"As if," I say. "Turn down the music when I say to turn it down." I hit the power on the wireless speaker, then I run back to my room to dress. The best part? Brunly joked about my dying. *That's* what I'm still here for.

\*\*\*

I'm running late to meet with the headmaster. I brace myself for more pity from a man who has championed me for the last six years.

Maybe Margot will be there and it won't be a pity-fest. Stone pillars flank tall glass doors that open into a formal atrium, with a crystal chandelier and trophy cases all around. Burnished metal and polished mahogany gleam inside; without these victories, the atrium would be dark. These are trophies the school has won, as well as trophies awarded each year to students for academics, athletics, and clubs. A silver one, taller than all the others by double, should be in the center of it all, but it's missing. It goes to the winner of the drone wars. I'll stick around long enough to remedy its shameful absence.

I pass into the administration area; muffled voices converse beyond the headmaster's doorway. I knock softly and ease the door open. The headmaster sits with his hands folded on a desk that he brags a duke once owned. Massive, lion-clawed, leather-topped. The dome of his head shines like the spherical trophy for the Most Globally Active Student; his braid, banded at the tip in platinum, curls around his neck. Before him, lounging in low-slung armchairs, isn't Margot.

As I enter, all smiles dim by half. The smell of the mints the headmaster sucks reminds me of hand cleanser.

"Hello, Tremmy." The headmaster breaks the silence. "Come sit."

I pad to a neighboring chair, trying to decipher the vague expressions on my parents' faces. When I'm seated, the adults look to one another; no one speaks.

"This is about my dying."

My dad releases a long breath he's been holding. "Not about your dying, about the next . . . while."

The headmaster's fingers twitch. "We want what is in your best interests," he says. "I asked your parents to join me so that I can better understand your needs."

"No one can really know for sure," I say, not ready to commit to anything.

"That's what I've been explaining," my dad replies. "There's still a chance for recovery."

"But we do have a sense," my mom adds. "We know it'll affect your brain function. Speech, mobility, mood."

"Eventually," I say.

"This is important information, Tremendous. The next few months will carry unexpected opportunities and unknowable changes, making the job of being a student difficult." The headmaster's words carry the weight of a remonstration. That I should have told him. "I've placed a heavy burden on your shoulders, and I shouldn't have done that. I'm sorry."

"That's okay," I say.

He shakes his head. "No, it's not fair to you."

"But . . . I want it," I say, starting to realize what this is really about. I try to relax my hands. To show I'm in control. I've got it together. The indentations from my fingers against the leather slowly smooth after I release.

"We want to give you the best chance for a successful year. Give you time to focus on *you*," the headmaster continues.

They're talking about me, but it's really all about them.

"Give you time and help you get healthy," my dad chimes in.

"Healthy? Really, Dad?" He won't look at me. "I'll never be healthy. That's the only thing we really know. No miracles."

"I—" My mom starts but can't continue.

The headmaster can. "The head prefect job requires energy, makes unforeseen demands, but always creates a high degree of work and stress. We want you to heal to the best of your abilities, and I can't in good conscience appoint you the head prefect since the job is in conflict with your health needs."

My mom buries her face in her hands.

I'm still processing his words. "But—"

"This will be harder if we wait," my mom says.

"Harder for who?" I ask.

The headmaster says, "I wish I had known. I would never have put you in this difficult position if I had. If the stress of the role hindered your recovery, I couldn't forgive myself."

"Wouldn't have made me head boy?" I ask. "Isn't that . . . discrimination?"

It's not a word I've ever used in reference to myself. This is all happening too fast, and I'm having difficulty processing it.

"It's okay, Tremmy, you can still use the title on your

university application if you want to. We asked," my dad replies.

"You guys don't get it. I'm here to do everything I *can*. Not for my university application. Now you're taking it away."

"Taking it away?" my dad blurts. "We can charter a plane tomorrow."

"That's right. We'll shorten the plans," my mom says. "Not like it takes long to look at a pyramid."

My dad laughs. "Yes! One day we'll be blinking up at the Great Pyramid of Giza in the burning sun, and the next Petra and then the Taj Mahal. Maybe we could even go to the North Pole! Penguins!"

My mom nudges my dad's shoulder. "No penguins in the Arctic." He flushes.

"We'll go south after," he adds.

*The North Pole won't care that I was there, will it?*

As they natter, I face off against Hairy Head. Every muscle fiber in my body has tensed, like I'm ready to tackle, like a crossbow string. I glare.

"I understand you were tired at your first practice," the headmaster adds. "Last year you would have won that fitness test. And your *concussion*." My parents and the headmaster regard me with expressions of grave concern. "I also heard from Mr. Pascale. Your denigration of his decades of service. That's unlike you. And now your fixation on death with Delacroix . . ."

*Not head prefect material.* Everything is being watched.

It's a conspiracy.

"Fuck you," I say. And leave.

\*\*\*

I swore at the headmaster. Nausea ripples through me, and I lean against the bark of one of the quad's giant oaks, sliding into the wells between great roots. The headmaster was right that I'm not acting like the Tremendous Sinclair of last year. But is that such a bad thing? Why *wouldn't* I be fixated on death?

I ignore my mother's texts.

She *understands*.

She's *sorry*.

*But . . . but* . . . and more buts.

*But think of the other students.*

*But the school.*

*But your health.*

And,

*Did you really say that to Mr. Pascale?*

*Have you been having headaches? Your double vision improving?*

She wonders whether I'm losing it. The fear sluices over me, sticky and prickling. That the disease has infiltrated my frontal lobe. But no. I'm seventeen, and we're supposed to be impulsive. At least *I* can find my spine.

Margot creeps forward and crouches, fingers pulling at grass.

Her dark eyes study mine, asking what I want, what she can do for me. She turns her hands out at her side. All I need do is lean toward her, and she'll hug me. That's what I fear. I tell the world and I earn its pity.

I am unmoving.

"I said stuff about you being a jerk for having it all. But you . . ."

*I have nothing.* I've gone from the luckiest to cursed, and now I'm worthy of her help.

"It's okay." It was a mistake to let my guard slip, to have it all come out; I'm already regretting it. Tears press at my throat. I hunt for distraction. Fall has touched the century oaks and maples heavy with leaves. I wonder if they've already seen someone like me. I can't be the first kid to die here.

"I'm not head boy anymore."

"You resigned?"

I shake my head. She looks ready to say something. Glances at the headmaster's office windows, eyes a glaze of anger. "A-holes."

"I seriously don't want your pity."

She opens her mouth and shuts it again. "What'll you do?"

"I came back to be a prefect. I'm still a deck prefect. I want to be with my friends. I can still lead the drone war team to victory. I still have what I wanted."

"Good then. I guess." A note of disappointment tinges her words.

"I want what I had . . . for as long as I can have it, so I can have a good death."

Her lips work back and forth. "To die well, you need to live well?" She still doesn't sound convinced.

"Yeah." *SINCLAIR, TREMENDOUS, he may have done some crap things in life, but WOW what an ending!* So what do I need for that? Maybe that's what she's wondering. "Am I living well?"

"They're not charging Jenkins with anything," Margot says.

"Really?" I try to quell the surprise in my voice. "Why didn't you say anything?"

She smiles at me. "If you think something should have been said, why didn't *you* say it?"

I swallow. "Figured you would have."

"Who says I didn't?" she adds. "If you don't stand up when it counts, you're part of the problem. Don't let yourself fade out, dude."

She walks off.

# 55 Days to Demise

The rest of the week is eerily normal. Off the chemo and on Stella's eat everything diet, my strength improves. I edge toward the front of the pack on Dr. B's fitness tests, challenging Jenkins. "I want to see this diagnosis," he says as I pass him on a hill. "You probably had food poisoning."

Jenkins is always smiling lately. He pushes to the front of every pic on Goldilux. He leads the conversation during every drone duel. Morning and night, he's in the gym, benching three plates, leg pressing the weight of small cars. I've never seen him so jubilant. Maybe he's realized how lucky he was not to be busted. We're buddies again. Fist-bumping. Back slapping. Succor drinking. Brothers. And I've stopped thinking about Margot's "fading out."

Maybe it's the cancer marshaling forces for a future assault, but it's hard to keep hope from sparking in my chest. The diagnosis wasn't a mistake, but maybe the treatment took? I'm a week off my scans. My mom keeps asking every day: How's the balance? Any lost time? Blackouts? Lightheadedness? Friends saying I'm behaving strangely? *Nope, nope, nopety, nope.*

Should I be planning on living longer? Living at all? Why

does everything change when I have more time to live? In my speech, I asked everyone to think about how they might change things if they knew they would die soon, but I *am* going to die soon and I still go back to my old way of thinking as soon as I have a good week. I wonder if I should keep calculus after all . . . maybe I should apologize to Pascale and to the headmaster. I feel so good that I avoid Audra and what she might be able to provide. People ask how I'm doing, and I say, "Great!" And I really am.

When Dr. B splits us up on teams for drone war scrimmages, she names Jenkins and me to lead. And no one cares if I've got a peanut in my head. Rumors swirl of a potential co-captaincy, and I can live with that. Well . . . for now. At the end of practices, Dr. B has us run through the electrified vines of the jungle obstacle. I let one brush my hand instead of using the armor to avoid the shocks. Electricity jolts through me. Pain dances along every nerve. I scream. I'm rigid for a second before regaining the use of my muscles, panting, clutching my chest where my heart skips and stumbles back into rhythm.

"It's a good idea to test the shock," Dr. B says. "Get used to it. You can fight through it. Do it again."

It's crazy, but I grab another vine. Screech. And need to pry my fingers off as the electricity throbs through my arm.

"Tough nut," Dr. B calls me. "Today's level is twenty percent higher than it will be during the race. Beat this, and you can beat it on race day. Use the vines as secret weapons."

***

Everyone is quiet as we enter Pascale's class. Last class had the first new material in twenty years, and no one knows what today will bring.

"Today we discuss the Argument from Ignorance," he announces. "Here we assume something is true because there's no evidence that it's not. A long time ago we might have said the earth is flat because there's nothing that says it's not. God exists because there's no evidence that He doesn't. The bridge must be safe, it hasn't fallen yet."

The rest of the class relaxes as Pascale sticks to the script, but the edge of my desk digs into my pounding chest. *Miracles can happen—there's no evidence they can't.*

"This can be powerful because it shifts the burden of proof. If I say God doesn't exist, you say prove it. It works particularly well as an attack. You're an idiot. There's no climate emergency. It's cold today! It's been colder the last three winters. If anything the planet is cooling. This argument is used by people who don't think critically. Which is to say, most people."

When Pascale turns to check his place, Margot nudges my elbow. "Should we complain again?" she whispers.

I shake my head and Pascale continues. "The Slippery Slope Fallacy is the next big one. If you legalize marijuana, people will smoke more of it, and that will lead to an increase in the use of cocaine and heroin and then crack, meaning most of you will be forced onto the street as prostitutes." He starts to laugh, catches sight of Audra's eye roll and laughs even harder. It wouldn't have been quite as weird if it wasn't written on the page. "Ha, always gets me. What this does is shift the discussion, forcing you to somehow defend a world where you're all crack whores."

He laughs again. But I can hear my mom saying, "Tremmy, I don't want to live in a world that euthanizes its vulnerable. Next thing you know, they're killing people just because they had a rough day. Is that what you want?" Audra notices me staring at her and smiles.

The final argument Pascale explains is the False Dilemma Fallacy, in which arguments are present only as black and white. In my new happy place I'm barely listening, but I remember it when it's used against me at my next doctor's appointment.

# 49 Days to Demise

The oncologist presses for more treatment options, calling it a strong recommendation. More tests. I like her, even though she's a bit crotchety and clearly thinks I can be immortal. She offers to schedule the scans earlier, since I am doing so well, and I explain that I'd rather not know—if I don't think about the peanut, the peanut isn't there. She respects that. My mom, who has been quiet and looks like she brushed her hair and slept for once, scowls.

"Tremmy, if the treatment worked, we should know. We can do more of it."

I lift my eye patch and my vision doubles. "Peanut is not gone, Mom."

"Please don't call it peanut . . . even if it has slowed, that's progress. What if one of these treatments would work? Ever thought of that?" Tendons rise on the backs of her hands.

I don't want to spend any more days in the hospital than necessary. "What's the likelihood that it has stopped or slowed?"

My mom grips her skull and rakes fingers through her hair. "We should run the tests."

"And I want one thing too, Mom."

She knows what I mean. "You can't blackmail me," she hisses.

I turn to the doctor. "How do I order doctor-assisted dying when I want it?"

The oncologist shifts uncomfortably. "I will write a referral to a child psychiatrist, a Dr. Balder," she says.

"Is MAID possible? I'm close to eighteen."

"My job is to heal you physically. Dr. Balder can explain MAID, but as a minor you cannot receive MAID."

"I've been looking into it," I tell her. "The Health Act allows mature minors to refuse or remove life *supporting* devices like respirators, feeding tubes, or other treatments that are keeping them alive. Kids can do this with or without the consent of their parents. Tell me I'm wrong?"

"That's true," she says.

"Right, so a dying kid can remove what's keeping him alive, but he's not mature enough to decide on an assisted death? What's the difference?"

The doctor says, "The killing part." Then she flushes and coughs at her glib response.

"Okay, okay, here's the thing though. Shouldn't it be the patient that matters? In both cases, the patient dies. In both cases the goal is to end suffering. In both cases there is no hope of recovery."

Perhaps it's having an ally in the doctor, because my mom doesn't shrink. She straightens and faces me. "That may be true, but it's different for the doctor in the case of removing treatment. In that case, *she* doesn't have to kill anyone, she only has to let the patient die."

"Fine, but that's okay for an eighteen-year-old but not a seventeen-year-old? It's dumb."

"They have to draw the line somewhere, and it's drawn at eighteen," my mom replies, and the doctor nods, both happy to wash their hands of the decision.

"It's a good conversation to have with Dr. Balder," the oncologist says. "He evaluates the capacity of adult patients for MAID on a regular basis."

I have time. Time being a relative thing. MAID requires the patient to wait ten days after making their decision—a reflection period. I imagine FAID would too. What if I wait until it's too late? I'm feeling okay, but I have tiny losses every day. I can feel it in my running. In my singing. In the space between breaths. Sometimes it feels as though for every ounce of muscle Jenkins builds, I lose the same amount. Like he's some vampire. "Isn't there a UN convention on the rights of children that doesn't allow torture? I'm pretty sure . . ."

"Eighteen," the doctor says. It's black and white. My mom smiles at the doctor. And, as the peanut flares like burning magnesium, I think, *Isn't suffering, suffering?*

***

One good thing came out of the conversation with the doctor. Art class is full of tears.

Delacroix reads my proposal aloud between sobs. She keeps hitting the paper with her hand. "This, this." She shakes it. "This is art. We will *all* do this. A collage maybe, Tremmy? Would that be okay?" Delacroix is the only teacher who refuses to use our last names, believing it to be elitist. "You are not your families," she once said. "You are you."

"That'd be cool," I say.

"*I* have to do his art project for him?" Jenkins objects.

"Only for however long you can hold your breath," I reply. That's the project. That I track the progress of my disease by drawing for however long I can hold my breath. In addition to the detailed self-portrait Delacroix had us working on, I've already done another ten while holding my breath. Just a little over a minute gives me time to add enough detail to make it me, even if it's a caricature of me.

"I don't want to work for you for ten seconds, let alone ten minutes." Gone is Jenkins's usual jokey tone, and I frown at its absence. Last time he was so serious, he'd been threatened with criminal charges.

"Ten minutes?" I laugh off my uncertainty. "As if."

He shrugs. "True, longest ever was nine and change."

"Wait. Really?" I ask. The longest I've *ever* held my breath is three minutes. Even Delacroix leans in, interested by Jenkins's revelation.

Jenkins draws a full breath and starts the timer on his phone. At least it shuts him up.

I toss him a pencil. "Why waste time? Draw something."

He hesitates, then starts sketching.

Minnie, the youngest in the class, stands and beats clay dust from her tartan skirt, from which hang a half-dozen rabbit feet. She grins. Always smiling. Before following me around, Audra followed Minnie. She's not even in our grade, only so advanced in her art that they allow her to do independent work—another scholarship student. What she does is disgusting though. Roadkill taxidermy. She finds dead things on the road, in the woods, or by scavenging from restaurant rat traps and then gives them new life in dioramas—little scenes in which the animals act like humans. Stella dislikes her because Delacroix convinced the headmaster that Minnie should be allowed space in the freezer for her creatures, so Stella gave up an entire freezer.

"My project this year will be inspired by fantasy and myth and by the animals themselves to create something whimsical. I'm thinking about using the phone fireflies combined with toadstools and making creatures that are parts of one another all mixed up, with the message being that we're all the same. The concept of race is a societal fabrication and next to nothing differentiates people at a DNA level. In fact, we have a ton in common with worms."

My fingers trace my head, my brain, and I wonder if that's true. I understand the sentiment. The school boasts kids from all over. Even among the prefects, Stack and Wang are Asian, Margot's black, Lily is brownish, Jenkins has some Slavic ancestry. But I'm certainly different from my friends, although there's little question that I'll soon be more acquainted with worms. The thought sends a cold shudder through me. I don't like the thought of rotting.

There's a sudden outburst from Jenkins. We sit stunned, realizing what has happened. I check my phone for the time.

"That's gotta be a world record," Delacroix says.

Jenkins shakes his head. His face is red as he gasps for air. "Only seven minutes. But I didn't," he gasps, "hyperventilate first. That makes a big difference."

Delacroix replies, "We'll have high expectations of your art, Franklin."

Jenkins reddens.

Everyone sniggers. *Franklin.*

"Let's see the sketch, Franklin," I say.

He holds it up. A skull with a snake squirming through an eye and back into the mouth.

I blow out a long sigh. *Everything is death.*

"What?" he asks. "You're the walking dead, and Minnie here's an animal mortician. What did you expect me to draw?"

His attempt to smile falters. And he draws long, deep breaths.

\*\*\*

The last activity of every week is choir practice. Our choirmaster is also the music teacher. I don't take music. I quit trumpet in grade nine, when the instrument failed to do anything beyond fart and squeak, but I kept singing. Singing can be threaded throughout your day, in the shower, on a hike, working on homework. It requires no band, only lungs.

Private schools have advantages over public. At a private school extracurriculars like cadets, or choir, or debating, can not only be socially acceptable, but celebrated. Of these, choir is my favorite— a weird communion that leaves me in a better place.

I can carry a tune somewhere between the higher range of a bass and the lower range of a tenor. It's not beautiful, but I can really belt it out once I know I'm in tune, and years of singing has improved my voice.

Mr. Johnston received a new conducting baton over the summer, a slim piece of lacquered rosewood ordered from a master craftsman in Kyoto. Super proud of the tiny stick in his hand, he uses it for everything, even when he's talking, poking and prodding the air to punctuate his words.

"VOG, middle C," he says, pointing at the ceiling. The organ plays a single note, and we all hum until Mr. Johnston nods. "This year the king is coming to hear us. The king!" He stabs for the roof. The king he means is the king of Sweden. Evidently there's a royal tour and he's a patron of the school. "We have five months to prepare. Are you ready to sing for royalty?" He rolls the *r*.

Recently I've started shuddering anytime someone mentions a length of time that I might not hit—*five months.* This morning I opened a new tube of toothpaste and needed to brace against the porcelain when I realized I might not live long enough to finish the tube. From here on out my life is a series of lasts.

Mr. Johnston points the baton at his face, widens his eyes and smiles in a way that looks crazed but that he wants us to mimic. It's a way of avoiding falling flat or going sharp.

"VOG, 'Africa' by Toto." With another swipe of the stick, the organ surges, brass pipes exploding with sound above the back of my head. It's the opening bars. Beside me, Merton smiles and says, "Please rise for the school anthem."

The stained-glass windows fracture sunlight into heavenly puzzles that fall on the animated faces across from me. Of the school's five hundred students, two hundred overflow the choir stalls. Almost anyone can sing, especially if you're like me and are prepared to follow. But there are exceptions.

Allister, a slight beanpole of a grade eight, starts a shaky solo. Last year his voice was pure gold soprano, delivering on heights that lifted the heart and the roof. But a boy's soprano is a fragile creature, and puberty has battered his, forcing it to crack and warp as he sings about storms.

He falters, and his voice stops entirely. Crying, he pushes past three students and hustles out. He'll be back in a few months after his voice settles on a range, but for now, at Mr. Johnston's nod, Jodie follows him. The music plays on. A small grief; life's a parade of them.

I know all the songs. Only a couple are religious, most folk music or pop, clapping rhythms, Adele, Bieber, Queen, ABBA. And I lose myself in the melding of voices, keeping a fraction behind so that I stay in tune. I sway.

When I open my eyes, the edges of color around the stained-glass panels quiver. Thousands of dust motes spark as voices rise, making me think of planets and celestial bodies. I feel as though I'm lifting, well-being floods me, the prickle of panic, a euphoric tingling.

*Any changes?* my mom's voice echoes.

Johnston's baton is a blazing sword. Halos, actual rings, surround the heads of the students opposite me. Their chins lifted, eyes wide, smiling. And then their eyes widen as mine roll back into my skull. *Here we go.*

# 46 Days to Demise

It was expected. Something like this. Perhaps not so soon after my last appointment, but expected.

I recover in the hospital. A bandage at my head hides stitches from where my forehead struck the music stand.

"Tremmy?" my mom asks as I turn my head. "Hey, hey."

"Ugh," I say. Tongue like burned toast. "Gross."

At my speaking, relief breaks across her face.

I assess. Wriggle my toes. First the fingers of one hand, then the other. No stroke. A seizure then. Smells of mint? No . . . antiseptic. My mom doubles, and I shut my bad eye.

Gone is the euphoria of singing, replaced by a hollow feeling in my gut. It's the hollowness of loss. A break in my voice. A jump-step in the fading. I try not to scrape too much at the scab of it. Beneath lies the black hole of panic. *Hell.* I'd started to believe. Hospitals are lodestones of lost time; it's why I hate them. I don't have time.

Tears press at my eyelids and finally trickle coolly across my temples. My mother's grip on my hand grows fierce. It presses at the intravenous port. The heart rate monitor pinches my finger. Other sensors suckle at my chest. There is strength in her hand, in fingers she complains cramp from arthritis. I'm jealous of her future pains. I hate that this dying part is really happening.

"I want a copy of the medical record," I say and face her, leaving the tears to run. Her head cocks, eyes screwing up. "For my classmates. I want to be able to explain what happened."

My vision blurs from tears as she replies, "Okay, Tremmy, I'll see what I can do. Can I get you anything else?"

I swipe my leathery tongue over cracked lips. "Water, and paper and a pencil."

Later she returns with a pen, no pencil. I sip water through a straw. The straw is plastic, and I sigh because I know that my continued living has sent another straw to landfill. I'm fading like Margot warned. I sip in a breath, hold, and draw.

# 44 Days to Demise

When discharged on Monday with a bottle of anti-seizure medication, my driver's license has already been revoked. They ran scans while I was there. That was the deal with my parents. I didn't have to see the result, but then I remembered my goal of exposing the school to death and asked for a copy along with the written report. It's amazing how reluctant doctors are to provide all of this. I overhear my parents arguing about whether I should know, but there's nothing more that can surprise me. I've seen my sketch, I know everything—eventually they cave.

Before I leave, I have to wait for a visit from a large, block-toothed doctor with a bedside manner polar opposite of the oncologist's. Where the oncologist hovers at the foot of the bed, often slightly turned to the door as if already partway to her next patient, Dr. Balder sits on my bed and holds my gaze.

"Hello, Tremendous, I am Dr. Balder."

"The psychiatrist," I say.

"You got it." That smile again. "How are you feeling?"

I sigh. "Better." Immediately after waking, I'd needed to go back to sleep. At least I can stay awake like a normal person now. "You know, for a guy dying of brain cancer."

His face is implacable. "The doctors tell me that you want to share your medical information with your friends. All of it."

"Yeah, we hide so much about death. It would be easier if it was talked about."

Dr. Balder nods thoughtfully. "I have to agree."

"You do?"

"Sure. Used to be that we were surrounded by death. War. Infant mortality. Kids died of measles all the time. It was pretty normal. Common."

"Now I'm special."

"Sure are. Death's a taboo subject, isn't it? Kids are sent away when we talk about it. You might have been told stories about what happened that aren't true. Dog went to the farm. Had to find a new home for kitty. That must be hard for you, not feeling you can talk about it?"

"Wait a second, you mean when my dad said Benji went to the farm, he really . . ." I laugh at Dr. Balder's expression. "Kidding! Who would name their dog Benji? You're right, though. It was hard, but that's not really why I want to do this. I want to do this for them."

He leans in. "How so?" I struggle to find the words; is my brain cancering out on me? "Anything you tell me is confidential, Tremendous."

I sigh. "I've been doing a lot of thinking because I'm, you know, dying. And it's made me think of stuff I've done—stuff that I probably shouldn't have. And I have to wonder if I wouldn't have already had those regrets and not done such stupid stuff if only I'd been around to watch my grandma die. Or my girlfriend. Anyone I really knew."

"How does dying change how you think?"

I snort. "Everything. I don't have time to change much. To make a difference. Maybe if my friends are there when I die, I can help them see how short this all is. What they're missing out on by not seeing that."

Dr. Balder's expression brightens with surprise. "Knowing death improves us?" He taps some notes on an iPad.

"Not seeing death means we don't ask ourselves the important questions," I say. "This all sucks." My hand sweeps the room and I relax back into the bedding. "But it's weirdly peaceful too." I blink at that thought. I've got nowhere to go or be. Not really. I like the way his intelligent eyes appraise me. "What's your diagnosis, Doc?" I ask, pressing my palms down on the bed to scoot higher.

"Thoughtful teenager with something to say. I'm prescribing a return to your friends and the confidence to persevere and ask the important questions three times daily."

I resist his infectious grin. "Yeah, on that point, what happens when I don't want to persevere? When I'm . . . done . . . ready to go?"

The grin vanishes. "Ah, yes. How old are you?"

"Seventeen."

"When do you turn eighteen?"

"Too late."

His expression softens, one hand scratching at the back of his skull. "Medical assistance in dying is a tricky topic for us doctors too. But until you turn eighteen, I'm afraid there's nothing to discuss."

"Then never."

Dr. Balder is now like the others, standing, turned part way to the door, and ready to go, but I don't think he's eager for the next patient. He's fleeing. His eyes flutter, and his spine lengthens before his loafers point back to me. "Would you like to sign a do not resuscitate order? It means that medical personnel won't use extraordinary means to save your life."

"I don't need my parents to consent?"

"No, but I'd recommend that you talk to them about it first. In the case of the DNR, I still need to consider your capacity to choose, but I have the sense that you're a mature minor, and the Health Act doesn't specify an age." He adds, "Except for MAID. There are no 'mature minors.' I'm sorry."

I swallow. "Yes," I say. "I'd like to sign the order."

# 43 Days to Demise

How do I accomplish what I said to Dr. Balder? How do I force everyone to confront death? I start researching interesting facts about it. Anything that might start people talking. The morning before class I sneak into the classrooms and graffiti the whiteboard screens with the information I've dredged up on death statistics. Death can teach us all sorts of stuff.

Here's the first: *In the USA, rich people live fifteen years longer than poor. Fifteen years!* I sign it, *Death Warmed Over.* I could've just posted it on Goldilux, but I have the feeling people are starting to ignore my feed. Death is too old-school.

I'm surprised, though, when my notes don't prompt any reaction. I'm expecting people to greet me as Death Warmed Over, but they don't—they're on their laptops or phones and ignore me. When I enter class, the writing on the whiteboard screen is gone, without even a faded shadow of the letters left behind.

\*\*\*

By the end of the day, I'm frustrated and ready for the only antidote that still works. The mud, the blood, drone wars. With a game scheduled for tomorrow, today we scrimmage. I didn't ask any doctor if I was allowed to play. There's no chance they could stop me anyway. As I head for the turf, I jog to catch up to Jenkins.

"Quit stalking my ass," he says, but there's something half-hearted about his mockery. I'm already breathing hard and can't come up with a reply. Instead, I stop and stare at him, and he flushes. "Hell, man, I thought you were gone."

He means dead. He's freaked out. "Can't get rid of me that easily," I say.

We lapse back into silence.

"What's up?" I probe the quiet. He's been distant ever since art class. Didn't come to the hospital, not that I expected him to.

He cracks his knuckles. Breath whistles from his nostrils. "You hear Wang's having another Flesh-Fest?" We start walking.

"Didn't his parents install cameras?"

"Audra has a hack to circuit them."

"Audra's freaking me out a bit."

He laughs. It's a shared laugh and it feels good. "Audra." He shakes his head, reminding me of the last time we talked about her.

"Haven't asked her yet," I say.

Jenkins looks about to say something when Dr. B blows the whistle. "Find your drone," she states, and everyone runs for theirs. "See you on the other side," Jenkins says.

"Jenkins, Merton!" Dr. B shouts as I reach the sideline. "Choose your teams."

I stand stunned. *Merton?* "She's giving you a break, Tremmy," Tonja says, holding a beast of a sentinel drone. Easily ten pounds and armored, bristling with weaponry.

"But I don't want one."

When Jenkins picks his team, he won't look me in the eye as he bypasses me for Stack and then Jodie. I'm Merton's fourth pick. Merton's. Fourth. Pick.

"You'd better not let me down," he says.

I don't plan to. But it has nothing to do with him. There's only one solution to what's happening. The only way I can clamber back on top. To kick everyone's asses. And most of all, Jenkins's platinum one.

Each team stands at their respective end of the field. As soon as a player's drone passes the finish line, they can start running the obstacle course. I'm losing wind, I know that. In contrast, Jenkins's armor strains to contain him. If I'm to win, I have to cross that line first in the drone portion of the race—by a lot.

I call my drone The Swallow. We have barn swallows around here, and when they're out at dusk eating insects, they fly in unpredictable directions, diving, swerving, curling in impossibly tight turns. Those turns are my offense and my defense.

"Power up!" Dr. B shouts.

"Ready warriors," both Jenkins and Merton order.

A light counts down. Red, yellow—eight-score of drone rotors whirr—green. I taste the sulfur of gas in the air.

With the goggles on, my swallow airborne, my drone leans forward as it hauls toward the first ring. One of forty rings that burst into flames. An enhancement that raises cheers.

"Tonja, skip the rings and cover the center." As general, Merton calls out strategy.

"If you put a second sentinel there, nothing can squeak past," I say.

"Follow your orders, Tremmy, and leave the leadership to me."

I sense his smirk as my face tightens with the heat from the rings. I curl through the first ring, drop into the second, lean back, and hurtle up, threading one of the higher markers, nearly clipping the metal tubing. My depth perception is off due to the eye patch. Without enemy interference, I'm clearing the field at a solid, if not record, pace.

"Incoming," Merton warns.

"Sentinel?"

"Suicide."

No wonder I didn't see it. Suicides are tiny and fast, but difficult to maneuver. I deke to the right, and it rips past, forcing me to loop back and take the sixteenth ring.

"Rope," Merton warns.

Ropes hit from above, so I swing low before hurtling back up, knocking off the seventeenth and eighteenth rings.

Tonja swears. "Sorry, guys, sorry. Missed him."

"Jenkins is at twenty," Merton says. "Tremmy, take him out."

"What?" If I take him down, it'll take *me* down. I'll be done. You never take out your own lead drone. "No way."

"Take him down as he hits the next ring."

Screw that. I hit the throttle and sprint for the ring, catching the flash of Jenkins's Green Machine as it, too, heads for the narrow opening. It's a game of chicken that neither of us can win. I start to yell, and in the distance, I hear Jenkins yelling too.

At the last second, before we strike, I drop power from one set of rotors and divert power to the others, flipping the drone as we reach the ring and passing through. There's a collective gasp.

"You missed him!" Merton yells.

"I got past him," I say.

Jenkins's machine missed the ring and is forced back.

"Now their entire platoon is after you, idiot. You can't win."

It's the challenge of being in the lead. I start laughing, swerving, cutting. I do a flip. But at the next set of rings, three sentinels are blocking the entrance. There's no space to thread through. Jenkins is following my own suggestion, essentially cutting off the enemy by creating an impenetrable fortress at a single ring.

"Go for it, Tremmy," Tonja says beside me.

"I give the orders," Merton says.

"Just do it," she adds. I catch Merton's scoff.

A second before I hit the sentinels, Tonja drops her drone like a stone, landing on the first sentinel, which knocks the second and causes the third to take evasive action, clearing the way for my finish. The last two rings are unguarded. The swallow whips across the line. I whoop.

Dr. B blows the whistle, signaling that I can start running.

"Go, Tremmy!" Merton shouts.

As if I'd be doing anything different.

I leap across several rubber islands surrounded by water and hurdle four small fences, needing to grab the top of the fifth and swing my legs up and over. I sprint across burning coals and climb the ladder up two stories, sliding down the opposite side, before another whistle shrieks—Jenkins is off.

The whistle sounds off regularly thereafter, ten seconds and two obstacles later. I'm closing in on halfway, surprised that

Jenkins has nearly hit halfway too, but then, he doesn't have a peanut companion. My breathing wheezes. Stack has stationed himself at the second to last obstacle. His job is to keep me from completing it before I hit the electric jungle, but one step at a time. I clamber through the windows of ten beat-up Audis before facing the Tower. A five-story cargo net rises in the center of the course. It's so tall that we have to clip in at each story for safety.

We reach the Tower at the same time. I clip in. Jenkins doesn't, and he's a few feet up on the other side by the time I catch him. I punch through the mesh, the fist catching him in the nuts.

He flies off. "Don't cheat," I yell. "And wear a cup."

He squirms on the ground for a moment, face thunderous, before surging back after me.

At the top of the first story, my fingers struggle with the clip. Jenkins hasn't bothered with his again, so we're face-to-face as we climb the second stage, neither clipped in. Spittle from his mouth flies to fleck my face.

"If you picked me, we'd both be winning," I pant. He keeps climbing, jaw muscles pulsing. "Say something," I say. "What the hell is wrong with you?"

He says down to me, "They've asked me to be head boy."

The strength nearly goes out of my fingers. The fight in me. I'm so lonely. Amborough has always been a unit. Each position I won—prefect, head boy, general—clinched my position as part of something bigger, maybe the center of it. And when I saluted, everyone saluted back.

We both hang, unmoving. "Harvard, Princeton, Brown, Yale." Jenkins hangs on his excuses, waiting for me to catch up.

"My mom thinks I can get in with head boy on my application."

It's not his fault I'm dying. "You should take it," I say, starting up, my hand out to shake his. We're three stories up.

He looks down and flushes. "I wanted you to hear it from me."

*They've asked me to be head boy.* He wasn't asking for permission. "What?" He's already accepted. "You know what they did to me." I jump and grab the netting three squares up. It's a technique I usually reserve for lower down, but now it's my spittle flying into his face. "Do you want to know why I stayed?" I ask. "Because I could be looking at lions in Africa right now if I wanted to." Jenkins stares through me. "I stayed because you're an entitled ass who doesn't think farther than the length of his dick or a crossbow bolt. I stayed to make sure you wouldn't be doing time for some crime. For you, man."

We both hang. Me, stunned by my admission.

"Then you should have gone." He starts up. Flies up. But I keep pace.

"No way." I shake my head, unable even to consider that I made the wrong call by staying here. "This is my gift to you. I'm going to die with you so you can realize that who you are is not what you want to be." Four stories. And I'm not done. "I'm saving you twenty-five years of documentaries, craft beer fests, binge-watching superhero shows, social media streaks, or whatever the hell comes into vogue when you combine AI and robots and VR with a rapey attempted murderer."

Jenkins swings a leg over the top. I hook my leg across. His expression suggests that I've given him the justification he was looking for. Maybe the headmaster told him that I wasn't in the right headspace for the head prefect role. That the school *needs* Jenkins.

"Aren't you the supreme saint suckass of suckasses. Too bad your IQ is that of beheaded tick. Didn't realize that dying gave you the right to be a raging suppository."

*Ad hominem argument.* Pascale's empowering him too.

"You're right. Dying doesn't. But I do have every right. Because I'm you. Because I *was* you. I was normal. Healthy. I was lucky to be better than normal. My parents named me Tremendous. I was excellent and an ass. And I had a really far way to fall."

Jenkins looks down. We both have a long way to fall.

"You may not have another year to live, but I do. Decades." His hands clench. "I have a future. I have succor to drink. Chicks to screw. Worlds to conquer!" He laughs. "I sure as hell won't be thinking of you when I do it."

I grab for his arm. He snatches mine and we grapple. "That's what I'm afraid of." His face twists in fury, shame, disgust.

"Robetty made me general too, in case you hadn't noticed. Stop trying to live on through me. It won't work." That thought sickens me. "Did you think they'd let a zombie be general?" *Straw Man Fallacy.*

The sky darkens, as if a cloud has passed over the sun. I hunch my shoulders, roar, and wrench us both from our perch. Jenkins's mouth has time to drop before I release. He topples backward. Carried by the drive of my thighs, I tumble after. Five stories. Screaming every story.

We hit. Air collapses from my lungs. My back folds. A whistle bleats. But the clouds continue to move in the sky, a sky blocked by Jenkins's hate-twisted face. Then his fist. It glances from my cheekbone.

Consequences will follow. But there's nothing that can be done to me. No one can hurt me. They've done their worst. They've taken it all.

# 42 Days to Demise

The knock seems to come soon after I fall asleep, but morning light ladles over my bed. I ache.

"Are you decent?" It's Mr. Bell.

Sun streams through the windowpanes. The choir sings. I'm disappointed in myself for missing practice. But maybe none of it is for me anymore.

I wear jeans, a T-shirt with the logo from the last 10K race I ran. My hair is a tangle. I rub my eyes. Trace my tongue around fuzzy teeth. "Yes, sir."

Mr. Bell creeps in, shoulders meek and face narrow as a mouse. I can imagine Mason House as one of Minnie's dioramas. Someone's jerking off. Five nod to music. A dozen are gaming. Another contemplates suicide or rolls weed laced with Fentanyl. An accidental overdose waiting to happen.

Mr. Bell glances back at the door and shuts it.

"I'm sorry, sir."

He cocks his head and lifts his eyebrows. "I would guess. I'm sorry too, son."

He remains standing, paws in front. "Want to tell me what happened?"

"Jenkins and I had a difference of opinion," I say.

"Not like you." His eyes are full of concern. But a lot of kids pass through this house. I'm not *his* kid. "That was very dangerous. What if you'd missed the safety mat? You're acting like a loaded gun lately." I peer at him, but he glances away, shifts back and forth on his feet. "As I understand your prognosis . . . you don't have a lot of time left. Perhaps this is making you impulsive?"

*Like a ticking bomb?* "I'm not a suicide bomber."

He waves the thought away. "Only saying that Jenkins has a lot to lose."

*And I don't.* "A lot has changed," I say.

"Yes. You've changed."

"Can you give me a break?" I ask.

"For the fight, yes," he says, but it's clear there's another shoe to drop because he sighs twice before adding, "but not for the sexual assault."

"What?" I swing my legs out of bed and jerk forward.

"You placed your naked . . . bottom on the head of another boy, a boy under your supervision," he says, looking away.

"What, the fart? Brunly? It was a joke."

"The administration doesn't see it as a joke. It is deadly serious."

"You're kidding. These guys have masturbation contests. They regularly sit on other kids' heads and fart. Five minutes don't go by without someone saying something about jizz, asses, dicks, or sex."

"Your role as deck prefect is to set the tone," Mr. Bell says. He's not as mousey, my confrontation only breathing strength into him.

"They do it because they're sixteen and stressed out, not because of me!"

Mr. Bell's face tightens. Everything I do and say is being watched and used against me. They're letting me off on the fight so they can let Jenkins off.

"In lieu of suspension—"

"This is—" I start to object.

"Or expulsion." He holds my stare, and I try to melt his skull with my gaze. "Administration has determined that you will be relieved of your prefect duties and will take a room on the lower deck. Effective immediately."

"Sir—" I say, but he points to a large rucksack stuffed under the bed.

Mr. Bell says nothing more but watches as I gather my stuff like some fired office worker who might steal intellectual property if left alone. *The administration* . . . this is coming from the headmaster. I shouldn't waste my breath. It's then that I realize the manila envelope with my recent medical results is missing. I search behind and under the desk. Nothing. When I'm ready, he grabs a crate of books as I lug the bag, marching me down the stairs to the first floor and then along a decrepit corridor to the last room. As we approach, I catch whiffs of bleach and mildew.

No one uses this room. The room at the end of the hall. Kids write ghost stories about this room.

A missed cobweb drapes the corner of the frame. "Would you stay here?"

He won't look me in the eye but opens the door and feels for the switch. The small solitary room receives no light, its

Lilliputian window out of reach of both morning and afternoon sun. A naked bulb illuminates a desk, a chair, and a narrow cot. It's a cage.

"Why not stuff me in the furnace room?" I ask. Mr. Bell's steps echo down the hall. I collapse onto the bed. It's hard. Everyone's a coward. No one's coming to comfort me. Outside the room, the world races on. I listen for the whistle of the drone war ref, but there arcs only a singular soprano. They're doing it to piss me off.

I push off the bed, slam the door of the dark cell behind me, and pound out of the house, breathing heavy, heart mangled. The person who did this sits behind a duke's desk.

"Hey," I announce as I enter the headmaster's office. He's with Pascale, and it's perfect. They both stand, tense and ready. Erect as dicks.

"You win, okay?" I slow clap them all. "I'm out. But I'm not letting you off so easy."

The headmaster pads toward me across velvety carpeting. "Tremendous, what's this?"

"This is my swan song. My last words before I die by way of vacation."

He opens his arms to me, offering the floor. Maybe it's because he has what he wants. He only has to wait me out.

"A few weeks ago, I was to be your head boy, the general of the drone war team. It was going to be an awesome year. Then something changed," I say. They both think they know what changed. "You did. I told you I was dying and I might as well have said I had leprosy." I hold up my hand to stave off dissent. "You need to look at what you fear. The tumor is in my head, but it's your fear that you're trying to excise from your heart by getting rid of me. Yours. You look at me, and you're ready to pee your pants."

Pascale smirks. "Very good, Tremmy, the Argument from Ignorance."

The headmaster stands, unyielding. "I'm sorry you feel that way, Tremendous. I wish you well on your travels. I hope you find what you're looking for."

I swallow at this. "No, *sir*, what I was looking for was at Amborough. All I wanted was a place to die well, where I wouldn't feel alone."

"A school is not a place for dying," the headmaster says. "It is a vital place. For the future. For the living."

***

My Amborough life lies crated and bagged and tagged on the floor. I've called my mom. Dad's on his way. He'll be an hour. They're excited. Looking forward to our trip. We'll be in the air soon, away from it all. I'm sending myself away so that the headmaster and teachers can tell stories about what happened to me. *Went to the farm. Found kitty a new home. Tremmy decided it would be best . . .* With classes on, I've got nothing to do but wait.

Crown molding runs across most of the ceiling. Former students have carved into them over the years with knives and protractors, their names and messages from the past. The oldest I spot is from 1914. Charles Chernin. He "was here." Is that it? A presence? Another Charles "sucks." Others "love." I recognize the name of another old headmaster. It's crossed out. I'm not the only one taking issue with authority. The most recent is from twenty years ago. I stand on the bed and use a pen to write in a corner. *Tremendous Sinclair, the ghost of Mason House, is here.*

At a knock on the door, I hop down and grab my bag. I bend to lift the two crates. "Gimme a sec."

The door opens to Margot. Her formerly long, black hair has been cut shorter, at an angle and streaked white.

"It's true," she says. "You're leaving."

The way she says "leaving" sounds a lot like "giving up." I drop the crates back on the bed.

"There's nothing for me here," I say. "I thought there was."

"What do you want?"

"To be general of the drone war team, head boy, deck prefect—"

"Those are titles," she says.

"I . . . wanted to die with my friends."

"But you're pissing everyone off."

"They're not being fair."

"Maybe." She shrugs.

"I make everyone uncomfortable."

"People don't like uncomfortable things."

"So they're isolating me."

"And you've let it happen."

"I haven't! I've fought everyone."

"Which is the same thing. If you want to stay, you need to build support, not kill it. People are afraid of death, right? So it's only natural that they try to oust you if that's all you're talking about."

I squint at her. Margot's eyes are on fire; she's leaning forward. I ask her, "Why are *you* here?"

"Because I know what they're doing."

"What do you mean?"

"Listen, when I want something, I don't go and ask a police officer for help with it. I don't go to the headmaster either."

I stare blankly. "I don't understand."

"When I first arrived at Amborough, I wanted to leave. I could count the people who looked like me on one hand. It was uncomfortable. One kid asked me if I had ever eaten anything but fried chicken and watermelon. Racism wasn't simply present; these kids didn't even know they were racist. Teachers were surprised when my essays were good and asked why I didn't play basketball. And they'll be surprised when I'm accepted to the university of my choice. There were a thousand reasons for me to leave. I was alone, like you feel now. But my mother taught me that it's at the point of discomfort where life gets important. That these were also a thousand reasons for me to stay."

"You're saying I'm like you now."

She squints at me, mouth falling open in disgust. "Not a chance." It's like a wall slides between us.

"Why not? My parents may have more money, but it's not like you're really poor. This whole dying thing puts me at a disadvantage."

Her tongue swabs the inside of her cheek. "You don't remember, do you?"

"What?"

"You were the kid, the one who asked me about watermelons." Shame shuttles into my throat. "And I bet you still don't know why that's so bloody racist." I shake my head. "Not my job to educate you. Before today, I would have plunked you with the trifecta of hate. But—"

"Trifecta of—"

"Rich, white, male."

"Oh. Don't forget cisgender."

"Quadfecta. I am black, female, straight, and middle class. I acknowledge my privilege, but we'll never be the same because you've never had to realize the god you're praying to doesn't look like you, and your neighbors have never worried that you were moving next door. You were right, though, about the school being mine. If I can't take ownership of it, I can't help change it. We both own this school. We both need to change it."

"But how can I change it? The headmaster keeps taking everything away."

"Like I said. Don't be knocking on the headmaster's door. Besides, other than taking your titles and crap . . ." A dismissing fart noise escapes her lips. ". . . no one's kicking you out. You're leaving. Stop being a tree. When Whitby couldn't enter the pool area with his wheelchair, what did he do? He got them to put in a proper ramp."

"It was Jodie who figured that out. With Wheelchair Day . . ." I cock my head. Wheelchair Day was fun. Everyone had a chance to wheel around in one to see what it was like. "Wait a second. That was Whitby's plan?"

"Whitby organized Wheelchair Day so kids could discover that parts of the school were inaccessible. Particularly the pool, which he'd already told the headmaster about the year before and nothing happened. When he asked them to improve access a second time, the students got behind him and the school did it."

It was a long way around to achieve what he needed. "But I don't need better access. I need people to stop treating me like I'm useless. To be fair."

"Why do you want to stay again? Most of the kids here are jerks."

"That's kind of why, actually. At first, I didn't want to die in some hospital bed. I wanted to go down in flames here. To die well. I still want that, but it's different now. The diagnosis changed stuff for me. Maybe it'll change stuff for them."

"Them. Like Jenkins." I don't deny it. "You want the jerks to see they're jerks before it's too late. People don't want to hear that."

"Nope."

"Do they deserve the chance?"

"What else is there?"

"We can take him down." There's history here. There's fear. Anger.

"He's my best friend."

She's calculating. Maybe she's recruiting me. Doing what Whitby did. Letting me see the system with my own eyes, waiting for me to come to the same conclusion.

"But I will get really frigging sick too." I scrub my face with my palms. The headmaster isn't the only one who is afraid.

"Nothing about the fight is easy. The problem with losing your privilege is you can't make mistakes anymore. You don't get to demand answers. You can't do what you used to do. That's how an attempted murderer is head boy and you get exiled for doing what you used to do as part of the system . . ." She pauses. "Ass-face-farting."

"You don't think I should leave."

She shrugs. "That's up to you. I fight the white patriarchy. If I leave, it wins. He wins, and the system continues. If you leave, all you'll be able to say is that you visited this school."

Never lived here. And I'll die in some hospital bed, crapping my pants. It's weird, but she's right. I've always been waiting for the next stage, waiting for high school to finish, so I can grab my university degree, and then join my parent's company's board of directors. I've never worried about the now. "You fight the white patriarchy. You fight me."

"Is it working?"

"Maybe."

"Good. We need co-conspirators too." She smiles. "In fact, it's all about that, really." She grabs my sketchbook, pauses when she spots the most recent fifty-four second sketch of myself, and then turns to a blank page and draws a big vertical rectangle. "Most of our world is set up like a skyscraper. Some lucky few start on the upper floors of the skyscraper." She draws me—maybe Jenkins standing on top. "They can challenge and change things because they hold privilege, but they don't because changing things means bringing the whole thing tumbling down. Most of us have to fight from the bottom to reach the top. People can see us coming and are pretty good at stopping us." She begins adding in more boxes around the skyscraper and then boxes on top of those boxes. "We need to be more like a city rising up around the skyscraper and choking it. It's too late before it realizes it." She must see my confusion because she tries again. "Next time you're in front of the chapel, check out the ivy." Ivy covers most the wall; tendrils latch stone and curl beneath the slate tiles of the roof. "It grows in whatever direction it wants. Be like the ivy, not like the tree. The headmaster will cut a tree down. You don't have time to be a tree. You need ivy. It grows fast and the headmaster will never see it coming." She tosses the sketchbook on the bed with the crates. On the page, the skyscraper isn't the tallest building anymore.

What if the stroke of genius my dad told me about, the one I need to wait for, doesn't need to be about business? Or making money? Maybe it's an opportunity to do something. Short, quick footsteps hurry down the hall; Margot turns to go.

"I have a favor to ask," I say. If I start to push back against Jenkins and all the other Jenkins-in-training for real, he'll never help me die. It may already be too late.

She stops. "I won't kill you. I'm a conscientious objector." Her fingers twist a cross at her neck. She once told me that I couldn't see God because I wasn't looking down for Him. Her eyes hold mine. "But maybe that's something worth fighting for. And against." She winks. It's so patronizing, but for some reason it fills me with warmth. "You've taken the first step, Tremmy. If you want to die here, then that's worth fighting for. Having the right to have an impact, the right to die on our own terms . . . that's something bigger than yourself. That's something."

There's another knock at the door, and Margot stands aside to reveal my dad.

Without Margot present, I'm not sure what I would have said. I'd come so close to being cut down in a single lumberjack blow. But she is here.

"False alarm," I say. "I'm staying."

***

Within minutes of my dad leaving, I receive a text from Dr. B. *You're benched for the game. Administration requires a doctor's note stating you're healthy enough to play.*

*Something worth fighting for.*

The muscles of my dad's jaw twitched when I told him I was staying. Anger. I wonder if he sees the trip as an opportunity to help with the fight. My parents want to help me. If they can't cure me, then they can give me beautiful experiences, tasting menus, and luxury spas. They can squeeze a lifetime of pampering into my final months. Isn't that what half the population dreams about anyway? But I have unfinished business.

As I climb the steps of the girls' dormitory, drones buzz as Amborough battles with our arch nemesis, Demonsfield. Evening has sunk sharp shadows over campus. I miss the first step and skin my shin. I swear and clutch it until the pain ebbs, my fingers coming away sticky with blood.

I grip the cold black-iron railing. The cancering out of things is growing worse. Thinking and walking at the same time causes me to stumble. It's happening. It scares me. Some parts of the disease don't. I can live with double vision. The loss of memory and brain power, though? That's as terrifying as losing the ability to breathe or swallow or close my eyes.

The girls' dormitory, unlike the boys', is only a few years old. No radiators clank. No air rushes through single-pane windows. The floorboards don't creak. The girls all have their own dorm rooms with adjoining washrooms. I doubt there are any jerk-off contests. I knock on Audra's door.

"Come in," she calls.

I ease the door open and step into the light of computer screens. A blackout curtain blocks sunset.

"What's another word for amazing?" she asks, eyes on her screen.

"Tremendous?" I laugh. "Why?"

"Can't believe I didn't think of that." By the strange formatting of the text, it looks like she's coding. "I need to change up my reviews. They're being flagged as fake because they're all the same."

"Why are they all the same?" I ask.

Her fingers rattle off a new line of code. "Because they are fake."

"Oh. Why would you post fake reviews?"

"Because I want to help pricks like Pascale, why do you think? Not everyone is as loaded as you are, Tremmy," she says.

"Ah." I'm distracted by the blown-up photos on her walls. They're not beautiful or interesting. They're of hospital entrances, old-age homes, and hotel rooms. The subjects appear random.

"I earn money for every review I post, and I can post about a hundred in a minute. I wrote a script that automates the logins, clicks, and posting. It was working well all summer, but Amazon is on to me."

"Awesome, wicked, excellent . . ." My mind does one of its fuzzies as I dredge it, but Audra doesn't notice and keeps typing in synonyms. "I can lend you some money."

"It's not only about the money. I like messing with the system."

On her desk beside a few scuffed laptops and on top of a brown envelope is an old-fashioned analog camera.

"You use film?" I ask.

"You can't capture the spirit world with digital pictures."

"Sure," I say, taking a closer look at her photos while really questioning if I want her in my inner circle of care.

She squints at me. "Look at that one." She points to a photo of a hotel room. Beyond the side of the bed is a nimbus of light that looks vaguely humanoid. A ghost? "A man was murdered here. I buy film that has a special silver rinse that captures angelic photons. I'm working on a digital filter, but nothing has worked so far."

*Yeah, because angels don't actually exist.*

"Oh, so you're trying to take pictures of angels."

Her gaze travels from my eyes to my forehead. "You'll have an angel around you any day now."

"You haven't seen anything though. Like on my shoulder or sitting on my head?"

"Not yet." Her eyes refocus on mine. "You may be joking, but how differently would you feel if you had proof of angels? Or any world beyond this one. Isn't that worth pursuing? Even if everyone would think you've lost it?"

"I'm sorry," I say. "I guess you're right."

"Pentobarbital."

"What?" I ask.

She spins in her chair. She's wearing what appears to be an ancient black corset. Her smooshed breasts bubble out of the top; her waist is cinched tight. She doesn't notice my noticing. "This is the first time you've ever knocked on my door. Word is out that you're planning on dying here. You're here to ask me for help, so ask."

There's a firm set to her jaw, and for the first time, I consider the option that she doesn't want to help. "You're the most interesting person I've ever met," I say.

"In a good way?"

I shrug. "In a way I don't understand. Odd, strange, weird."

"You're good with synonyms."

"Angels, corsets, and fake Amazon reviews . . ."

She grins. "I'm like some gothic, spirit-hunting hacker."

"I'd read that book."

"Really? I'll code AI to write it in an Anne Rice style," she says, face falling serious so that I don't really know what I'm nodding about. "If you want my help to be immortal, I could hack Dr. B's server and borrow her algorithm for VOG and code you into AI using old essays you've written as source material. You'd live forever."

"Not really me though," I say.

"Call it a subset of your consciousness."

"No, I mean, I plagiarized most of those essays."

"Then pentobarbital."

"What's that?" I ask.

She raises a scoffing eyebrow. "The drug you use to kill someone." I shuffle back and forth on my feet, feeling as though I've let something nasty into my life. "I can get it for you. My parents kill animals all the time." Her eyes shine with curiosity, and I bite down a shudder. "Ten thousand dollars, whenever you want it. Five thousand if I can be there when you use it. Free if I can do it. That's the gold package."

I nod. This is what I wanted, isn't it?

"One more thing," she says. "I want access."

"Access to what?" I say, taking a step back.

"I want to be able to take photos of you."

"I don't believe in angels."

"Doesn't really matter, does it."

I consider. "Guess not."

"So?"

I mull the permutations of how this could go. She wants to snap a few photos of me. She likely has already. *What harm could it do?*

"Deal. I'll let you know which package I go for."

"Great, first photoshoot is today." She grins. "Take off all your clothes."

Audra waits until I am down to my undies to tell me she's kidding about *all* the clothes. The photoshoot doesn't take long because the film she uses is expensive—hundreds of reviews a roll. She strings a black sheet across her wall—so the angels will really pop—and takes four pictures. I simply stand, expressionless, for the first couple, before I realize I might as well have some fun, so I pretend to be a model for the last two.

"You really think you'll find an angel?"

"Tremmy," she says, "I know I'll find an angel. I want to discover at what point the angel finds you."

***

Amborough lost the drone war. Demonsfield isolated Jenkins and knocked him out early. The other team could have walked the obstacle course and still won. I'll admit to enjoying his pain. That Jenkins played after our fight on the Tower, after I was benched, proves everything Margot said was true.

"Heard about the game, sorry," Margot says, and then smiles at the heaping pile of pasta Stella dumps on my plate beside a smaller-than-usual glop of caviar.

"Stella thinks gluten is the cure for cancer." Stella winks as I slide down the cafeteria line, letting in Margot, who selects the vegetarian option and both the challenges: escargot and chitterlings. Today's theme is the digestive tract. Margot always takes the challenge foods.

"Have you noticed that the boys here are all called by their surnames and the girls by their first?" Margot asks as we collect cutlery.

"Hadn't thought about it, but you're right. Maybe it's a legacy of it being a boys' school?"

"I think it speaks to how we value men over women. Society does it with naming bridges and buildings too."

In the dining hall, we sit at one of forty long pine tables, each large enough to seat a dozen. A couple of staff bus dishes or bring cappuccinos to students.

"Cappuccino? Latte?" a young dude asks, sliding a flickering candle between us. By his complexion and accent, I suspect he's one of the Syrian refugees the school sponsored a couple of years ago and continues to employ.

Margot's face darkens. "No, thanks, Mohammed." After he moves on, she adds, "We can get our own coffee."

"Gives them jobs though, right?" I suggest.

"That's neo-colonialist bull, and the fact you can still think that is why I have to work so hard not to hate you."

I tap my head. Brain cancer. She can't really hate me.

Whitby rolls up with a tray in his lap and takes the head of the table where the chair has been removed.

"Fraternizing with the enemy," he says to Margot.

"Enemy?" I ask.

"I'm scared of people who want approval for something that

encourages disabled people to off themselves. FAID, you're calling it?"

*Does everyone know?* "That's Pascale's Slippery Slope argument."

"Yeah, well, it's one backed by facts too. In some countries people with mental illness can ask for medical assistance in dying. What if one day people here can ask for it for no better reason than they don't want to live without the use of their legs? One person's unbearable suffering is all another person may have ever known, and it won't make it easier to get ramps installed."

"Yeah, well," I say, picking at my food. "It's not a question of *if* for me, but when."

No one has taken a bite yet. Margot pries a slug out of its shell, keeping silent about her reasons.

"It won't work, you know," Whitby says. His hands jerk the wheels of his chair back and forth, front wheels lifted as he balances on the rear ones. It's like he can't sit still. I force my eyes away from his legs, just bones wrapped in fabric.

"What won't?" I ask.

"Margot says you're trying to show this is all normal."

"Death?"

"People avoid me, too," Whitby adds.

"Why would they do that?" I flush because I'm guilty of being uncomfortable around him. The question isn't about other people; it's about me.

"They don't want to see themselves. Everyone could become disabled in an instant. Like most people become disabled while dying."

"So when people look at me, they see their mortality."

"Only Narcissus was truly comfortable looking in the mirror," Margot interjects.

"It's why it needs to be done. People need to get past it," I say.

"It takes a lifetime," Whitby replies.

"That's what I've got."

"No, man. No, you don't." Whitby swallows. I bite back anger. I said I want people to speak the truth to me. "It really sucks."

"It. Death sucks?" I ask. Whitby's eyes widen. I burst into laughter. "You're telling me." It feels good to laugh, and the laughter keeps pouring out uncontrolled. Finally, I wipe my eyes, stifling a laugh still trying to escape. "Sorry. And I'm sorry I avoided you too."

"Hey, I—" Whitby struggles. "You don't have to go around asking for forgiveness for the things you've done."

I glance at Margot, who reddens. It reminds me of how I used to tell Jenkins everything. "I'm not sure I can, even if I wanted to. Most of my regrets include alcohol. Blacking out. Saying stupid things. Threatening or scaring people who didn't deserve to be scared. Six months ago, I was at a tournament in Hong Kong, for rugby, remember? We were staying at a hotel and had gone out drinking. The doorman was this tiny Chinese man. When we got back, someone joked that he looked cute. They took selfies with him. He stood so still. Taking it. I wanted a reaction though, so I pressed in real close until he was breathing into my sternum, his doorman cap perched on his head. I smelled the tobacco he smoked. Still nothing from the guy. I grabbed the fabric of his shirt and crotch, heaved him over my head, and roared. I felt so strong. Like I was a king." I shut my eyes, recalling the terror on his face, his screeching. I treat Swiper better than I treated that man. "I can't apologize to him. I can't believe I did that to another person."

"You're smiling, you know," Margot says. "You do realize that."

I go cold. She's right. "It seemed funny at the time."

"There's an unfortunate truth that privilege is often synonymous with assholery," Margot says.

I snort, starting in on the macaroni. Stella has infused the sauce of aged gouda with white truffle and I moan with pleasure. "Working on it. What about you?"

"I have regrets, most particularly diving into a certain shallow end." His hand jitters, knocking his fork against the plate. I've never heard him talk about how he became paralyzed.

He starts to say something but stops, then says, "I'm surprised picking up that guy and shaming him for a funny photo is your biggest regret. Didn't you cut the brake lines on some kid's bike?" Whitby asks. "Stephens's bike. After he drove his Humvee across your parents' flower beds."

"No one proved it was me," I say. "And who would have thought he wouldn't try them until he was already racing down a hill." But it's close to what Jenkins did with the crossbow. I struggle with the memory. I'm not smiling now.

"That's messed up," Margot says, expression uncertain. Any more and she might argue I'm beyond saving.

Whitby isn't done. "Was that the night you tapped your dick on the head of—"

"Yes, okay!" I say. "I've done stupid ass things." My shout rings out, and it's a moment before the clink of cutlery covers my heavy breathing. "A lot of stupid things."

"Okay, okay," Whitby says.

"You can't change the past, Tremmy," Margot says finally. "The only thing you can change is the future."

Margot's been chewing the same snail for a minute.

"You know those are basically just miniature colons," I say. She spits it out and I laugh. "I guess we're all done with assholes."

# 41 Days to Demise

I bury myself in death, picking up where I left off before tackling Jenkins from the Tower. I want the whole school talking about death. I write on the whiteboard screens using the *Death Warmed Over* tag.

*Only one percent of North Americans are dead before they turn eighteen.* Balder was right. Death is now a rare thing for the young, at least here and in my circle.

*The average life expectancy across the world is sixty-nine, but that varies based on where you were born and to what family. If you live in Sierra Leone, your life expectancy is forty-seven, but in Japan it is eighty-three.*

*The three most likely ways to die as a teenager are accidentally, which includes motor vehicle accidents, poisoning or drug overdose, or drowning; suicide is the second most likely cause of death; then homicide. Usually by a gun. The reasons are the same for boys and girls. Cancer doesn't even hit the top three.*

*But that's only in North America. It's totally different if you look at the worldwide statistics. Most female deaths are due to pregnancy and childbirth. Yep, that's teenagers. Then suicide before car accidents. After that comes diarrhea.* I'd prefer a brain tumor over death by diarrhea.

*In most African countries the leading cause of death in teens is HIV-AIDS.*

But, as with my earlier attempt to generate conversation, no one talks about any of these statistics. Every morning I write them on whiteboards, but it's like they never happened. I attend classes. Learn to argue. Sketch portraits of myself. And struggle to figure out how to manage a pain in my head that explodes in flashes of white and sulfur. No one discusses death, except in the whispers about mine at a safe distance. Jenkins doesn't say two words to me. He swaggers around the school, convincing parents to send their daughters here with his blistering smile and new sandalwood deodorant.

# 30 Days to Demise

Last night, I discovered a whole new statistic; I'm surprised by it more than any of the others. Excited by it because it forces me to think, so it will force others to think too. It's a depressingly cool statistic called DALY—or Disability-Adjusted Life Years lost. The main causes of DALY in Africa? Depression, road injuries, iron deficiency, HIV, and suicide. So, say in Zimbabwe, of a hundred thousand total years of life, over eighty thousand of those years are spent either dead or so disabled that they are considered lost. If only twenty percent of a life is worth living, then the real lifespan in Zimbabwe is about fifteen years. *I'm old.*

Only one kid this week, *one kid*, asked me if I was Death Warmed Over, and he went into class early yesterday to pick up some homework he forgot. Someone has been following me. I'm tired of wasting my time.

This morning, well after the cleaners have polished the floors, and staff have sharpened the pencils and straightened the materials at our desks, it's nearly silent. My footfalls echo through the halls. The marker squeaks as I write on the whiteboard screen.

*Researchers use DALY to measure Life Years lost due to all forms of disability. What if we used it to measure Life Years lost due to*

*First World problems? How many years are lost due to YouTube views? What about social media, partying, or hangovers?*

I add a second statistic, convinced that no one has seen any of them yet.

*The average life expectancy in the USA is seventy-eight, but if you're very poor, you can expect to live fifteen years less than if you're very rich. Bet you're glad you're very rich.*

I inspect my handiwork.

It's still the most shocking statistic I've found so far and bears repeating. Growing up rich, I didn't really realize I was rich. I see Mohammed and Margot and Stella, and I know everyone isn't like me, but I assumed they had *enough*. And I assumed that everyone has the same opportunities. I'd never have thought I'd get fifteen more years of life—not that *I* do, but people like me do. Jenkins will. That I was lucky. In fact, I remember thinking that expectations were set even higher for me, so *I* was the unlucky one. But the reality is that the rich are way more likely to end up rich, and those born poor are more likely to end up poor. There's not a lot of trading places.

I add a question to the board. *Should income be correlated with life expectancy? What should a year cost?*

After I'm done in one classroom, I run to the next and write the same things. This is my habit, but after hitting my third classroom, instead of continuing on down the hall to the fourth, I duck into the stairwell, run down the stairs, sprint to another stairwell and then skulk to the top of it to revisit the classrooms where I've already written my notes.

The first whiteboard has been erased. I dip into an alcove with a water fountain and slow my breathing. Moments later, I hear the quick patter of footsteps. I swing out, but they've already entered the next room. I wait in the hall for the culprit to reveal themselves. It only takes a moment. Jenkins leaves the next class and then hustles on. At the door to the fourth class, he stops. I haven't made it that far. There's nothing on the whiteboard. He swears.

"Buddy," I manage.

He stands, shoulders slouched, chin lowered.

"Why are you doing this to me?" I ask.

"Headmaster."

"Headmaster, what? He doesn't want me writing on whiteboards?"

"He says it's not healthy for you. That you're sick. Need to spend time on yourself, on getting help."

I charge up to Jenkins so that my chest is level with his. He straightens, and I realize I've either lost some height or he's grown. "I'm *not* healthy. I *am* sick. Every time you erase that stuff, you're wasting my time. DALY. You got that?"

"I'm head boy—"

"Not some lackey who needs to do the bidding of the Hairy Head!"

"I need this," he says. "I need to stay head boy."

"Why? So you can get into the top business school instead of the second best?" He swallows. "Have a spine. He can't remove the head boy every time he doesn't like something." Jenkins's eyes shift with uncertainty, and I put my hand on his shoulder. It's been a long time since he's let me touch him. "He can't do that. Let me do my thing. Sleep in this morning. Miss your alarm. I'm only trying to start a conversation."

After a minute, he nods. "Okay, Tremmy."

He walks away, but before he hits the stairwell, he turns. "Correlation isn't causation," he says.

"What?"

"Income and life expectancy. They might be correlated, but it doesn't mean being poor causes . . . Poor people are poor because they're less educated. So they don't eat well or exercise or stay on top of their medical appointments and stuff. So they die young. It's not because they're poor."

*Affirming the Consequent fallacy.*

My mind flashes back to before the party. When we met the two boys playing ball and Jenkins had said that they were sad, that he was the best part of their day. "Are you kidding me?" I ask, realizing he wasn't kidding then and he isn't now. "They're less educated because they're poor, not poor because they're less educated."

"Maybe the poor should go back to school."

"But that costs—"

"No one wants to hear these death facts, okay? Talking about death doesn't stop it from happening. I didn't become a better person after I saw my dad with his face blown off!"

He shoves open the door to the stairwell and hammers down the stairs before I can finish. It's true, what he said. In some ways that was when he became more self-destructive. But there's a difference, isn't there?

I restart my rounds.

This time, though, I change the question. *Should being poor be a death sentence?*

An hour later, when I walk into the World Issues class,

Pascale is responding to someone's question about whether the media is a form of state control.

Halfway through the class, Pascale has moved on to a news story about AIDS, and I flip through Ken Niving's transcript and can't find the spot. Margot leans over and asks, "Where are we?"

"Off script," I whisper back.

A smile plays at my lips.

\*\*\*

"It's brave," Delacroix says as I work on my breath-sketches. More pictures of myself. Narcissus and his mirror. Beside me, Minnie sutures the head of a rat onto the body of a cat.

"What's brave?" I ask.

Audra stares at me from across the paint-splattered floor.

"The photoshoot." As I'd entered class, Delacroix had been in a heated discussion with Audra. "You *are* okay with Audra's project?"

"Oh that. Yeah, I guess." I hadn't realized it was her art project too.

Delacroix exhales noisily out her nose and grips my shoulders. "To bare truth. Very brave."

Audra dusts her hands together and then leaves, as if she's pretty much done for the year, which I guess she is.

\*\*\*

As I'm eating lunch, Mohammed walks past, delivering a cappuccino to another student. On his way back he stops and leans down. "How many years live Syrian?" he asks in his accented English.

"What's the life expectancy of a Syrian?" I close my eyes, remembering my research. "Seventy, I think."

"And Canada?"

"Eighty-two."

"Good, I am Canadian," he says with a wide grin. We bump fists. It's weird to think he might have more years to live simply by immigrating to Canada. I can imagine everyone in Sierra Leone rushing for the border in order to live a dozen extra years. But the same could be true of the poor in the United States, who'd be much better off to come to Canada as refugees than stay where they are. Is an early death a valid reason for applying for refugee status? We talk about war refugees and climate crisis refugees, but not life expectancy refugees.

Mohammed's fist bump encourages me to keep at it.

*\*\**

*Meet me in the chapel.*

The note is taped to my door. I glance around, wondering when the note went up. It's signed with an *A*.

I draw heavy, slow breaths after slogging my knapsack over to my bed. The room smells musty with a touch of burned hair—probably from someone's electric heater. On my desk is the envelope with my medical record. I glance around, as if I might be able to figure out who had been in my room and why. What else might they have stolen?

Did someone find the envelope and drop it back? Had someone taken it and returned it? Maybe someone afraid to ask questions? Maybe it had always been there and I'm only losing my mind.

I crumple the note in my hand and head for the chapel.

The chapel is always open during the day, and I don't know why I don't spend more time here, even ignoring what happened the last time I was in it. It's managed to retain a sense of sanctuary, with VOG an ever-present witness. Maybe it's the expectation of silence and stillness.

Light scatters through the stained glass, painting the pews in glorious fall colors. I don't see *A*—Audra. I slide into the smooth oak choral pew. Someone has left a black music folder with the hymnals, "Amborough" embossed in gold lettering across its front. Inside must be the sheet music the choir is working on for the king.

I clear my throat, don't bother opening the music folder and start to sing the school song. For a brief moment I don't recognize the voice as my own. A thin, tinny sound. I wince and shake my head as it fades. *Dies.* There are so many parts of me that are dying. No one tells you that. That I'll die in a hundred parts before the last breath comes.

"VOG?" I ask.

"VOG is listening."

"Play 'Africa' by Toto."

The organ answers, and I lean back and breathe. Music connects me to others, but it also makes me feel small. I want to feel small.

Audra steps from the shadows of the balcony above. "Take off your clothes." Light winks from her camera lens.

"Here?"

"Churches are great places for ghosts and angels." She points to the red carpeted stairs before where the altar would have once been—a place of christenings, weddings, and funerals. And that's when I understand why I'm drawn here. The chapel is a place that understands beginnings and endings.

I slide out of the pew and strike a sultry pose on the velvety carpet.

Audra takes a picture from above. "Shirt."

I pull it off as she jogs down the stairs, heels echoing against marble steps worn by a hundred years of heels. I'm drenched in sunlight, feeling ever smaller as I shed skins. The shutter of her camera blinks a second time.

"VOG off," she says.

"VOG is listening."

"Do you think you're getting close?" she asks.

"Close?" I glance down at my prominent ribs, at the pock and needle marks, the tattoos of medical monitoring.

"What are the doctors saying now?" She's near. Near enough for me to spot the greedy curiosity in her eyes.

I pull my shirt back over my head. "I don't know yet. But pretty much anything could trip it." Audra squints, then holds up the camera and its silver film. Like a vulture high in a tree, the lens eyes me, wanting to pick my bones. The cost of pentobarbital feels high. If the headmaster is ready to send me into the desert, Audra is following and waiting. No better. As she frames another picture, I drop to the floor onto my knees. Arms, legs, head judder.

Audra screeches first with surprise and then delight. Her shoes clack against marble as she rushes forward. I swoon to the carpet. Stairs dig into my back with each writhe. My eyes have rolled back, and I reach toward the ceiling as if seeing something.

"So beautiful," I whisper.

*Click, click, click, click.*

"Yes!" Audra says. "Yes." *Are those tears?*

"Hold me," I say.

Then my arm drops.

I swallow my breath. I can't hold it for long now. Can't hold the smile back either. I let my tongue hang cartoonish. And giggle.

Audra's face is purple, tear streaked. "You owe me a roll of film."

"Worth every penny," I say. For the laughter.

"I'll enjoy watching you die."

And then I'm alone again.

So, alone. "VOG?"

"VOG listens."

"Play something happy."

# 28 Days to Demise

Wang's four-story mansion rises out of an old-growth forest, tree trunks as thick as the full-on Greek columns that flank the front door. Doric columns? Ionic? There's a joke about that but I forget it. The columns serve no structural purpose. They're decorative. It's a theme that starts here and never seems to stop.

"Divinia," the party-hostess announces her name. She takes my hand as she swishes in her sheer gown, leading me through a near colorless home. Home's the wrong word. Homes have chipped paint, missed dust balls, and antiques that don't quite fit in, handed down from grandparents or picked up on now-forgotten travels. The carpets have faded wine stains from when an aunt tripped over a stray toy and spilled her Châteauneuf-du-Pape reserve. We arrive at a miniature coliseum at the back of the building, which holds a circular pool surrounded by matching sandstone pillars, buttressing a glass dome. The Romans could have staged sea battles here; instead, a hundred kids joust and duel with foam lances and swords on surfboards.

"Enjoy the party," Divinia says in a sultry whisper and swishes away.

Unlike a Roman smorgasbord, with its platters of grapes and

fish and wine, Wang has pizza and beer and bottles of tequila lining the tables. Old Tremmy could get messy here. New Tremmy isn't that interested. I wonder whether I should send for an ambulance and have it wait at the end of the street. A few kids are smoking from a bong. It bubbles, the glass fogging with yellowish fumes. One girl snorts as she tries to hold the smoke in. Everyone else giggles.

Nobody is thinking, DALY drifting away with the pungent smoke.

As I arrive, Wang steps lightly from a rope swing and says, "No one is allowed in here with pants on," before recognizing it's me. Another kid launches from a zipline strung across the ceiling and dives into the pool, narrowly missing one of the jousting platforms. Near the tables, girls and boys in swimsuits turn. Seeing me, Wang's face drops. "Oh, hey, do whatever you like. Pants. Fine. Whatever."

Margot was right. I've pushed everyone away, but that's why I'm here tonight. To rebuild something of what I had.

"Thanks, Wang," I say, reaching down to grip both my pantlegs. "But I'm a big believer in rules and regulations." I yank. The pants tear along their Velcro seams, and I rip upward so that I'm holding them in my hands, the lower half of me nude except for a golden Speedo, sparkling with sequins.

There's a pause and then a roar of laughter.

"Disco banana hammock!" Wang screams. "Tremmy is back!"

I haul my shirt off and the cheering dies down. My chest and arms look like a poorly taken care of coffee table. Needle tracks from the last hospital visit distress my arms. Suction cup rings from electrodes dot my chest like coffee stains. "Where's the tequila?" I ask, and the cheering brightens.

I'm two shots in when Jenkins appears. We haven't spoken since the hallway, but letting me write my declarations has me hopeful. Without being asked, he pulls off his shirt and pants to show off his sculpted, spray-tanned body. The silence this time is awe-tinged. A vein snakes across corded abdominals. AC/DC fills the humid air, and it's his theme song now, not ours, as he flexes and slowly turns to reveal his back to the crowd. Across his shoulder blades is scrawled a tattoo. *Who Rules? Wang Rules!* I laugh despite myself.

"Tell me that's permanent," Wang yells.

"It'll stay there as long as you rule," Jenkins replies. "Speaking of which, who wants to challenge the undisputed dueling champion?" There's a sudden lineup. "Three hits wins."

I glance down at the knapsack I brought and pull out a life jacket. I don't want to die due to a seizure, not tonight in this pool. I'm fairly confident they'd say, "It was a good way to go, what he would've wanted."

The life jacket is yellow and has a duck head at the back.

Brunly shouts from the hot tub. "Put that on, Tremendous, and no one will ever look at you the same again."

"You mean this crown?" Slowly, carefully, I slip my hands beneath the glorious vinyl. I lift it to the ceiling, gazing reverently. "Tre-mmy, Tre-mmy," a chant begins, and I grin. Rank rubber slides over my head, and I wave my hand like the British queen does. Then I pinch the duck bill so it quacks. If I'm wearing a life jacket, I'm owning it.

As I head to the buffet spread, I stop. To influence anything, I need to participate. "Franklin," I call. He pauses as he engages his first opponent. "I recall beating your ass last year." I jump into line behind three others.

"I want to see this," Merton says as he offers me his spot and lets me ahead. Seeing me, the others part too. On his surfboard, Jenkins falters in his battle against Tonja and takes a jab to the ribs. He grunts, then with three sharp swings he hits Tonja's thigh, chest, head. Three touches and she's done. It happens so fast that Tonja keeps fighting.

"You're dead," Jenkins says. She sags and walks off the surfboard like it's the plank on a pirate ship.

"Up next, the nearly dead." Into the water I go and climb on the surfboard. It wobbles under my bare feet. The cold rips through me and with it sprouts a field of goose bumps. Jenkins has a distinct advantage, having had time to acclimatize to the footing.

"The dead jokes are growing old," he says.

"Like I never will?"

He brandishes his weapon. "We don't have to do this."

"The swords are foam. Get over it, you're not going to kill me," I reply. "That can come later. But I hereby waive the three-hit rule. This is to the death. No one wins until one of us has fallen in. Deal?" I add, "Unless I drop dead of natural causes. If that happens, we call it a draw."

Jenkins nods without smiling, and we cross swords. "On guard!" he shouts.

His first swing is two-handed, slicing from the bottom up, driving me back along the board so that its tip lifts. I windmill my arms and throw myself forward on to my knees. His blade whacks me on the shoulder, sending me and the board sliding through the water before I manage a lucky block with my blade, arcing it blindly back over my head.

I recover to one knee and then stab forward. But he's ready, cracking his sword-noodle against my head so that my ears sing. Like a whip, the sword snaps back and clips the other side of my head. With my balance off, sight blurred, it's already over. The surfboard rocks, and I step off, but somehow manage to step onto his, surprising him so that he needs to grapple my arm for balance. It offers a moment of respite, and I strike his chest with the pommel. His muscles bunch and surge, and then I'm tossed, flailing, and flop back onto my board.

The next hits come fast, smacking down with all his weight again and again and again. I try to recover under the barrage, but it's too fast and too heavy.

"Yield?" he screams. "Yield? Yield!"

The rest of the pool is silent except for the slap of foam against my back and the echo of his shouts. Blows rain until he delivers a chopping cut to my ribs that unbalances me and sends the board flipping.

I swim to the side and hand the sword up to the next guy. Behind me, Jenkins breathes heavily. "I tired him out for you," I say to the next competitor and roll out of the pool.

Last year it would have been an even fight. A week ago, maybe I could have won a couple points. I'm beaten. Red blotches bloom across my sides and, I imagine, my back from the strikes. Despite the shuddering cold, my face heats. I don't know why I was trying to keep up with him. Is this me being Margot's tree again? Rooted. That tree was hacked down by a foam noodle. So much of me still wants in. The party chatter picks back up again with the slaps of another swordfight. Music thuds. Laughter comes from the hot tub.

The hot tub fits eight, but twenty kids are buried in it to their chins. Water sloshes over the side.

It overflows as I slide into the slick flesh, smooth skin rubbing over my legs. Hands beneath the jets' bubbles find knees, and I am pressed up against pairs of legs. It has been weeks since I've really felt excited about anything between my legs or anyone else's; this cancer has made me less of a sexual being. Another death. Hot bodies mirror my thoughts, reorganizing so that no one is touching me.

"Nice life jacket," Jodie says with a scowl. "Very safe." Wet hair frames a pale face. Eyelashes form pretty triangles. Her makeup has mostly washed away in the pool. She always looked better without makeup. Without the foundation I can see her freckles. She looks more human.

"That's me, Tremmy the safety duck," I say.

Across the pool, Jenkins has abandoned dueling, nursing a beer while eyeing me, sizing me up, but there's little more he can cut away.

"Why don't you ever call yourself Tremendous?" Brunly asks.

"I would," Stack says.

I shrug. "It's a setup, isn't it? Say I start out tremendous, where am I supposed to go from there? That's the best I can be. I can only go down."

"Like Jodie," Stack says, sticking his tongue into his cheek.

"Shut it, Stack." Jodie splashes him in the face.

"Yeah, Stack," I say. "Seriously."

Jodie stares at me hard. *Surprised?* "Tremendous," she says.

"Right, I forgot who I was talking to," Stack replies, wiping his eyes. "I'm not allowed to say anything jokey."

"How about don't be a dick?" I ask.

"Yeah." Jodie laughs.

Under the water something snags my ankle and, as Stack surges like a hippo out of the water, I'm dunked underneath. I roll and then come up sputtering.

New nearly naked kids take Stack's place, moaning as they settle into the heat.

"Stack's right." Merton squints at me. "Hey, Wang! Did you even invite this guy?"

Wang, over at the tequila bar, pauses as he salts his hand.

"Not officially," he says slowly.

Jodie sits silent.

"Shouldn't we keep it Amborough? Those who intend to finish the year," Merton says. "Wouldn't want anyone to get hurt."

I straighten, and Merton laughs as the duck head pokes out at him. I face the challenge of his eyes. Aside from the music, there's silence. How is this building support? "You're right, man, might want to move away. I'm like an exploding bomb."

Merton swings his legs over the side and joins Stack.

Brunly leans toward me. "You're letting him get away with that? At least fart on *his* head."

"I reserve head farts for good friends, Brunly." I settle into the tub, water up to my chin as I slide down. "We needed some room. Stack and Merton had to go."

There's laughter.

"I totally didn't report you, by the way," Brunly says.

"I know," I say. "But I still wouldn't do it again. I'm an ass for doing it."

"It's the Mandela approach," Lily says. I hadn't noticed her.

"How's that?" I ask.

"Nelson Mandela's, Gandhi's too. They didn't think anger was ever a valid response."

"Forgiveness then, right?" I say. "I'm not so sure I'm a big enough man."

Jodie's eyes have glazed over, and she keeps sighing. Finally, she groans and follows after Stack. Her bikini bottoms have slid between the crack of her butt. She adjusts them as she walks.

Lily scoffs, but it's evidently not due to my staring. "Forgiveness is a construct of the patriarchy," she says. "We're expected to grovel to God and get absolution. Go to confessional, pay into the collections basket. Forgiveness is transactional. Perfect for institutions like the church."

"Deep. You sound like Margot," I say. "Except for the church-beating."

"Thanks!"

"I need to test the tequila," someone else says, leaving.

The hot tub empties further as three more kids follow.

"Go ahead and set off your bomb," Brunly says as he hops out too. "You guys keep talking and there'll be no one to hit."

A kid nearly misses the hot tub she's so drunk, and then slides between Lily and me. "Hi," she says. "I'm like, really drunk."

Across the pool Jenkins smirks at me as he chats with Jodie. She keeps stealing glances my way. Each time she does, Jenkins's expression grows more intense. He clinks a shot glass with hers, offers up salt on his arm to lick off and a lime between his lips to suck. Red-faced and cheered on by her girlfriends, Jodie tucks her hair behind her ears and then puts her hands behind her back. She licks salt from Jenkins's bicep and drinks the shot using only her lips. But, when she goes to take the lime out of his mouth, he holds her elbows, holding her to his lips.

Friends cheer and clap.

I want to leave. Something tells me I shouldn't.

# 27 Days to Demise

It's two o'clock in the morning, and I've done enough shots to count as a round of chemo. Over the course of the night, I had seemingly deep conversations with a half-dozen people. I already forget who and what about. Drunken Adjusted Life Years lost. I stagger through the house in search of a place to crash. Kids are strewn around like beer bottles; the lights are on everywhere and I can't find any switches, everything being voice activated but keyed only to the voices of Wang's family.

I mimic Wang's low pitch. "Lights off."

"I'm sorry, I don't recognize you. Please find a family member to use the system."

I walk in on Stack humping away at a woman with huge sloshing breasts and iridescent eyes. I blink and realize it's not a woman, it's Wang's older brother's sex robot.

"This is awesome," Stack says.

I really hope I'm drunk enough to forget this in the morning. As I yank the door back shut, I face Jenkins. He shambles down the hall, arm outstretched and bleary-eyed.

"Tell me you have a condom," he says. "Even that really old one."

I pat my swimsuit, as if it might have pockets. My jacket's downstairs by the pool.

He pales. "Crap. Maybe I can pull out."

"Who's the lucky mom-to-be?" My foggy brain slowly recalls that I'm angry with him.

He licks his lip and says, "Sorry, man, she likes me."

"Every girl likes you." He smirks agreement, but why the apology? "Wait, Jodie?" I'd caught the way he held her, the looks at me, both of their looks at me. The hall sharpens.

He doesn't deny it.

"Jodie's totally blitzed. She looked too wasted to walk earlier. I wouldn't touch her," I say, offhand, like I'm saying I need to avoid gluten.

"Well you're not really you anymore, are you?" he asks.

I struggle to tease apart that sentence. "You're right. Maybe I would have, but it's still wrong. *You* shouldn't touch her either."

"Such a hypocrite." He pushes me in the chest and wheels, tottering back toward the door he stumbled out of.

"Seriously, for your good and her good too, man."

"My good? Screw you for thinking about me," Jenkins slurs at the threshold.

"She's drunk. You're drunk."

"Equals out."

"She wasn't excited about you kissing her poolside."

"Seems convinced now."

"Convinced." I blink. Fully alert.

"Yeah." He opens the door.

"You can't convince drunk people of anything. Don't do this."

He starts to shut the door. There's only darkness beyond.

This is like the crossbow again, but a different kind of bolt. I put my leg through the doorway, and he slams the door on it. I cry out, fumble for a light switch, and catch a table lamp and find a pull cord.

The lamp flickers. Jodie lies on the floor. Her top's off, but she's facedown on the carpet, drooling as she snores. She doesn't even flinch as we crash into the room.

"Still think she wants anything from you?" I ask.

He squints at me. "Cockblocker."

"You serious?" I point. "She is not prey. Not prey. She's a person. You are a man. Act like one."

"What are you talking about? I wouldn't have touched her like that."

"Okay, Jenkins, *buddy*. Like you weren't going to fire that crossbow either."

"Buddy . . . try worst enemy. You try to keep head boy from me, you're angry I'm drone war general—alive and you're rotting away, hoping we all start dying." He grabs his shirt and charges.

I brace for the hit, but he brushes past.

*Boom.*

I go off.

I bite my lip, pull a blanket from the bed, and drag it over Jodie, before shutting off the lights.

I barely reach the washroom before I vomit. I vomit fresh, red blood.

\*\*\*

My stomach knots and knots again. I moan, bite down on my finger. Somewhere, dishes clink. It's morning. After a few breaths the spasm releases and I wait for another. It never arrives.

I roll off a white leather couch onto a fur carpet. Polar bear? Faux polar bear? I imagine vomiting blood over it, and I remember the toilet. My head pounds, each pump engorging the tumor, the tentacles of tumor. I don't need a doctor to tell me that vomiting blood isn't a good sign. Tequila likely didn't help. I'm done with tequila. What do you regret? *Most of my regrets include alcohol.*

Bodies litter the living area, which has been cleverly designed to include a number of comfortable places for conversations. Teenagers fold over chairs. They snore. I needn't have worried about barfing. There's plenty of that around, the air sour with bile. I search for a bathroom and bump into Jodie, who's on her way out of her room, the blanket I placed over her around her shoulders.

"Hey, Tremmy," she says quietly, cheeks rose colored.

"Hey, good sleep?"

She mocks barfing and smiles, but the lights are out in her eyes. Before she turns away, she asks, "Tremmy, do you know if . . . if Jenkins and I . . ."

"Did anything?"

She nods.

"Don't think so."

Relief washes across her face, and then she sobs.

"It's okay, it's okay," I say.

"I thought, I thought . . . he'd—" She cries out again, body spasming with agony. Over her shoulder, Jenkins watches from the shadow of an alcove, his face tight.

"Nothing happened, Jodie, I swear. I was there."

Now the relief is Jenkins's.

Jodie sniffles, brightening. "You know, when you said you were sick . . . I'm sorry I was scared of you."

"And now?"

"I'm not scared anymore."

I place a hand on her arm, and she flushes before heading to the washroom.

From his shadow, Jenkins gives me a thumb-up. He doesn't see that I stopped him from raping Jodie. He thinks I've kept him out of jail. A second time.

# 26 Days to Demise

I spend Sunday in bed, recovering from a hangover, silent about blood. Because blood is bad. Blood means tests. DALY lost. Instead, when my mother isn't hovering, I surf the internet and decide it is likely a stomach ulcer, an ulcer that could easily have been exacerbated by the tequila.

I'm not doing well. The knives of brain-pain slash at more regular, more frequent intervals. The portrait I sketch is barely recognizable as me. I can hope that my shortness of breath is due to the hangover and vow never to drink again, which makes me laugh, so I add sex and driving and wonder what comes next. The laughter hurts.

"Let me check your forehead," my mom says, opening coffee-colored drapes to a steely day. I snap the lid of my laptop shut. "I wanted to take you out to lunch."

I've lost too much time already. I know how to be rid of her.

"Why won't you support MAID for me?" I ask. She shuts her eyes. The fingers of her hand, ready to cup my forehead, fold into the palm. "Do you want to see me suffer?"

"That's unfair. Murder is wrong. You're asking for murder. No more of this, please."

"But it wouldn't be if I were an adult?" I ask.

"Tremmy, I've thought about this more than I want to." She sits on my bed. "I don't want to answer this question, Tremmy. It gives me too much power. I'm tired. I'm struggling. If I say yes, how much is because *I'm* suffering? Because I failed?"

"I'm asking you to give *me* the choice. Don't you think I can choose?"

"I don't understand why this is important to you."

"Because it takes away the dying part. It means I don't have to worry. That's the gift."

"We will manage the pain, Tremmy. I will be there for you."

"There's a reason MAID exists, Mom." I don't trust the system to take care of the pain. *I don't trust her.* "What about that part between when you can't manage and death? What will you do then?"

Her hands clench in her lap. "What if you could have gotten better?"

*The problem of miracles.*

"I don't believe in miracles, Mom."

"Maybe I do!"

"Don't you think a miracle would have happened by now?" But then, she doesn't know about the blood. "We'll talk after the next scans, Mom. Then you'll know."

Her eyes waver, and her thumb caresses the top of my hand. "Okay, sweetheart."

*Doing nothing is still a decision.*

# 20 Days to Demise

A pall hangs over Amborough in the days that follow Flesh-Fest. Midterm exams come and go. No one expected me to take them. Without a doctor's note to clear me, I'm still relegated to the bench during drone wars and, with my right leg dragging when I'm tired, this won't change. My singing is a feeble whisper. My drawing time dwindles. I dwindle. I'm left out, sidelined; it's as if everyone in Margot's race has surged ahead of me, well beyond my finish line. Uncatchable, unreachable. But, in all of this, I see one more chance, a baton handed back from the generations of students who have gone before.

# 13 Days to Demise

Private schools are filled with traditions. Some include the entire school. Some the junior years. Some are for seniors only.

Last year, when I was a junior, we competed for the best decorated deck in the runup to Christmas. Deck decorating is an apprenticeship in thievery. Our prefect split us into three groups, because three of us had been allowed cars on campus. Each car was to troll a different neighborhood. Our job was to sneak onto properties and borrow Christmas paraphernalia.

We unplugged red and green security floodlights. We unstrung rainbows of LEDs from towering pines, running around the tree as silently as possible with snow squeaking beneath our boots in the dark. We stuffed gigantic blow-up Santas and Frosty the Snowmen into rear seats, deflating them as we pushed. We were Grinches, and we laughed, taking photos of where everything needed to be returned.

When the teacher-judges walked onto the deck to evaluate, our prefect, already glowing with pride, threw the switch on a power bar. The lights of the entire house flickered with the surge, and then ours blazed. Two snowmen, one Santa, and a giant Rudolph all inflated as we sang "Jingle Bells." Projections of snowflakes whirled across the walls and ceiling. We won. The teachers never questioned where we had collected such an eclectic mix. And after, no one cared about taking the goods back to their owners. Wang returned the baby Jesus to the local church's nativity scene, but only when we started to joke that he was headed to hell if he didn't.

Borrowing became stealing. It may have been wrong, but the houses we stole from were mansions; we knew their losses wouldn't matter, because it wouldn't have mattered for us. It wasn't exactly Robin Hood style, but we hadn't felt like we were stealing from the poor either. They'd get new decorations. Or their dad would yell at their groundskeepers for not chaining the decorations down. It was a joke.

Tonight is another tradition entirely. Tonight is Pumpkin Night, and it's my chance to be a part of Amborough again.

In many ways, Pumpkin Night is both worse and better than burglarizing dozens of homes and churches. In one night, we decorate campus with hundreds upon hundreds of pumpkins. Pumpkin skulls will be driven through every tine of the wrought-iron fence surrounding the school. Hundreds, maybe thousands, of pumpkins, pulled from farmers' fields, from Loblaws and Walmart stores after midnight, will decorate the campus.

There's no pretext of borrowing anything. We drive to farmers' fields to collect the pumpkins from them. But what we steal doesn't have any real value. No one is selling pumpkins after Halloween. We visit supermarkets where the bins of pumpkins are left out, often still brimming. Having access to my pickup truck, I'm a much sought-after driver this year. Maybe I've only been reluctantly included, but I am included, and I'll take any connection on offer.

"But I can't drive," I say to Stack and Audra.

It's the first time I've admitted it. My truck rusts in my spot, where it has sat idle for weeks. I'm as likely to leave campus unconscious as conscious. License or not, I shouldn't be driving. "Do you want me to be driving when something weird happens to my brain?"

Stack stares. "No, no, sorry. Guess not."

"But I'm coming still. Don't trust you guys not to drive my truck into a ditch."

"I'm never learning to drive," Audra says. "Self-driving cars are where it's at. Until then, there's always the bus."

"Bus? Good one. No one's that poor," Stack says. "But I can't drive stick, and I don't know anyone who can. Maybe Wang's chauffeur?"

"What about Margot?" Audra asks.

"She's boycotting, says Pumpkin Night is stupid," I say with a shrug.

"It's tradition!" Stack cries and gives me the first fist bump I've had in a week.

"I'll drive," Jenkins says from the door. Stack and Audra look to me to fill the lengthening silence. "Yours is the only pickup. We need it. And I learned stick by driving that beater with your dad."

And whether it's an excuse or an olive branch, I don't know, but I don't have time to care. He's been nicer to me than ever since Flesh-Fest and Jodie. "We've got our team then," I say.

"Sick," he replies and walks on.

Pumpkin Night is a poorly kept secret, with the housemasters ignoring obvious preparations of warm jackets and head lamps and walkie-talkies. We'll spend the first few hours after lights-out collecting pumpkins and the final hours before dawn decorating. It's also a night of pranks. Last year, the seniors pulled out the tables and chairs from the entire dining hall onto the front lawn, and we had breakfast served outside. This year I know Jenkins plans on placing a pumpkin on the top of the chapel's cross. It's been tried many times, but never successfully. Each year has to be crazier than the last.

At dinner, every senior, with the exception of Margot, asks for coffee. Near the end of the meal, she leans back, balancing on chair legs, lifting her head from where she buried it in a book and whispers to me, "We can't afford mistakes, Tremmy. Can't."

But she's wrong on this one. Pumpkin Night is approved disobedience and has been for decades. "You have a good sleep, Margot."

Back in my room, Jenkins holds a slip of paper that details our territory. I recognize Lily's handwriting. We're on pumpkin pickup in farm country north of eighth line.

"Epic," Jenkins says. "I took an Uber up here a few days ago and marked the major pumpkin patches." He unfolds a map with highlighted circles. A couple farms are crossed out in red marker. "The pumpkins are too close to farmhouses," he explains.

"Ready?" I ask, grabbing the fob for my truck.

"Born ready," Jenkins replies and fist-bumps Stack before shouldering the gear.

"Ready," Audra says.

"Can you even lift a pumpkin?" Jenkins asks her.

"I can kick your ass, twig," she replies, and I laugh, sliding across the mattress to high-five her.

"Mothership, this is Scrooge McDuck, over," I speak into the walkie-talkie.

"Mothership reading you loud and clear," Lily replies.

"Scrooge McDuck is on the move, over."

"Ten-four, may the Great Pumpkin have your back."

I squelch twice to signal affirmative.

In the truck, the cold leather of the passenger seat seeps through my jeans. Jenkins starts it, a Silverado with the six-liter V8 engine, crew cab. It's jacked up on raised suspension and oversized tires.

Jenkins keeps the headlights off until we turn out of campus and then hammers the gas pedal to the floor. The engine pauses before roaring. Jenkins, Stack, Audra, and I, we all whoop—this is everything I love about Amborough, everything I love about life. Wind from the open window rushes through my hair, I am free. Alive. One. Last. Night.

Stack pulls a bottle out of the bag and I take a swig and cough and splutter. "What is that?"

"Cognac. Rémy Martin. My mom loves the stuff."

"It's gross." And I cringe at the memory of blood in a toilet.

Stack takes a swig himself, eyes watering as he wipes a hand across his mouth. Then takes another. "It gets better as you go."

It's not long before we're beyond the lights of the city and on to gravel country roads. The headlights cut through an icy fog. The in-dash GPS shows us nearing the first pumpkin patch. Jenkins turns off the lights and radio, and we drive in a hush. If there were any stars or moonlight, they're well buffered by clouds. Drizzle and a scattering of sleet falls on the windshield. The distant glow of the suburbs frames tightly wrapped hay bales.

"I love hay bales," I say. Jenkins scoffs.

"You and Monet," Audra says. I stare back at her. "Monet? The painter? He had a thing for haystacks, painted dozens of them."

"Why?" I ask.

She shrugs.

"That's stupid," Stack replies. "I'd paint naked chicks."

Audra taunts. "Real, or naked robot—"

"Who invited this bitch along anyway?" Jenkins asks. In the silence, his eyes flick up to the rearview mirror in search of support.

Audra replies, "Sounds like someone doesn't like being the only one who can dish out—"

"Shut up, shh . . ." Jenkins says and hands me a powerful head lamp. Another half a mile up the road, the lights of a farmhouse burn through the mist.

Audra mutters, "Such an ass."

Tires crunch in deep gravel as Jenkins pulls onto the shoulder. I lean out the window to scan the field. A halo of light shimmers at the edges of my beam, but within the center of the blaze is a mess of green and browning vines. Nothing orange. No pumpkins.

"You have the right place?" I ask.

"This place was full of pumpkins. I don't know what happened."

"Halloween, I guess," Stack says and laughs.

"It's not funny," Audra replies. "We need pumpkins."

I scan deeper. Among the tangle of vines lie a few pumpkins.

"Well, let's grab what we can," I say and hop out of the truck. The bottle of cognac sloshes once more before Stack, Audra, and Jenkins join me. We split up, each heading for different pumpkins. The soil is crispy with frost on top and muddy beneath, making footing treacherous in the rutted field. The scent of rich earth fills my nostrils. I jump to vine clumps for traction, but these too are slippery with mold.

The first pumpkin I grab for is slimy with rot, but the second is firm, with only a few soft spots. We don't need any to win county fairs. As big as my chest, I lug it back to the truck, while the others have collected two each—even Audra, who might be trying to prove herself to Jenkins.

"Let's see if the next patch is better," Jenkins says. "We can always come back."

I roll the pumpkin into the truck bed, where it thuds, and hop back into the passenger seat. Stack gives me the thumbs up and takes another swig. "If you pass out, I'm leaving you behind, man," I warn.

He laughs. "Audra can carry me."

But no one's laughing after we hit two more pumpkin patches, both of them nearly bereft of fruit. Soon we're sweating and tired, the truck bed only a quarter full of hard-fought pumpkins, half of them spotted with decay.

"I'm trying the farm on eleventh line," Jenkins says.

I consult the map, and it's one of the crossed-out pumpkin patches. "Maybe other crews are having better luck?"

We all know that's not true. The complaints have crackled over the radio all night. Evidently early frost ruined the crop.

Audra says, "How close was the pumpkin patch to the farmhouse?"

"Does it matter? Do you want this to be the worst Pumpkin Night ever?" Jenkins asks.

"No!" Stack roars and takes a swig. "No pumpkins, no Pumpkin Night."

"I won't be head prefect on the year Pumpkin Night sucked," Jenkins shouts.

"Right," Audra mutters. "What's the worst that could happen?"

Jenkins turns onto eleventh line.

As we near the pumpkin patch, the problem is obvious. A large two-and-a-half-story farmhouse abuts a field. A field full of pumpkins.

"Jackpot," Jenkins whispers.

"Thank you, Great Pumpkin," Stack shouts, and I hush him. "We have pumpkins," he hisses into the radio. Team after team chimes in with congratulations. "We are the champumpkins, my friends."

Jenkins shuts off the lights. The glow from barn security lamps shines down on the field. It's a lot of protection for a pumpkin patch. Paint flakes from the dark farmhouse.

"Two thirty in the morning. No one is awake," Jenkins says. "We can do this."

"I say we drive right up to it," Stack replies.

"No way," Audra says. "Farms are quiet. Any engine noise will wake a farmer. We do this from the road." The field is set back a hundred yards.

We all look silently at the jumble of pumpkins.

"You only live once," I say.

"Easy for you to say," Audra complains. "Farmers own guns."

Jenkins laughs. Stack drinks.

And then we're out and running, avoiding the gravel, keeping to the grassy center of the farm lane. As we slip past the house, I half-expect a dog to growl, but then we're into the patch. I take the biggest, fattest pumpkin I think I can carry and haul it back toward the truck. Stack, who has finished a third of the bottle, straggles.

"Again," I say, patting smooth corrugate orange skin. Jenkins sprints ahead.

Audra gives me a questioning look, and I shrug before whispering, "We need pumpkins. Badly."

The pumpkins are big and the truck fills quickly. After the fourth or fifth pumpkin each, and no sign of anyone home, we all start to relax, but my right leg is leaving a furrow where it drags.

"This one looks like Jenkins's ass," Stack says.

I start to say something about Stack's face or Jenkins being an ass, but then I spot the pumpkin, and it has a perfect ass crack. "Actually, that is a great ass."

"I'd slap that ass," Jenkins says.

"I'm pimping out that pumpkin," I reply.

"Tremendous pimps pumpkins for pumping," Audra says. "That's so awesome."

Laughter bursts from me. I immediately cut it off even as it echoes off the gray boards of the barn. A cat scrambles across a sheet metal roof. "Sorry."

But no farmhouse light switches on. Our breaths blow frostily with relief. The swig of cognac I'd taken burns in my chest. I'm lightheaded as I roll another pumpkin into the back of the truck.

It's after three o'clock and I'm tired and giddy. At the edges of my vision, shadows shift and the icy fog surrounding the security lights shimmers weirdly. At first, the shadows reach through the cracks in the barnboards or shift feline behind the leaded panes of the farmhouse windows. Audra and Jenkins are unaffected, jogging back for pumpkin after pumpkin. Stack can barely keep on his feet. But the darkness folds in on me, one pumpkin at a time, from the edges in. As I trudge and drag myself back into the muddy patch, my head is yanked lower by the heavy dark.

"You okay, dude?" Audra asks.

"Looking for angels again?" I reply.

"What did you say?"

"Angels."

She stares at me for a second before heading back. "This is the last pumpkin," she says to Stack as she passes him.

"Right, baby," he says. "Baby, baby, baby . . ."

Jenkins is nearest the truck, when someone asks, "Which of you boys will be paying for those? And all the other years' too!"

It's a second before anyone realizes what's happening.

"Run!" Audra shouts. "And I'm a girl!"

Jenkins swears. Stack drops his pumpkin and sprints. Even drunk and covering three times the distance due to his swerving, he's faster than the farmer who scrambles down porch steps. I watch disconnected, like one of the black shadows tunneling my vision.

"Tremmy!" Audra calls.

The truck starts. My head sags and I can't lift it. The large pumpkin, half buried in a nest of moldering vines, begins to sparkle like Cinderella's right before it becomes a carriage. The edges of night start another darker fold.

"Tremmy!" someone hollers.

The truck engine revs. The gears grind, then the clutch pops.

The craggy face of the farmer pushes into my line of sight. An angry, tired, disappointed face. "What's wrong with you, boy?"

The pumpkin is cold across my belly, like a clean, fresh sheet.

"Chrissy!" the farmer shouts, as a truck engine fades, "Call the ambulance. Little prick looks like he's dying on us."

# 10 Days to Demise

Some things I have learned only because I'm dying.

*From VOG: The dust motes in the chapel are bound by the same science that binds the rings to Saturn.*

*From Pascale: It is far more probable that I am part of a simulation than that I am alive at this moment in time on this tiny planet.*

*From Stella: Ice cream is worth living for.* It's more important than vengeance.

I have no time for vengeance. Bothering with living at all is a leap of faith. The forces that govern the small things in a system also govern the big.

The longer you stare at a hospital ceiling, the more shapes you discover in the water stains. The people currently around my bed are not sharing all of their thoughts. I know it. I know it when my mom doesn't look me in the eye. I know it when my dad laughs too hard at some dumb joke about the food, which actually isn't that bad.

I can walk still, but barely. Enough to avoid a catheter. The tumor presses on everything from my motor cortex to the optical nerve. I can't feel it. It manifests in the weird shadows. The shimmering lights. Stars. I once read that some kid, nicknamed Bubble Boy because he had to live in a bubble, had asked to see the stars before he died. I wonder how satisfying that was, or whether he would have been better off leaving it to his imagination.

Fatigue is the enemy. No one told me I'd be so tired. But I've been here for a few days now and I don't think I'm getting any better. I've tipped down the slide, and I'm on my way.

"He shouldn't go back," my mom says. "The germs at school will kill him." *Right, unlike the hospital.* "He'll stay home." *What if I want to see the stars?*

A young doctor knocks hesitantly, perhaps a resident, maybe newly minted. "Hi, Tremendous," he says. My mom's fingers squeeze at my hand as though she's massaging a heart back into rhythm. "Your doctor wanted me to explain the results of one of your tests. Have you been having any stomach pain? Vomiting blood?"

When I don't respond right away, my mom leans into me. "Have you?"

I nod. "Yes." I cough and clear my throat. "After the party, but I'd been drinking and . . ." I shrug. "Does it matter?"

The doctor smiles. "Not unless you want to bleed out?"

"No," my mom says sharply, and the doctor straightens.

"Then it matters. You have a stomach ulcer. Likely a side effect of the earlier round of chemotherapy."

"What's the treatment?" my dad asks.

"A course of antibiotics."

"Wait," I say. "I can die from this?"

The doctor shrugs. "If left untreated."

"And I can refuse treatment?" The doctor might be beginning to clue in because he turns to my mom for help. "Without my parents' consent?"

"Why would you do that?" the doctor asks.

"Have you read the rest of my chart? The part about terminal cancer?" The doctor nods. "If I wanted to let myself die before the cancer got me, I could do it." When the doctor still registers confusion, I add, "You *have* read the rest of my chart?"

"Yes, yes. But it would cost you . . . months, and we have an easy cure for this."

"Tremmy." My mom's eyes quaver with desperation. I imagine her picturing me standing on the guardrail of a highway overpass. But this isn't suicide. No one is doing the killing.

I lie back and stare at the ceiling, languishing, reveling in the decision. It feels good to have options. To have control, even if that control is to let blood fill my stomach. "Are we past talk of miracles now?"

She hesitates. "No. I don't think so."

"Why?"

"Because *every* moment is precious. Because I'm not religious and I believe there is only one life."

*She'll never be beyond miracles.*

"But this isn't about you. This is about me and what I want, what I believe. It's about you letting me go . . ."

The truth is, life, for me, is still worth living. But what if I don't have another chance to control the process of death? What if this is the only chance I have to go quickly and easily? And this is why MAID for minors is important, so I don't have to let myself bleed out to circumvent arbitrary rules. "Okay," I say.

"Give me the antibiotics. Then let's get out of here."

"How about we see how you're doing tomorrow, Trem," my dad replies while tapping out a message on his phone.

"What'll be different tomorrow?" I ask. Except my life will be one day shorter.

"We'll have more results, from the CAT scans. Treatment options. The doctor thinks we might be able to shrink some of the tumor."

"No, Dad, if the treatment saves me any time, I'll have to spend the same amount of time sick."

His stare pleads. "But alive."

"That's not really alive. Not better." It's not like I have an aversion to hope, but I don't have time for lies either. "Take me back to school," I say. "I really want to sleep in my own bed, away from the beeps and the blood pressure checks at two in the morning." I miss the distractions of deck pile-ons, pranks, the rhythm of school.

"Your own bed is at home, Tremmy," my mom says.

My dad pats me on the wrist. "We'll check with the doctor."

My mom follows him out. I don't have my phone and haven't been online for the forty-eight hours I've been conscious. The lack of connection has left me in this anxiety-inducing limbo, where I have no idea if Audra and the others were caught. If my truck is okay. How spectacularly Pumpkin Night ended. I don't dare ask or I might get them into trouble. I remember the farmer, and then nothing else.

With my parents out of the room, I unhook the heart rate monitor so that I can go to the washroom without an audience. My lack of balance forces me to stop each step, get my bearings, and take another, all the while keeping my eye on the doorknob to the bathroom. Walking for me is a bit like yoga's Warrior Three pose, where I need to focus on something unmoving so I don't fall. Except I'm not balancing on one foot, I'm trying to walk without collapsing. I grab for the doorknob, miss on the first try, and catch the steel handle with the second. I take a deep breath and shuffle for the islands of porcelain. I grab on to the sink, swing around, pull down my pants, and collapse onto the toilet. The seat's so cold I gasp. Then I see my underwear.

I shat my pants.

I stare at it for a long moment before taking the underpants off and dumping them in the trash. I clean myself up. I'm sick. I've been unconscious. People crap their pants when this happens. It's crappy.

It's over. I can live with this. It's over, but not time.

After cleaning myself up, I linger at my reflection. I'm lean, but not hollow-cheeked. I'm pale but not pallid. I've got long, wavy brown hair, tousled by sleep. It's my eyes that are dying. Glazed, dull, and lonely.

"Tremendous?" It's a nurse from the hospital room.

"I'm good," I say through the door, forcing cheer into my voice.

Heels clack away. I open the door and repeat my unsteady hustle back to the bed.

When I wobble, I lean down to grip the chair beside the bed. Wedged between the seat cushion and the back is a phone. My dad's phone. It must have popped out of his back pocket. I toss it on the bed and then complete the patient transfer. Finally, I sit on the mattress and swing my legs back aboard, taking a second to feel for the phone's smooth glass beneath the hospital gown. I key in a password that hasn't changed in years and log into my social media accounts, hoping to see some pictures of Pumpkin Night. Relaxing into the feeds.

I smile as I scroll through images of pumpkins on fences, on pillars, one on the top of the flagpole, and shake my head at the one all the way on top of the chapel cross. I have seen a lot of Pumpkin Nights, though, and something about this one seems half-hearted. Other Pumpkin Nights had cleverly carved pumpkins, the headmaster's car buried in pumpkins, his car recreated out of pumpkins, the headmaster as a pumpkin effigy, the entire teaching staff carved into pumpkins. It's like the students stopped before the creativity fueled by alcohol, weed, and lack of sleep really kicked in.

I've got messages too.

Jenkins: *Sorry, man! I had to save everyone else.*

Audra: *If I'd known you were in trouble, I never would have left. I'm sorry. I owe you.*

Stack: *No matter how bad you feel, I'm pretty sure my head hurts worse. If I find this Rémy Martin, I'm kicking his ass.*

Jenkins: *You see that, Tremmy? You see that?* He's sent another photo of the pumpkin on the cross. *Epic.* Is he sending the photo to make me jealous, or is he sharing a triumph? A second photo reveals how he did it. Jenkins hovers with a jetpack. *A jetpack.*

Margot: *I can't believe they did this to you.*

My dad goes a shade paler when he spots me with the phone. "Hey, Dad."

"Hey . . ." He's acting weird, staring at the phone.

"You know what I want?" I ask.

"No, what?" He steps back, shoulders bunching.

"Ice cream. Rocky Road." His eyes shut, and he smiles.

My oncologist removes the smile just as quickly as she enters and flips the screen of her tablet around, saying, "We have the scans back." She pauses, and we're either supposed to clap or hold our breath. "They are showing significant progression in the tumor." Her finger brushes a bright white area of the brain. "This here, at the occipital lobe, has nearly doubled in size over the last two months. That's why you're having issues with balance and losing consciousness."

I can't see peanut as peanut anymore. I imagine a squid. It reaches down with its cool, slimy tentacles and grips my stomach. Its beak feeds on my lungs, stealing my breath. A pressure in my butt suggests I might crap my pants again, also not an inappropriate reaction.

"Wait," I say. Her finger has drifted to another part of my brain, on the right-hand lobe. "It doesn't matter."

"There are treatment options," she says.

"Radiation, surgery, drugs," I count off on my fingers.

She lowers the tablet to her side. "We can be highly targeted in our treatment."

"No side effects?" I ask.

"Side effects can be expected, but—"

"No thank you."

"Tremmy." My mom grabs my hand. "Treatment—"

"What's the success rate?" I challenge.

"We can reduce the size—" the doctor begins.

"It's buying time. No cure." I'm being argumentative. Of course, there's no cure. No one is talking about miracles anymore. Miracles are no longer a problem.

"No cure," the doctor agrees.

"Do I have any new horror that you'd like to share?"

The doctor glances to my dad and then back to me. "There's a strong possibility that—"

"Wait. I don't want to know. I don't want my imagination to know." My disease is better left to my imagination. No more squids. One is enough.

The doctor nods.

"I don't want a prognosis either. Six weeks, three months. Let's say short." She doesn't object. "Let me out of here."

The doctor steps to the side of the doorway and motions. At first, I think she's waving me out, but Dr. Balder stands in the door. It's a circus. I have the kraken in my head, and no one is listening to me, and I am going to crap myself and I want everyone out for that.

"I'm glad you're here," I say. "Do me a favor?"

"If I can," he says.

"Will you assess my capacity to give consent for MAID as if I'm of age."

Dr. Balder shakes his head, but I don't wait. I have the DNR forms in my room at school. I know what he needs.

"Mom, Dad, doctors have these special forms they have to fill out when they're meeting with patients who want MAID. I have answers, okay?"

Everyone is shaking their heads now.

"You all decide if I have the capacity to consent." I swallow and hurry on. "I have a stage four brain cancer, specifically a rare form of diffuse intrinsic pontine glioma, which means it is inoperable and malignant. My condition is terminal, and I will die of the brain cancer or complications related to it. I have no reason to doubt this diagnosis. I have had second opinions.

"There are several experimental treatment options for my tumors. None of these will cure me. If successful, experimental treatment may increase the time I have left to live. From weeks to months. This is the optimistic scenario. Some of these treatments have caused death due to heart attack and stroke. All cause nausea, hair loss, fatigue, dizziness, and more. I have refused these treatments because, on balance, I do not see they are worth the risk. I am instead requesting medical aid in dying so that I can be assured that I won't die in intolerable pain. That I can have control over the time and place of my death. That I can avoid the final stage of my disease, which can include loss of ability to swallow, speak, breathe, and hear. I am refusing alternative treatments. I understand that MAID will end in my death. And that death is a permanent condition. I am not being influenced by my parents to desire MAID. I am not being influenced by my friends to desire MAID. It is my personal choice."

I stop. My mom is sobbing.

"No more miracles, Mom," I shout. "Did that cover it, Doctor Balder?"

He's staring at his black shoes.

"I will request a homecare consult," the oncologist says.

"Homecare?" I ask.

"Palliative care," the doctor clarifies.

My dad looks through me, shoulders slouched, gaze blank.

I move past the obvious—that this is happening, that

everyone has accepted I'm actively dying—to the logistics. "They can come wherever I want? Like to my school? I board there."

"They go anywhere and everywhere in our community."

I sniff. "Okay."

The doctors leave. My dad's Adam's apple bobs as he packs the few things he'd brought me. Toothpaste. Another new tube. What a waste. How many tubes of toothpaste does the average human use? A couple hundred? Not many.

"Will you finish that?" I ask. He holds up the toothpaste with a questioning look. "Yeah, the toothpaste. It's a new tube. Will you finish it?" At the pain twisting his face, I wave the question off. "Why would you? Why would you want the weird reminder?"

He zips the bag and pauses. "Everything will be a reminder, Trem. And I want it to be. I would never waste anything of yours, and I cherish every moment we are together."

It's the first time I've heard him admit that I'll be gone. I didn't realize how much I need his surrogate well of hope. I push back deep into the mattress and pillows.

My mom folds my clothes neatly on the bed. Folds my socks, new underwear, a shirt, jeans. Folds them even though she knows I'll need to put them on. Finally she stops and shakes the crease out of the jeans.

"Tremmy, I don't want to say goodbye." The clump of guilt in my throat silences my question. "And . . . if one of your friends helps you die, I will personally charge them with murder."

*So that's how it's going to be.*

We all sit for a second in silence, listening to my breathing and to the beep of a machine. "The school called," my mom adds finally with a measure of dread. "The headmaster wants to meet with you as soon as we arrive."

"What else can he do to me?" I ask.

\*\*\*

Hairy Head plays with his ponytail, which swooshes past his chin. "You're expelled."

"For what?" I ask, glancing to my parents for support, but their faces betray nothing. "You knew?"

"The farmer is pressing criminal charges," my mom explains.

"For stealing rotting pumpkins?" I ask. "The whole senior year was doing that!"

"You . . . you were caught."

"So you're expelling me?" I'm shaking between my parents, facing the Hairy Head. I'm an outflanked drone with three sentinels closing.

"Tremmy." My mom touches my shoulder. I flinch. "They don't want you dying here. The parent council had an emergency meeting. They are worried you are distracting their children from studies at a really important time. A parent has complained too. One of the big donors."

"It is school policy to expel students charged with a criminal offense," the headmaster explains. Black and white.

"Of stealing compost," I say. "Jenkins was charged with attempted murder."

"Never charged," the headmaster notes.

Pain shoots through my skull. The headmaster rakes his fingernails across the tumor. "This bites."

"It does. I offered the farmer payment," my dad says. "But he wouldn't take it."

I search for something to say and don't know if it's cancer fuzzies or rage that prevents me from coming up with the right response. Instead, I simply let my mouth run. "What do you have against me?"

It's as though the headmaster is shot. His face flushes; fledgling jowls jangle. He levers himself from his chair and moves across the room. He recovers slowly, a hand on the silver vase on the mantel. "Tremendous, I have done nothing—nothing—but support you for the last six years. And I only want what is in your best interests. Be with your family. Focus on your medical needs." He shakes his head. "And, you must agree, sexual assault, fights, criminal charges—your staying has not gone well."

I can almost hear Margot making chainsaw noises as he cuts me down. A chainsaw I put in his hand. *Can't afford mistakes.*

"What are you afraid of?" I demand. *You don't get to demand answers.*

Hairy Head turns to my parents for help. I brush past the headmaster. When my elbow touches his, I dust it off as though it's filthy. His expression purples.

"Tremmy!" my mother says and points out the door.

"I'm not leaving," I say.

"Then you will be charged with trespassing," Hairy Head replies.

"You're being awfully hard on him," my mom says, and then I realize she's talking to me. I whirl in the doorframe and fall on my side. My parents rush for me, and I hold up my hands. "He's known you since you were eleven, Tremmy. Remember when the older students were bullying you? The headmaster spent hours with them and you. Took you under his wing. You are not seeing that he is still trying to protect you."

"You know what, Mom? I'm focused on me right now. His life expectancy is looking pretty darn good."

She bends, reaches out like I'm Swiper, skittish and hiding under a car. "That's part of it too. You're not supposed to die. You're not only you. You're the aggregate of dozens of people's hard work and dreams. Your dreams, sure, but theirs too. Teachers . . . parents . . . aren't supposed to outlive their students and kids."

"You want me to feel sorry for him?" I ask, genuinely confused now.

"People become teachers because they believe that the greatest influence they can have is to teach kids like you. To shape you. The more kids they shape, the greater the impact. Whether you like it or not, people had high expectations of you."

The collection of kids he's shaped gloats down at me from the wall.

"I didn't ask for that," I say.

"You may not have asked for that, or any of this, but you dying . . ."

"Means it was a waste of their time." I'll never hang like the head of some deer on the headmaster's wall with the other students. I'm no longer worth collecting.

"A piece of them goes with you. The closer they are to you, the bigger the piece."

"Was I a waste of time then, Mom?"

She stares, blinking back tears. "God, no." She chokes. "You're the best thing that has ever happened to me. But this is *hard*."

"I'm the one who is dying, Mom. Me."

"I know, baby, and I only wish it could be me. We'll get through this together. I love you. I'll be with you. It'll be fine." She says this last bit without looking at me.

I stare at her. "I'm seventeen years old, Mom. And I'll never be fine again." I slowly pick myself off the ground, batting away my mom's reaching hands.

"Where are you going?" she asks.

"To fight."

\*\*\*

Outside the school gates is a small convenience store stocked mostly with chips, chocolate, and soda. It also has everything a student needs for a project, or to stage a protest.

I purchase two pieces of white Bristol board, duct tape, and markers. At one o'clock, I find a dry patch of pavement in the sun and set to work. I write:

TOSSED FOR TRADITION

DENIED FOR DYING

*Because that's what this is about.*

With the duct tape, I create a sandwich board that I hang over my shoulders, and then I pull out my phone and record: "My name is Tremendous Sinclair. I have been expelled from Amborough College because they don't want me dying there. I will be protesting this injustice in front of the school until I am let back in or until I die, whichever comes first."

I post it to my social media feeds. A car drifts down the school drive. I block the exit. The driver honks. I point to my sign and peer into the window and see Mr. Bell on the phone, mouth jawing, hand incoherently waggling at me.

I take a selfie before the car, smiling. Post it. Then I slow walk the rest of the way across the entrance before he accelerates away.

Soon after I post, Margot arrives. She runs across the field toward me, a field she plays field hockey on, and stops halfway. Peers at me. Starts running again, only to stop outside the gate. I can't set foot inside. That's private property. The vast swathe of land Amborough purchased for next to nothing from some farmer over a century ago. It's not for average citizens. It's not for me.

"Tremmy," Margot says, breathless. "I saw. I'm so sorry."

I want to cross the fence but can only stand on the other side. "Why?"

"I convinced you to stay, and now . . ."

*It wasn't worth it.*

"You warned me, and you were right."

She stumbles forward into my arms, tears on her cheeks. "But I don't *know* anything."

"What are you talking about? You're the strongest person I've ever met. Adults included."

I miss her heat when she releases me. I realize I'm cold all the time now.

"I don't actually know what I'm doing. Most of the time, I'm just holding on." She flushes with her admission. "Maybe you wasted time . . ."

I smile. "Maybe no one knows what they're doing. Maybe there's only people who do things, and those who do not."

"Yeah, but sometimes I wonder, who am *I* to try to change things?"

"Who are you not to? I mean, somebody has to." Her eyes connect with mine and hold them hard. "None of this would

217

have happened without you, and now I'm trying to convince you it is right. It's like a weird loop. None of us know what we're doing, but maybe by doing it, we reassure each other that it's okay and we can all keep fighting."

"What if we're wrong? You're dying and could be out traveling the world, or on a beach, under a palm tree."

"The palm tree isn't missing me. And I don't miss it."

I point to my sign. Her eyes scan it. I turn for her so she can read the back. "Nicely inflammatory," she says.

"I thought so."

She claps me on the shoulder. "The headmaster really has it in for you. This expulsion thing is ridiculous. The teachers watched everyone as they unloaded pumpkins. They all know what we do. They saw."

"I know. But I was caught. Made a mistake."

"They're banning the tradition."

"Good."

"What do you mean, good?"

"The farmer was right. I shouldn't have been stealing his pumpkins. Even if they were rotting. I don't think I should go to jail for it. I don't think I should be expelled for it. Doesn't make it okay."

She studies me for a second. "Got any more Bristol board?" I shake my head, and she runs to the convenience store.

"Tremendous . . . Tremendous!" the headmaster roars from where he strides across the field. I glance over my shoulder, too surprised to believe he's yelling at me. His face looks as though it's inflated; his cheeks pucker and his head shakes. "What have you done to her?"

He stands fifty yards away, but I move back.

"To Margot?" I ask, looking over my shoulder toward the convenience store.

"Margot? No! To my daughter!"

I blink. "Daughter? I didn't touch your—"

"You know exactly what I'm talking about! I won't be blackmailed."

He spins on his heel and stomps away.

Across the road, Margot stands waiting, wide-eyed, for a gap in traffic.

She hurries across. "What was that about?"

"The headmaster thinks I have his daughter. Why?"

"Didn't she die seven or eight years ago?"

"Right. Then how would I have . . .?" I go cold. "Oh no." I know where his daughter is.

I send a text to Audra. *Was it you?*

She sends back a devil emoji.

*Give it back.*

She replies: *I shouldn't have left you. He'll cave. He'll let you in. Not like this. Put her back.*

She sends a sad-face emoji.

"What is it?" Margot asks.

"I can't say," I reply. On the headmaster's mantel was no trophy, no silver vase. It was an urn. Audra stole his daughter's ashes. I shake my head and force down the smile. "Do you know how his daughter died?"

"Leukemia, I think."

A weird mix of compassion and anger flushes through me.

Margot's marker has been squeaking as she works on her

poster. Finished, she holds it up. It reads: *Tremendous Respect.*

"I'm feeling a little like Wilbur in *Charlotte's Web*," I say.

Margot shudders. "Makes me a spider." We stand together as a few cars pass without turning onto campus. "You need to post more if you actually want this to work."

"I was wondering if I'd ever see my five minutes of fame," I reply, handing her my phone.

"This is Margot Allan, we are at Amborough College, where Tremendous Sinclair, high school senior, has been expelled. What are you protesting here today?"

The weight of the camera lens probes. "Uh . . ." Margot waves me on, nodding encouragingly. I glance down at my sign. "Basically, the administration is using a school tradition as an excuse to get rid of me."

"And why are they *really* getting rid of you, Tremendous?"

"I have brain cancer, and I've been fighting to remain at the school while I die."

"You have brain cancer and you want to die in school," Margot says. I nod. "Why would you want to die here?"

I draw a deep breath. "This is my home. My real home. It's where my friends are. Where I hope someone will help me."

"Are you talking about Medical Assistance in Dying?"

"There's more. I think everyone hits a point in life where something happens. They're in a car accident, maybe. A friend hurts herself. A parent dies. Whatever. Something that really strikes home. That makes you think about life and who you are and what you want to be. And the closer you are to it, the bigger the hit. I might as well use mine for something."

Her head shifts forward on her neck as she peers at me. "You want to be the car accident. You want to have an impact on your friends? Is this about you too, then? That by them being better, you somehow are too?"

"Is that not true? I mean, if they go on and help others instead of hurting them—" It reminds me of Hairy Head's wall.

"What do you mean, hurt?" Margot asks.

I swallow. "Use people. Assault them. Kill them."

"You have friends capable of that?"

"I am capable of that."

Margot lets the video stretch in silence.

"If you can stop that, that's something, Tremendous."

"I don't have time to change."

Margot's eyes are shining. "But you have, Tremmy. You have." She lowers the phone.

Margot turns to me and says, "No one knows what they're doing, huh?" And laughs as she slow-walks across the driveway in order to block Pascale's exit.

No one joins me after Margot leaves. I am a tree. A few students stand and point from the other side of the field, not wanting to approach. Those who pass by on the way to the store walk quickly, looking down at their phones.

A half hour later, having backed up student-pickup-traffic several blocks—honking, some yelling, some *kindly* telling me that "You're not doing yourself any favors"—the headmaster's Cadillac windows power down.

I step in front of the car.

Through the glazed windshield, the headmaster's expression is stony as I complete my traverse of the entry. Bugs have splattered the SUV's silver grille. I can't help but empathize.

"You done?" he asks when I return to the side.

"I didn't take her," I say.

His eyes betray nothing and emotion surges in me. I can't tell what kind; it's dizzying heat, occluding. "How did your daughter die, sir? I heard it was cancer." Horror flashes across his face. The window starts to power up. "Did she die in pain? Is it because you don't want to be reminded of that? Is that why you're trying to get rid of me?" The window is up now, and the tint reflects the evening sun. *I'm right?* "Because that makes sense, sir. No one wants to see their child die." The large SUV doesn't move. "A death doesn't have to hurt so much. I believe that. I want that. I don't want to die in this driveway or in a hospital bed or home alone. I don't—"

The SUV surges forward and hurtles down the road and away.

# 9 Days to Demise

Last night I had trouble falling asleep. Each time I almost drifted off, I jerked awake, as if something hooked my sternum and yanked. It happened dozens of times, until I began to fear trying.

I wake the next morning with a nasty cough. Cancer wears everything down. More often than not, it's the pneumonia that kills you. My throat gurgles with chunky goo. I stagger from wall to wall to the sink, where I cough some up. It's thick yellow, but not bloody. So there's that. I reel back from the reflection in the mirror. Flesh is melting from my face, stretching skin taut over bone.

"You're staying home," my mom says.

"Same as dying." My reply echoes in the tiled washroom.

"It's not the same. And the forecast is for cool temperatures and rain. I'm not driving you."

Abandoned to my own initiative, I scramble three eggs and microwave six pieces of bacon. While it sizzles and spatters, I swallow a handful of Tylenol and Advil. I force-feed myself the last disappointing bites, my sense of smell having withered overnight, and order an Uber. I step out beneath slate gray skies before my mother even knows what I've done. The driver leaves me at the school gates. A few cars have slipped through, but I'm not the only one here. A half-dozen adults stand, toes of boots punching through the thin cracklings of ice that have formed on puddle tops.

*Supportive parents?* I don't see any designer labels. Cars honk as they pass. I wave tentatively. A news truck grinds over the gravel shoulder and stops. I rub my hands for warmth.

"Honk to save Tremendous!" some woman shouts.

"What?" I say and unfurl my new sign. It reads DYING TO STAY.

"Save Tremendous!"

The use of my full name is the first clue that something is wrong. Even with the eye patch, my vision is blurring on me today, and I struggle to read their signs. Words carefully printed on stiff foam boards, with picket-fence post grips for easy lifting, read, *Save Our Children. Care Not Killing. Kill Pain Not Patients.* These are pros.

These people aren't here to support me. They're here to *protest* me. I can't help but wonder if Margot knew this would happen when she created the video post. I stand before them, feeling small and tired. But, with the arrival of the next car, I begin my slow walk amidst honks and cries for my safety. It's not long before the Tylenol and Advil begin to wear off, and I wonder if I can persevere for the full day.

"You've got fans."

It's Jenkins. Seeing him, my eyes sting. "None of mine. They want to save me, literally and figuratively."

"You see the comments on your show?"

The video post I shared didn't quite go viral, but special

interest groups trolled it. I was called "emotional." People asked where my parents were. And wrote me off as a criminal. Sure, I had some support too, but it was mostly "poor boy" stuff.

At another honk, I give them the finger. "You protesting me too?" I ask Jenkins. His being here, whether for or against me, boosts my energy.

"It was my mom," he says. "The parent that complained." I jerk around, everything swings, and I bend to hang my head between my legs. Thankfully Jenkins doesn't touch me. "I'm sorry. I didn't ask her to complain. If it helps, I had this huge fight with her about it."

"Why? She thinks I shouldn't have the right to die here?"

"She called you a troublemaker."

*I'm a bad influence.* It has nothing to do with my dying, even though the headmaster managed to twist it that way. "You tell her about how you took the head prefectship."

"Not sure I need it anymore," he says. "I can't go to any Ivy League school. My mom won't support me."

I pause, wipe spittle from my lip. "That's a big fight."

"Told her I didn't want to go into the family business. Not yet. Want to take a general arts degree and see if there's anything that can actually excite me."

"Really?" The family business is a billion-dollar construction company. "You'd be guaranteed to be rich."

"Joining the company would be like you taking that trip around the world. I would be dead already. I may end up in the business, but I want to know that's what I want. The business may be a good thing, and I know I'm crazy lucky to have options. But knowing it's what I want changes everything."

"Choice."

"Like this?" Jenkins asks, pointing to my sign. His eyes widen in sudden understanding.

"So why are you here?"

"I saw your video. I know it's about me." Jenkins waits, perhaps hoping I'll deny it. "Remember how I said I was searching for some kind of oppression?"

"Yeah."

He flushes. "I have no idea what it's like to be on the bottom. I sure as hell don't think I'd rape anyone. And I don't want to believe I'd kill anyone either. And maybe that's the problem. And maybe I'll never find the fight I'm looking for. Maybe I'll never find it if I'm only looking at myself. It's about being a buddy."

"An ally," I say.

"Yeah, an ally."

I take what feels like the first full breath I've taken in weeks. "So what should we do?" I ask as another van load of protesters shows.

"In all instances, the best course of action when faced with opposition is mockery," he says. "Have any more Bristol board?"

I hesitate. Jenkins has disappointed me so many times. I've let him back in so many times. And he's let me down when I needed him. But the ship is turning too. He's changing. An arts degree? Refusing his mom? He hasn't admitted to doing anything wrong, but he's open to a difference in perceptions.

I shake my head and point to the store. He jogs across the street; someone honks, and he laughs at them. When he returns, he has already made signs. "What do you think?"

The first reads *Swerve to Kill Tremmy*.

I laugh. "I'll stand close to the protesters. Maybe I can take a few with me."

He shrugs. "They all think they're doing the right thing. Tough to blame them."

The second reads *Tremendous Expiration, Please Stand By.*

We earn our first honk and cheer.

The news camera approaches us, a slim, narrow-faced reporter behind it. I tense. "Tremendous Sinclair, how do you feel about what has happened to the farmer who charged you with stealing his pumpkins?" she asks.

"What do you mean? What's happened?"

"Your trolls have taken down his website and downrated his apple-picking farm with over a hundred one-star reviews."

I swear. "What? I didn't—"

"Is this retribution for the charges against you?"

"I didn't review anyone . . ." Audra, crap. Her automated review service could easily be turned against someone like this. "I have a message for anyone who thinks they're helping me. I plead guilty to the charges. Downrating the farmer isn't cool at all. I stole. He charged. I ask anyone who posted those fake reviews to take them down. To the farmer, I'm sorry. I'm sorry I stole your pumpkins. I'm sorry that these people are hurting you in my name. It's not . . . not cool." The reporter lowers the camera. "Please put that on the news?" I ask.

"That's for the editor to decide," she says.

Not good enough.

I text Audra: "If it was you, delete the reviews." She'll know what I'm talking about. "If it's not you, can you fix it?"

The protesters weave in front of the school gates, slowing the progress of cars. They've usurped me, which I guess was their plan. "You coming?" I ask Jenkins.

"Where?" he asks.

"The only thing better than a protest is a march."

"Yeah, buddy, even though it's like walking with a no-legged, castrated two-year-old."

"In defense of castrated toddlers everywhere, I'm even slower." I smirk as we start, and we're joined by half the protesters. They don't even look at us, but I let them join in. The more the merrier. We lift our signs. Now we're blocking all traffic. And it's amazing how few people it takes to disrupt the system.

Jenkins shouts, "Kill to care! Automotive assistance in dying." We dodge a car skidding out to pass us.

"Don't murder your friend," a matronly protester wearing a white peasant blouse says.

I've heard them shout stuff like this all day, but Jenkins pales when he hears it and whispers, "Friends don't kill friends. That's fundamental."

She touches him on the shoulder. He scowls at her and she backs off. Then he sees my desperation. "Margot won't do it for religious reasons," I say. "My parents won't because . . . I think they'll wait until it doesn't matter anymore. Audra wants to because she's Audra. I need a *friend*. My friend. Strap me into your jetpack and let me fire off until the fuel runs out."

We stand in silence for a minute, listening to the honking, watching the shiny faces of the protesters watch us. Jenkins says, "When you first told me about MAID, I . . . I saw my dad. I saw him on the ground again." I start to say something, and he shakes his head. "I saw you, like how I found him."

I shut my eyes to the pain in his face, but I can't avoid the pain in his voice. "Sorry. I hadn't thought of that."

"I do. All the time. Can't sleep sometimes. I think it's why I drink too much. Why I do stupid stuff . . ." He shuts his eyes. "It's harder for me to think about, harder to talk about, not something I can do."

"You're not dying."

He starts marching again. I stagger to keep pace. "Why can't you do it yourself?"

"I have brain cancer. I don't know what will happen. I could become paralyzed. I could go crazy."

Jenkins shrugs. "We both know it's too late for that."

"Not now, man. This isn't a joke. Listen, I probably won't need you. I'll probably be so hopped up on drugs nothing will matter. But I don't want to do it too early either. If I can give you the signal or if I'm wasting away to no purpose. Do it. I have an idea how."

"He'll lose his soul," a protester whispers.

"No God wants people to suffer!" I shout and then start coughing, really hacking, and the protesters back up a step. Jenkins places his hand on the small of my back as I bend and cough. "I don't want to die alone, dude. Not alone. I don't want to stroke out at night or go heaving my guts into a toilet."

When I straighten, Jenkins won't look me in the eye. "I won't let you die alone," he whispers. "I'll help you. But you need to be at school when you go."

# 8 Days to Demise

I post on social media. "If you think I should be allowed to die in the place of my choice, please come support me at the gate. #TruthtoPower."

Evidently the Truth to Power hashtag was a good choice. The first person to repost is a local politician and activist. "Tremendous!" is his only comment. I don't know if he reposts everything with that hashtag, and this barely took him a moment's thought, or if he believes strongly in my cause, but it's something. The result is a hundred shares from his supporters, something noted by the news station feed "Terminal cancer patient garnering Tremendous support." And, for the first time, I give thanks to my parents for my ridiculous name.

Today, my mom drives me, but we hit traffic with four blocks to go. We're not moving. "Something's going on," she says.

"I can walk from here." I ease out of the car, and my mom powers down the window.

"You'll be okay?"

I reach through the window into the seat well to pull a gift from her. A cane. A really cool cane that helps me to understand why Mr. Johnston loves his conducting baton. It's sleek black wood with a gold dragonhead handle. Between the dragon's teeth is a pearl and, in the eyes, rubies. I love it. Don't love that I need it, but I love it. I wave it at her, my way of saying *all good*.

"Tremmy," she says, following me as the traffic crawls. "I want you to know that I've never protested anything. Never spoke up. I'm proud of you."

For a few car lengths I am feeling so good I don't need the cane at all. After half a block, I am glad for it, and as I approach the gate, I hobble. And grin. In front of the school, not walking back and forth but linked arm in arm, is half the senior year with signs. *We Walk Out Until He Walks In.* I'm proud of the fifty or so people stretched across the pavement. A few months ago, I might have been embarrassed by it. I might have rolled my eyes and calculated the combined salary of all those people sitting in cars waiting to enter versus the cause of one unlucky kid. Now? Now I agree. I support it. I deserve to have my voice. Everyone does. Lily, Margot, Audra, Whitby, Stack. Merton? They cheer when they see me.

As I cross the road, weaving through cars, I sing, "He Who Would Valiant Be." Someone picks it up, and then everyone, and I arrive shaking with the effort, sucking in breath every bar.

On the opposite side of the road, the anti-MAID protesters stand silently and listen.

"Speech!" Margot calls.

I grip the cane with both hands, leaning heavily on it. "Um . . . thanks," I say to everyone. I flinch at Margot's withering stare and blow out a deep breath to try again. "Some say walkouts change nothing. Well, some people have not met us." For a moment I'm back at the podium in the gym with nothing but a blank, cancered-out brain. But only for a moment. I find Jenkins in the crowd and focus on him. "I've been thinking about obituaries. Everyone's going to die, peeps. Everyone. And everyone deserves to die well. It's taken me a really long time to figure out what dying well means."

My mom jogs up the gravel shoulder and links arms with Jenkins.

"To die well, I need to move past my shame and regret. And to realize that all I can do is be better. I've made the mistake of trying to reclaim what I once had. But that privilege often comes at the expense of others. I know I'm asking for another privilege. But I also know I deserve this one. Everyone does."

There's cheering, and Margot blurs, but it's not cancer; it's a deep, welling gratitude. The cheers dwindle into silence. No one says anything. I won't leave it like this, so I chant. "Let. Me. Die. Let. Me. Die."

And it's quickly taken up. And, as I shout and grip my cane and pump my fist at them, I ask myself, are these the people I want at my funeral? And the answer is *yes*.

Two hours later, without a single car through the gate, I receive a text. At this point, our numbers have swollen into a legion. We've passed the time with more singing. My voice has gone hoarse. Younger kids play tag. A few schlep cappuccino orders from the dining hall. Others duel with fireflies or use them to order takeout.

"It's the Hairy Head," I say to the gathered students. They cheer. "He wants to meet."

I lift the cane like it's a sword and everyone follows behind me, slowly, as we squelch across the loamy battlefield to the pillared school entrance. My supporters leave me at the door.

"Good luck, Tremmy!" someone calls.

"Don't take no!" calls another.

My mom lifts a thumb.

It's weird, but I sense the weight of them. They're lifting me up, but also holding me to my course. Every one of us holds power. Power together. But I walk on alone.

The headmaster greets me at his office door. I slide into an armchair and cut off a moan. Everything aches. I wipe cold sweat from my forehead and then cough into the crook of my elbow.

His face is grim, his fingers caged. He leans forward and says, "Mr. Arnold has dropped the charges."

"Mr. Arnold. The farmer?" I slip deeper into the leather, gripping the dragon head tight. I hadn't realized how tired I'd become. "He saw the video?"

"It appears your apology was accepted."

Poised on the mantel is his daughter. On the wall, among the collection of rich and famous, there's a new photo; something tells me the headmaster hasn't noticed it yet. It's me. Naked but for my underwear, lips kissing air, at the chapel's former altar. The Hairy Head must take my stunned silence as thanks.

"Your expulsion is withdrawn, and you are *welcome* to return to school. There is one condition, however." I wait for it, tearing my focus from the skeletal boy on the wall, knowing I must look even worse now. "The school is not in a position to accommodate your medical needs. It is not a hospital. As soon as outside help is required for your care, you must agree to leave."

That stage is not far off. Days. Maybe a week or two. But the firm set to his jaw suggests he's consulted legal opinions on the matter. I consider the crowd outside. The photo. Have I already won? The school's position isn't unreasonable. But is it right?

Before I go, I point at the silver urn. "Hope was her name, sir?"

"Yes, Hope," he says.

"I'm sorry for your loss."

"Thank you." He nods, his hands unclamping and running over his lined expression, no longer the big, hairy dome head but a father who lost his baby girl, his hands now tugging at a remembered ponytail.

As I open the huge doors to exit, the crowd waits on the limestone steps. I bask for a moment in the sun and silence. Beyond, ivy grows along a limestone wall.

I cough. "I'm back."

A cheer erupts. I lift my cane. They quiet.

"Until I need outside help."

We disperse solemnly. Everyone has a sense of how little time is left.

# 7 Days to Demise

This morning, I went to art class and drew another last gasp. Fifteen seconds isn't much time to draw, particularly when your brain isn't churning at full speed. But every classroom had a message on their whiteboard screens. Not one in my writing. Ours was, *Welcome back, Tremmy!* But others were interesting facts. Discussion topics. A few jokes. Even a riddle.

Delacroix made the mistake of asking who forgot to shower this morning. Everyone glanced around awkwardly until she flushed, realizing that it was me. Because my dying smells. I'm leaking. I, of course, smell nothing.

"It's okay," I say. "But let's create a bill of rights for the soon to be stardust, okay?" Delacroix was too embarrassed to say anything, so I kept talking. "Here's one. Farting is a sign of life. We can all fart. Fart up a storm. Next time you fart in public, you can shrug and say, better than dead."

Margot lets one rip that echoes. I high-five her. Everyone laughs. "Next. Ask me anything. Silence is when I am most alone. That's when that shadow of death's in the room." Audra glances around. I can tell she wishes she had her camera. "The dying are still people. I haven't changed, not an iota. I want to participate. You guys play basketball? Put me under the basket and pass me the ball every once in a while."

And that's why I guess I'm here right now. I want the ball, one last time. That's privilege, to have a bill of rights, I know, but now I understand that I deserve this privilege and I know how to fight for it.

After class, I confront Margot. "You knew the protesters would come. That's why you wanted to post that video."

"We all have our responsibilities," she says. "The reasons why people opt for assistance to die are tracked." She counts off on her fingers. "Loss of autonomy. Inability to engage in enjoyable activities. Loss of dignity, including control of bodily functions. Burden on family and friends. Inadequate pain control or concern about it. None of these are acceptable reasons. You're a child—you've never had autonomy. You fart on people's heads. You've participated in jerk-off contests—dignity can't be your priority. Burden on family—only if you're told you're a burden. Finally, inadequate pain control really means inadequate palliative care. Manage the pain and MAID for minors is unnecessary."

She's right about some things. About how, even after I've started crapping my pants, I still want to live. This isn't an abstract question about dignity for me. "Did you know that pain in the brain is really hard to manage? What happens when I can't swallow?"

I hate the compassion on her face as much as I fear the scalding agony of the pain I've felt. But she still has an answer. "I read a study where participants were told they would be given an electrical shock. Half the group was told that it would be painful. The other half were told it wouldn't be. They were then all asked to rate the level of pain they felt. Those who were told it would be painful rated the pain twice as high as those who were told it wouldn't hurt. The shock was the same in both cases. The study proves that pain is highly subjective. What one person thinks is unbearable may be entirely treatable. Especially if we tell them it's not so bad."

"That's pretty . . ." Mean, bad? I've lost the word. "Patronizing."

She flushes, gripping her pendant even tighter. That's the problem. No one on the other side of this equation can possibly understand each and every situation. Margot missed my reason.

"It's okay," I say. "I have backup. I think."

Margot looks pained. "Tremmy, I know he's still your friend, but I wouldn't trust Jenkins."

"For FAID?"

"For *anything*."

\*\*\*

That evening, as I sift through other last gasps and struggle with Margot's arguments, I start on the last of my art project. I cue up the firefly so it hovers a foot from my face.

"It's no secret that I want some help in dying well. I don't think I've been asking the question right. Let me show you instead."

And then I set to work, animating my last gasps into a sequence. Intercutting it with photos I asked Audra's permission to include. I drew the same thing every time. Almost a hundred drawings. In class, I used charcoal and oil pastels. Outside of class, I used pens, pencils, and pencil crayons.

When the video is ready, I send the video to Delacroix with the title of the piece, "Time to Say Goodbye."

But it's not for Delacroix.

# 6 Days to Demise

The next morning, I wake to pain.

It starts as an aching in the front of my head. And grows. By the end of the day, my skull's ablaze. Agony. My sheets blur. Double. The pain redoubles. The throbbing obliterates sound. The tumor crushes something really important. My fist pounds my pillow. I squirm, teeth clenched, sweating until I find a position where the pain subsides to embers. I slap at the side table, find a bottle of Advil, shake several into a palm, swallow them. Wait. It's fighting a forest fire with a squirt gun.

Footsteps pad down the hall, and then knuckles rap at the door. "Busy," I say.

But the door opens. Audra pokes her head in. I'm naked, crouched on my bed in a cold sweat. "Loss of dignity," I say. My laughter that follows stabs at my temples.

"Should I get Mr. Bell? Call 911?"

"Don't . . . say . . . anything," I reply. I know what an ambulance visit will mean. Going home. Or to some palliative care ward. She nods. "No pictures either," I say and groan.

She layers on the comforter. The pillow muffles my thanks. Maybe the painkillers are kicking in because I'm able to breathe steadily once more. It takes several minutes, but eventually I unfurl. Audra's still there, sitting in my desk chair. She's wringing her hands.

"You don't have to leave," she says.

"Tell that to the . . . cancer."

"Amborough, I mean," she says. "I know how to keep you here."

"Angels and miracles?" I reply.

"Not quite." Her eyes dart to the door. "Blackmail."

"*What*?"

"I know something the headmaster won't like. Won't want to be made public. You can use it against him."

However long I have left, if not spent here, will be spent alone at home with my parents, or on some ward somewhere with nurses and the odd visitor. I know that despite what friends say, despite their best intentions, few of my friends will visit. I want to be here. I start to shake. After a moment, I'm back under control. "What do you know?"

"There's a death pool." She flushes and stares at her entwined hands. "It's like a fifty-fifty draw, but to win you need to guess closest to the date and time of your death."

"A gambling ring," I say. "A horse race but I'm the horse?"

"Yeah, and it's hosted on the school's servers." Her hands are flipping back and forth.

I remember her fake reviews. Her need for money. Her crowdfunded assassination attempt. "You didn't?" But I know the answer. She even mentioned it in art class, when I'd talked about students working out my prognosis.

"All this publicity helped. Went through the dark web like—"

She snaps her fingers. "I shouldn't have, but now I've already spent the money and can't stop it."

"Audra," I say. "My medical records?"

Her eyes shut tight. "I borrowed them. But I promise to be better. Those negative reviews? They weren't mine, but I buried them in five stars. He's got the number-one-rated farm in all of North America, maybe the world."

"It's amazing? Awesome, wicked, excellent?" I try to laugh.

"Tremendous, even," she says. "It was so weird. All this did something to me. This morning, in the mirror, I saw something . . ."

I don't know what to think. The death pool is gross. Profiting on my death. But also entrepreneurial, right? I start to laugh and then cry out in pain. Finally, I ask, "When?"

"What?" She looks up, eyes full of tears and confusion.

"When's the most popular date?"

"Oh . . ." She bites her lip. "Twenty-seven days."

"Morning or night."

"Early morning."

My crowd-sourced expiry date is in less than four weeks. The throbbing brain suggests I'll be lucky to get there.

"How can the death pool help me?" I ask.

"Pascale placed a bet."

I sit up a bit. "Pascale gambled on when I'll die?"

"And I doubt the headmaster would like that to be public."

I think. "Wouldn't he find out you were behind it?"

Audra shrugs. "I shouldn't have done it."

"You could get in deep trouble."

"I can cover my tracks so no one will know who it was. You'll have what you need."

I would. But not how I wanted it. Besides, I believe Audra when she says she'll do better.

"No, I don't think so," I say. "But can you let Pascale win, even if he chose the wrong date?"

"Let him know you know?" Her shoulders sag, maybe with relief, maybe with expunged guilt. She stands and goes to the door. "I can do that."

"Audra, remember the pentobarbital?"

"Say the word."

"Word. Keep it handy."

She pumps a fist. "It's on me. Gold package."

I smile. "Thanks, Audra."

After dressing, I shuffle to the dining hall, taking breaks every soccer field length. Stella cooks me some oatmeal, which I eat a few ashen bites of before my stomach cramps and I quietly vomit in the bathroom.

My first class is art, and I'm finding it difficult to sit upright, let alone draw anything.

"Take a sick day," Delacroix says. "Try again tomorrow." It's probably best not to be too visible in this condition. Maybe tomorrow *will* be better.

I leave the art studio and slowly hobble back to Mason House, using two canes, dragging my right leg, shredding the toe of my loafer. Halfway, I stop and turn toward the windows of the headmaster's office. Partially obscured by the windowpane, his moon face watches.

I foot-drag on. The weight of defeat on my shoulders.

# 4 Days to Demise

The next day was better, and I made all my classes, but the following morning I'm woken by more pain. It's early, the time when everyone expects I'll die. Dark through the windows. Sleet prickles at the glass. For the next several hours I fade into sleep, only to be jolted out by shocks of white agony. And when I wake in the light of day, still not hungry but knowing I have to eat, I text Audra. I text Jenkins.

*I've got to go.*

*I need help.*

And I'm pretty sure the death pool's estimate was way wrong.

*** 

Audra slips into the room first. With her is a leather satchel and camera.

"Wait for Jenkins," I manage.

She nods and snaps a photo.

Soon, footsteps creak down the hall. I relax.

Soon.

But it's not Jenkins. My mom. Audra sighs heavily under her suspicious gaze. "Dad's on his way."

After that, it's a line of friends. Lily, Margot, and Stack crowd my bed. Jodie comes and leaves, both ways in tears. "Not dead yet," I told her as she left, but it didn't seem to matter. It doesn't, I guess. It's goodbye. My head hurts less with everyone around. If I can't die, I don't want to leave.

While my mom's keeping busy packing books and clothes into milk crates borrowed from the kitchen, Lily's reading a note from Stella.

"Bambino," she reads with humor in her voice, "Should I be pinching your cheek while reading this for authenticity? Okay, okay. Bambino, I will miss you. I've watched so many of you boys grow up, but never one so quickly. I'm proud of you." The note came with a bag of fresh pasta and a carton of Rocky Road ice cream. I keep a spoonful down.

When Audra snaps a picture from where she crouches in the corner, my mom frowns at her. "It's okay, Mom, we made a deal. There's good light for angels this morning."

I watch through the window as my dad arrives and backs the truck close to the entry. My mom's head jerks up with the bleeping of the truck in reverse. "He's here," she says, and waits while *everyone* grabs a milk crate, and I'm left alone with an empty room. Skull pounding. It happened all at once, like they couldn't wait to be out of my room. And still no Jenkins. The air feels close and humid with breath and bodies. With the ghosts of them. Cracks in the plaster run across uneven walls. I've stared so often at the moldings around the ceiling, listened to the clank of the radiators as hot water gurgled through them like chains. It's an aged place full of phantoms. And now I'm to be one of them.

My father's girth fills the doorway.

"Ready?" he asks.

I shake my head. "No."

He sits on the mattress beside me, hand rubbing at my back. "It's not over."

But it is. This is me with the plane boarding. Ticket in hand. The last call. But I am not allowed to let the doors close without me. That's not an option. Not the deal I made. "I'm ready to die now," I say. Fat tears fall on my lap.

"Come on, let's get you home." He hauls me to my feet. Three months ago, he wouldn't have been able to do that, but now he does it with ease. His arm arcs beneath my armpit. I fumble for my cane but miss. In the hall outside my door are other seniors. They reach out tentatively as I pass, faces sober, lips mouthing whatever they hope may be appropriate. "Bye. See ya, Tremmy. Sorry, Tremmy. See you later. Good luck."

*Good luck.* I snort at that. Outside, the sun has whisked behind clouds. The headmaster steps from around the corner of Mason House, sees me, pales, and appears to gather himself. He's remembering, I can tell, remembering what his daughter looked like before she died. The violence disease wrought on her body.

He offers a slim-lipped smile, along with his hand. It takes me a moment to adjust my balance but, eventually, I clasp it, seeing no reason not to.

"I hope you get your wish, Tremendous," he says. "It was a pleasure to have you here. You will leave a big hole." *In the fabric of reality.*

"Thank you, sir." There's no time left for recriminations. I simply don't care what he thinks anymore.

The guy behind him. Him I care about. The drone war team crowds behind Jenkins. "Sir, the deal was that Tremmy has to go if he needs outside help, right?" he asks.

The headmaster's eyes shift, calculating. "Correct."

The victory lighting Jenkins's eyes contrasts with the anguish in his downturned mouth and the determined jut of his jaw. "He doesn't need outside help. He's got us."

"Jenkins," I say, "it's okay, man. It's time. This is the dying part."

"No, Trem, I've been a terrible buddy for months. I can be a good one for a few days."

"Weeks," I say. "I might have entire weeks." Everyone looks to me. "What? Just saying."

"Weeks then," Jenkins continues. "I'll take care of him. We protect our own. We keep it Amborough."

"Tremmy needs twenty-four-hour care," my mom says, stepping in front of me.

"We'll take shifts. All of us," Jenkins replies.

I can't see Jenkins or the team through my tears, but the headmaster growls. "I can't allow you to do this."

"Mom, don't worry," I whisper, wiping at the tears, "I need you too. This doesn't cut you out." She understands because her chin dips and she steps away.

I've never seen Jenkins taller; it's more than that, though. He looks like a head prefect. "Sir, Amborough has always professed to be in touch with the rest of the world. You're always saying we should help people. That we should think beyond ourselves. Amborough sent students to Africa to build schools. Why can't we take care of our own? Why is it easier to hop on a flight somewhere?"

"Homework. Other obligations. You don't know how to care for him," the headmaster objects, counting off on his fingers. "It's a horrendous duty." *His baby girl.*

"What do you need, Tremmy?" Jenkins asks. "Food, meds. I know how to poke a needle, sponge bath, what else is there?"

"Washroom," I say.

"I'm not wiping your ass." He chuckles.

"If you're doing this," I say, drawing a deep breath before continuing, "you may actually have to wipe my ass."

He sobers. "How long?"

I shrug. "Not long." Pain lances through my skull and I gasp; my father's grip on me tightens.

"Twenty-four of us. One hour each. For three weeks." Jenkins marshals the forces.

Out of ammunition, the headmaster nods to my mom.

My mother turns to me. "Is this what you want?"

"Yeah, actually, it is."

Still, the headmaster appears ready to say no, or perhaps defer the decision, which is the same thing.

"I accept," Mr. Bell says. He stands at my shoulder. "I can't think of a better way to teach these kids compassion and empathy. It's a big hole in the curriculum. We'll post a schedule outside Tremmy's door and repost it online." He holds the headmaster's stare.

"*Ex nihilo nihil fit,*" Jenkins says.

The headmaster nods, then he starts to say something and stops, shuts his eyes, and says, "Okay."

I grimace through white light, trying not to let on that I can't see. "Thank you, now let me lie down."

The gauntlet of boarders welcomes me back. I'm handed from one person to the next through the door and down the hall to my room, where I collapse onto the bed, and it's like coming home after a month at summer camp. I feel safe and lifted up and as though I can sleep for days.

And I will try.

The last person to touch my forehead I know from the remembered brush of her fingers.

"Mommy," I say. "This is time to say goodbye."

She hushes me, but at my triggering words, the firefly projects a tiny screen on the whitewashed wall.

On the screen pile all the photos I took of the "last gasps" I've created over the past months. They flip slowly with my voiceover. "This is my self-portrait," I say. "I could only draw for as long as I could hold my breath. That was the rule. I had two minutes to draw the first three portraits. A minute fifty-five for the next." They roll, nearly identical. "This is healthy Tremmy."

Up comes a half-naked picture of me. One of Audra's. "How'd that get in there?" I laugh, but of course, I put it there. Changes to the drawings begin to appear. "For these drawings, I had a minute forty-five." A photo of me on the chapel's red carpet follows, then more sketches. "Here's after my first big seizure. A minute ten left to draw." My face has lost a bunch of detail. It's gained a forehead wound. In the next photo, I'm noticeably thinner. The first time Audra showed it to me, I fought nausea. It's also absent angels. The images roll like an animated sequence.

By the time I'm reduced to forty seconds of drawing time, it's hard to recognize myself. "If you really know me, you can see it's me. See, long, messy hair. Blue eyes. Goofy smile."

"But . . . this . . . this . . . and here." Audra took this last picture yesterday morning. She placed the light high so that it created shadows beneath my ribs, and pools in the depths of my cheeks. I'm skeletal. But that's not all. Gone is my vibrancy. My animation. I am inanimate. My mother gasps at it. "And this final drawing." I hold on to the frame. The drawing is of a shaky oval with some jotted eyes. "Mom?" I ask in the video. "Do you recognize me in the drawing?" My mom's cries are heavy and heaving. "Who could? It's a potato with some eyes. A vegetable. That's me at the end. You get it now?" I ask, my voice strong and clear. "It's not about dignity. Or being a burden. Or subjective pain. It's about not being. At the end, only a few dashes remain. And when you think of it that way, it's not much to let go of. It's not much to ask for."

The video is over and still my mom sobs. I'm fading, quiet, struggling to stay awake.

Finally, the fingers are back at my forehead.

"I love you," she says, tracing a finger from one temple to the other. "Give your mom a kiss?" Her cheek presses against my lips. Then her lips are at my forehead.

"You made me," I whisper.

She curls warm into my side. Sobs. "Goodbye, my love, goodbye."

# 3 Days to Demise

Disease dictates my days. I eat when it lets me. Rocky Road only. I sleep at random times. The poop thing happens less and less. That's my body shutting down. A bonus for the cleaning crew. My parents check in. We're into the mechanics, though. Done are the deep conversations. In good moments, Jenkins piggybacks me across campus like I'm some little brother. To the river. To watch dawn. To see the stars or feel the rain. Only the pain builds. Pain meds nauseate me. I try to watch movies and television shows. I ask for everyone's favorites and binge in bed nestled with my mom, sometimes my dad, sometimes Jodie, Margot, Stack. Audra drops by with her leather bag again, and I tell her *not yet*. There's a dreamy moment with Jenkins and Margot wedged together up against the wall, closer than I would have believed possible. My hearing diminishes. My vision fades. But Margot presses into that wall like she's trying to climb it, while Jenkins smirks, huge and hulking.

My speech slows.

Still there are little things. The feel of hands as someone washes my face. Hearing the choir sing in the chapel. My mom visits with the cat and presses her to my ear so I disappear into her fur. My dad's tears mingling with mine. Cheek to cheek. The needles hurt less when my friends are here, except for Margot and Jodie, who for some reason suck at giving needles. The best at it, the gentlest touch, is Jenkins. He's the one who ensures I have everything I need. He's the one who helps me with my bath, at first piggybacking me into the basement showers, complaining that I always want to see his naked ass, and then a couple days later bathing me in bed, with warm water from a basin. I'm like a lizard, needing to leach heat to move, and I move as little as one.

We're all waiting. And I've waited long enough.

# Day of Demise

Today, after the bath, when I'm thinking of the coolness of the air as it draws the last of the moisture from my skin, I find my voice stronger.

"Remember . . ." I say, but it's a long word. Lots of syllables and tough as hide.

"It's okay, dude. I will," he says, and I shake my head to try again.

"Remember . . . your promise?"

The towel rasps over my forearms before he says anything. "What you thinking? A pillow over the face?"

"Pento . . . barbital. Audra."

"Either I help you, or you do it yourself and it'll be messy, is that it?"

I turn my head toward him, even though I can't see. I've been having small, regular seizures and hope I don't have another, because I have trouble remembering anything after. We both know there's nothing I can do for myself. I'm the potato drawing for real. But the pain is also real. The seizures are real. I'm spending minutes of every hour awake. I've noticed people coming and going without ever knowing who was there, like I'm an open casket at a funeral.

"Promised," I say.

"Yeah," he replies, his voice shuddering with emotion. "And we'll do it right. I remember you talking about how the process works. You've made your request. I know you, and you know what's happening, so I think we're past the consent stage. But there are protocols to protect you, right? A reflection period. Now we wait. How long was it?"

The bastard. "Ten days."

"There you go, buddy. You hang in there ten more days and I'll take care of things."

I try to shake my head, but don't think I manage it. Ten days . . . it's more than my lifetime. I have no energy for anger.

Later. Margot returns. They think I'm sleeping. "How is he?" Jenkins answers in a way I don't see. "Sad," she says.

"Yeah," then he adds, "don't take this the wrong way, Margot, but that stress eating you're doing is putting the pounds in the *right* places."

*It's what he said to Chen.*

There's a sharp intake of breath. "You're such a dick."

"I'm teasing. You look good. We're a good team."

I shudder and they both come over. Jenkins pries open my eyelid; his hand rests on her shoulder. They're both leaning forward, and his gaze travels from me to the open hang of Margot's shirt. My eye shuts. I quake again, but it's not the cold, or pain, or a seizure. It's knowledge. I made a mistake. Jenkins hasn't changed. Will never change. "You, okay, Tremmy? Need something?" And I can see him at university, a quarterback, a business student in his senior year signing up to welcome first years, watching for the hot ones, the ones who don't know they're hot yet, who will be most *grateful* for his attention.

*JENKINS, FRANKLIN, died at the age of ninety-seven, leaving a legacy of harassment and abuse, never having had anyone stand up to him or question him. "My father was the greatest," say his sons.*

"Get Audra," I say.

"You go," Margot says. "Let me take over for a bit."

Jenkins hesitates, and then leaves. Margot doses my eye with a lubricant, and she blurs for a minute, but the medication eases its itchiness and gives me ten minutes during which I can open my eye on my own.

"This isn't fair," she says. "I was starting to crush on you." I don't believe it. There's not much left to crush. "Spend another day with me, Tremmy. One more. And then another, okay?"

She guesses why I want Audra, but she can't guess all of it.

Audra arrives, and I flick my fingers until Margot understands. She rubs my hand, and says, "Endings are the most important parts."

"Yup," I say, and she leaves.

After loosening the string of her small leather sack, Audra proceeds to extract a syringe and a bottle. She tugs at my arm. "I've been watching YouTube videos."

"No, Audra," I say.

"You chickening out? Jenkins said you want it done."

Agony cascades through my skull and, when it ends, I've forgotten what I'm doing. Something hooks into my arm. *Think of a fish. If you jerk the line too hard, the hook comes out.*

"No."

"When, Tremmy?" Audra asks.

I think. "New plan. Hack Dr. B."

"I'm listening."

"Electric jungle. Boost voltage."

"Ah, you mean the amperage," she says and waves off the clarification. "I can do that. But dude, I thought you were afraid of pain. That's a harsh way to go."

"Bad?"

"Worse than anything you've *ever* felt."

I draw long rattling breaths. There are finishes far worse than pain. "Do it. Cover your tracks."

"Gotcha. When?"

"Watch the feed. You'll know." Audra takes a photo. "And Audra . . . can you have the trail lead to Jenkins?"

Her laughter echoes down the hall as she leaves.

Margot returns and hugs me.

"Eye," I say, and she lubricates it again. "My firefly." One appears above my face. "Margot, thank you."

She hesitates. Nods. "Thank you." And leaves.

Every word has a cost, but slowly, I say, "SINCLAIR, TREMENDOUS, AKA Tremmy, died after a fierce mortal combat with the big 'C.' Tremmy is survived by his loving parents. He went to Amborough College, where he was a privileged jerk who stole, exploited, and bullied. Who, quite frankly, deserved what he got. That guy? He left the world a better place as he left it."

---

*That's right. The truth sets me free.*

---

Jenkins jokes as he swaggers down the hall, returning.

"Call police," I tell the firefly. It needs to run. "Track me." It slides away to hover in a corner.

"Hey, buddy," Jenkins says as he skids to a stop in the doorframe. "Half expected you had Audra do the deed." *Is that disappointment?*

"See the stars?" I ask.

"You want to see the stars?"

"Drone light show. In the war zone."

"Giddy up." He jostles me onto his back. I wrap my hands around his neck, and he grips my legs with the sides of his arms.

Fresh winter-touched wind runs through my hair, and although I can't smell, the air here feels thick with oxygen. The firefly darts, a pinprick of light six feet above.

"You're lucky. Clear night," he says.

We stop at the benches near the field. "Closer," I say. And we shift down onto the turf, past the trough. Past the cold black coals of the fire walk. "There." The electric jungle. "So I can stand."

He tests a wire-vine and relaxes when there's no shock. In the far distance, sirens wail.

I wrap one vine around a wrist. Then another around my second wrist. I smile at Jenkins when I'm standing, held by the vines twined around my forearms. The wires bite, taking my weight. Somewhere Audra is working, watching the feed from my firefly. Recording.

"Looking good, Tremmy," Jenkins says.

Around us gather more fireflies, dozens of them. This must be Margot's doing. She always could put things together. The drones curl and sweep, a touch of magic on a hellish night.

"You're my best friend," I say. "I wanted to drink the succor of Zeus with you . . ."

Jenkins winks. "Me too, buddy."

"I'm sorry." Jenkins eyes me. His chin swivels toward the steadily rising sirens and scattering lights that remind me of a party a lifetime ago. "Thank you. For your mercy. I know you didn't want to do this. I couldn't have done it without you."

"What do you . . ." But the expression of betrayal on his face tells me he's answered his question. "You're setting me up."

*Run, rabbit.* I nod to the fireflies, to all of them, head tilted to the stars.

And then the night lights. As the current runs through me, the school song rises, and whether the voices of Amborough students soar or it's a hallucination from some part of my brain, I don't know, but the song twines with Jenkins's screams and the echo of the sirens as they come for him.

Drones streak like comets. The pain rides momentous. And, for a moment before what happens next happens, I have peace. A crescendo.

Cut off.

*Click.*

# Thank you, dear Reader.

If you enjoyed this book and would like to review it, please do, wherever you make purchases. There are no greater gifts to an author than reviews and word of mouth.

You can find me on Amazon, Goodreads, Facebook, Instagram and Twitter. I love to talk.

If you'd like to hear about new releases and take part in giveaways or opportunities to act as an advance reader, please sign up to my newsletter on my website or via my Facebook page. You'll get a free secret book that you can't get any other way (and it's a much lighter read!). :)

# Acknowledgements

In response to one student's question about how to live life authentically, the philosopher Martin Heidegger said that we should spend more time in graveyards. This is that book for me. But the truth is, I learned little from graveyards, and far more from the lives of the people who, in their life's final months, shared their stories online. *Thank you.*

Writing this book presented numerous challenges, and I would never have finished it without a lot of help. I want to thank my editor Catherine Adams of Inkslinger Editing for her brilliant insights. To Jessica Holland for her copyediting wizardry. And to Stephanie Parent, also of Polgarus Studios, for proofing and final thoughts. Quintus helped me get the Latin right. *Gratias tibi ago.* Erin Murphy and Elizabeth Law, you won't know this, but you provided encouragement at an important stage. To Martin Stiff at Amazing15 for the spectacular cover, and Glendon Haddix for the glorious wrap. Jason Anderson, I rely on your formatting skills—thank you. To my early and critical reader, Deborah Gomes, thank you so much for your time and big mind.

A writer is nothing without his community of fellow writers, so to the Odfellows 2016 and Jeanne Cavelos of the Odyssey Writers Workshop, and to the Sunnyside Writers Group, thank you, thank you all.

To my daughters, who inspire me to be better every day, thank you for your support and encouragement with this book. To my wife, who receives the roughest, crappiest drafts of all and still manages to find something within them to keep me going, you have my heart. If all we need is one person to believe in us, thank you for being mine.

And to you, reader, thank you for choosing this difficult novel above others. It wasn't easy to write. I hope it was worth it for you to read.

## About the Author

Michael is an award winning author who lives in Ottawa, Canada. His dozens of graphic novels, novels, and early readers have been published by Orca Book Publishers, Rubicon Publishing, and distributed by Pearson Education, Scholastic Canada, and Oxford University Press. To learn more about Michael and his projects, visit his website at www.michaelfstewart.com.

CPSIA information can be obtained
at www.ICGtesting.com
Printed in the USA
BVHW080342260321
603216BV00001B/5